Robak in Black

NOVELS BY JOE L. HENSLEY

Robak's Run
Fort's Law
Color Him Guilty
Robak's Fire
Robak's Cross
Outcasts
Minor Murders
A Killing in Gold
Rivertown Risk
Song of Corpus Juris
The Poison Summer
Legislative Body
Deliver Us to Evil
The Color of Hate
Grim City
Robak's Witch

WITH GUY M. TOWNSEND

Loose Coins

ROBAK
IN BLACK

Joe L. Hensley

ST. MARTIN'S MINOTAUR
NEW YORK

www.minotaurbooks.com

Library of Congress Cataloging-in-Publication Data

Hensley, Joe L.
    Robak in black / by Joe L. Hensley.—1st ed.
      p. cm.
    ISBN 0-312-24109-7
      1. Robak, Don (Fictitious character)—Fiction. 2. Trials (Murder)—Fiction. 3. Trials (Arson)—Fiction. 4. Indiana—Fiction. 5. Judges—Fiction. I. Title.

PS3558.E55 R58 2001
813'.54—dc21

                                  2001041962

First Edition: December 2001

10 9 8 7 6 5 4 3 2 1

For Charlotte Brown Eyes and another time and place

ACKNOWLEDGMENTS

For Kath and Mike, Doctors Sue and Pat, and
other swimming pool advisers

ROBAK IN BLACK

I

(NOVEMBER)

In the Beginning

JO BECAME ILL just before Thanksgiving. That happened during my fifth year of being Mojeff County circuit judge.

We were recently moved into our new home with its Ohio River view, getting adjusted, liking it. The summer before we'd moved had been the best time for us since an early two weeks of honeymoon time in a beach motel at Grand Cayman years before.

We'd taken son Joe and wandered Canada in July, mostly sightseeing, impressed by the big, clean cities of our northern neighbor. We didn't drive far or fast on any day and most late afternoons found us in a motel with an indoor pool for swimming-fanatic Joe. We were well enough off financially for him to have his own motel room while we had ours.

I'd allowed my life to appreciably slow during that vacation. When I returned to work I didn't rush back into a heavy trial schedule. Instead I concentrated on keeping up with routine court matters, doing the things that a judge seeking reelection next year needed to do, dissolutions, estate work, the things that kept my local bar happy and the docket up-to-date.

Jo, on our return, went back to her own routine, that being good golf, lots of ladies' bridge luncheons, and evening parties, the last with both of us invited. Plus she was president of the library board and held memberships in half a dozen other local organizations.

She was bursting with health, strong and vibrant, a stunning woman.

We were into the small-town life of Bington, Indiana.

I knew I loved her and believed she loved me.

I'd decided during vacation that being a judge was something you could do either full-out, as a few judges did, or at the lower speed most of the trial judiciary seemed to favor. I settled back at three-quarters ahead. I kept up religiously with the routine and, now and then, when an interesting case came along, I pursued it.

I'd had times in my life when all I had enough hours for was work. I found I didn't want to move at that pace anymore.

Jo liked the schedule. It made extra time for both the two of us and the three of us.

Then she became ill.

In its first hours Jo's illness seemed to be a cold or some kind of hard flu. First there was high fever. Then there were bad aches and strong pains. The sickness mutated and became a raging heat bomb. It colored her usually fair skin red, reflecting the fire inside her. It was accompanied by severe muscle pains. Her blood pressure jumped high, then skidded low, and she went in and out of consciousness.

All I could do after we arrived at the hospital was sit by her in an isolation room and hold her hand. The doctors didn't want me to do that, but I pointed out that I'd been with her when she became sick and had stayed with her at all times after. I also told them that our son had been exposed to her for he had been in our bedroom the night before discussing his high school adventures with us.

The disease both puzzled and alarmed my medical friend Dr. Hugo S. Buckner.

"What's happened to her, Robak? You and your son haven't caught it yet and so maybe something toxic she ate or drank or breathed made this happen. Think, Robak."

I thought hard and told him all I knew. I did my best to answer his questions. Where had we been in Canada? Well, mostly Toronto, Montreal, and Quebec, but that had been four months back. Did I know any place where Jo might have been recently exposed to any sickness, even someone's bad cold? What exactly had we been doing the past two weeks? Had she cooked and eaten any locally caught fish? Could she have gone swimming in the Ohio River or eaten fish taken from any other area river, creek, or lake? Had we purchased our vegetables and fruits from roadside stores? What canned foods had we eaten? Had she toured the local Macing Drug Company at its fall open house?

I had to ask others about the last question because it set off a small alarm inside me, but I soon found she'd not done the tour.

I remembered nothing that helped Buckner. I tried hard because I knew he hated sickness and death far worse than any sin.

I recited her schedule. There was nothing important or out of routine. Some parties, most recently an annual golf banquet at the end of the season. Jo had collected two trophies. Who had been there? Other golfers, a large crowd of them. And before that banquet there'd been lots of bridge with various groups. Some civic and club meetings including her library board meeting.

Questions, answers, frowns. Nothing appeared to be suspicious.

And yet I was suspicious.

All this was happening as Jo's life burned away in high fever.

I told Buckner I'd awakened early the first morning of her sickness. Outside I'd heard a cold rain scrubbing more of the autumn leaves out of the trees.

The night before, a Tuesday, we'd each had two small glasses of merlot at the crowded country club bar, then gone through a dinner buffet table with perhaps a hundred others, both of us drinking iced tea with the meal and eating sparingly. We'd gone

3

home after the golf ceremony, talked at length with our son, Joe, about his excellent report cards and his piano playing and the perils of being a high school sophomore infatuated with three or four girls.

We'd then turned down the furnace, kissed as chastely as we could manage, and switched off the bedroom light.

"It's hot," Jo complained beside me in the early morning. She wasn't talking to me, but instead dazedly explaining her problems to the room around her. She looked up at the ceiling, breathing quickly, and eventually sensed me lying next to her.

She said: "My ears are ringing like church bells, Don. I feel ghastly."

She arose looking as if she'd had far too much to drink the night before. She walked into the bathroom, showered a few moments, and came back to stand beside our bed.

"I've got a sick something that's built a blaze inside me," she said. "I took my temperature before I had my shower and it was over a hundred and three. I hope you and Joe don't catch this bummer. It hurts inside my head and stomach and my throat is raw. I feel bad all over, outside and inside."

I looked her over. Her face was flame-red, her fine hair lay wet and lank from her abbreviated shower. Her eyes were dull red and lost in their sockets. She was unlovely, something hard for her to be.

"Tell me what you'd like me to do, Jo. Like, I maybe could call Doc Buckner to come to the house or we could meet him at his office. If you feel you need treatment right now I could drive you to the hospital emergency room. We could probably meet Buckner there. You decide."

She looked down at me. Her hands were crimson and her lips were only slightly more red than her fevered face. She shivered with the beginning of a chill.

"I guess the emergency room." Her voice held something in it I'd never heard before. She was afraid.

She normally shunned doctors and hospitals.

4

I became afraid also.

I woke son Joe and told him where we were going and why.

"Should I go along?"

I didn't think he wanted to go, but he was willing if I wanted him to or thought his mother needed him there.

"It only needs one of us to get her there and you've got basketball practice after school today. Isn't it the last practice before Thanksgiving vacation? I'll call our voice-mail number after the emergency room doctor sees her and let you know what's going on. Check the phone for a message when you get home. It's probably just a virus or maybe one of the hot Asian influenzas that have been around this fall. I mean, the kind people can't seem to easily get over." I tried to make my voice sound more confident than I felt.

I helped Jo out to my eight-year-old Ford, holding tight to her arm, leading her through the rain. The last of Indian summer was gone and another unpredictable Indiana winter was soon to come. It had turned cold early, then warm, then cold again. The leaves were nearly all down. I could look down our denuded hill and see the Ohio River at pool stage. The brown, sparse lawn bore ruts, smelled dead, and I thought we might have to reseed in the spring.

Jo's almost new Olds was parked in the pull-off spot in the asphalt driveway. There was a basketball hoop above the open door of our two-car garage. We parked both cars away from that door to make room so that son Joe and his boisterous rooster pals could drive under the basket and whoop all the way into the empty garage.

I drove Jo to the hospital emergency room. Soon Doc Buckner was present as were lots of nurses and other doctors moving here and there, fast.

It got worse. Jo's temperature continued to climb.

They put her into isolation and covered her body with tubes and needles. They gave her shots and pills. She slept fitfully. Soon she didn't recognize me even though I thought her eyes sometimes saw, followed, and then discarded what she saw.

5

The doctors watched and talked softly among themselves. Son Joe and I waited. They rolled her in and out of rooms and placed her under complicated machines. They took X rays and CAT scans. They put her in ice baths.

There was a time on the second night when Buckner thought they'd lost her, but they got her back. Her heart stopped for a long moment and then was started again. They talked about a ventilator, but then decided against it.

Had she died that second night I believe I would have questioned the undiscovered cause, but not vigorously. A virus. A new Ohio River influenza. A dark, weird something coming at my Jo from out of the changing disease world, scythe in its bloody hand. We humans have managed to dirty the world around us and now medical things are uncertain and changing because of it.

Instead she lived. She lived after a fashion and in a different way, wounded deeply, but still alive. She was young. She was strong.

She lived.

During this time Joe and I were spending most of our time pacing and worrying in the private contagion waiting room located near Jo's isolation unit. I'd ordered Joe away, but he hadn't followed my orders. Because he'd also been exposed to whatever Jo had Doc Buckner had taken his side. We'd all then smiled at one another, allies.

For days we saw few people other than doctors and nurses. The medical people who visited our room wore masks, latex gloves, and white gowns. Friends coming to the hospital to visit Jo were turned away, not allowed to see any of us. Flowers arrived and were kept in the hall or placed in other rooms in the hospital. There were dozens of get-well cards and letters. They were left unread and unanswered although later we did politely answer all.

"What is it, Pop?" Joe kept asking me, at times teary-eyed. "What's got Mom?"

I knew nothing to tell him.

For a long time no one would even guess for us what was wrong, not Doc Buckner, not the other doctors who were helping, not the lab people.

Buckner said softly that he thought it might have been some allergic reaction, but then withdrew that answer. He also mentioned our huge local drug company, Macing Drugs, with the thought that something there might have "escaped." If it was that way it had only escaped to attack Jo.

"Don't hold me to anything," Doc said. "There are some alarming allergies I've read about in the medical journals and Jo's symptoms resemble some of what I read. And there's some high-powered stuff they work on at Macing Drugs. Lots of locals work there."

Whatever it was, Jo was sick. Lots of people get sick. Lots of times the sickness is communicable. We found out that what Jo had wasn't readily communicable.

Flu, crazy new viruses, pneumonia . . .

New ways for people to die.

Guesses.

I kept wondering if there was anything I could have done to prevent the circus that was now occurring around Jo, Joe, and me. I went over and over things, remembering small details.

Nothing useful came to me.

I got two lawyers from my old law firm to send a letter threatening to sue the country club for Jo in a kind of *res ipsa loquitor* suit. They obtained a list of guests for that golf banquet night. I studied the list and tried to remember if anyone had been there who wasn't on it. They also got a list of employees who worked at the club that night, but that didn't lead to much, either.

Libbie Macing, from the drug company, was on the guest list. She and Jo might be enemies because of me, but that feud was inactive and now twenty-plus years old. Now they played golf and cards together. They weren't close friends, but they weren't enemies, either.

Joe and I tried to get used to the sour smell of Jo's sickness. At first I wore the mask they gave me and Joe wore his. Soon neither of us wore masks, but instead dabbed Vicks near our noses.

The smell became ever present in our clothes.

They packed Jo in ice half a dozen times.

Buckner shook his head when I asked about that.

"The fever inside is trying to cook her, Don. Her brain can only stand so much heat. Her temperature has to come down. We're treating her symptoms, not having identified her disease."

Eventually the fever did come down. Some. Then more. Then it returned to almost normal.

Judges pro tem ran the business of the court and the superior court accepted all new criminal charges. Civil cases and hearings awaited my return for trial dates.

Joe and I ate the hospital food that was delivered to us or carried in by us to our solitary waiting room. It soon mixed with Jo's room's smells and made us nauseous. We had our clothes cleaned and we showered at home, but the smell was ever present when we entered Jo's room.

Hooded, gowned, and gloved doctors and nurses watched us, waiting for us to become ill, asking us questions about how we felt, taking our vital signs. Then they told us we didn't need to wear the masks and the gowns. They muttered things about past incubation periods (I asked for what diseases).

They still wore sterile uniforms.

We remained well.

A wet, heavy snow fell outside on the tenth of December. It became icy and the snow froze and more fell on top of it. Winter came in dead earnest.

On the twenty-second hospital day Buckner said to Joe and me: "She seems stabilized. The fever's gone and has been gone for five days. She'll likely live, but she'll never be the same as she was. I'm sorry about that. We'll just have to wait and hope about how much she can come back from the state she's in now. For at least the near future, after she's finally released from the hospital, she'll need a lot of assistance."

"She sees me and Pop in her room and sometimes she smiles up at us," Joe said. "She tries to talk."

"My guess is that part of her brain still recognizes you. Has she said anything to either of you?"

"No," I said.

8

He knew that. Why was he asking it again?

"We'll try to locate a place for her," Buckner said. "You two can't take care of her without at least semiskilled help. She's incontinent, for one thing." He shook his head and I saw he had tears in his eyes. "No way."

"What did she have? Tell me what it was?" I asked for the hundredth time.

"I'm not sure. We took blood and urine and did tests. We sent specimens off to various labs. We've found nothing in our hospital lab reports that explained her problems and we've heard nothing yet from any other lab. We may find out something and may find nothing. What I'm saying again is that our lab tests were puzzling and didn't pick up anything definitive we could blame for the onset of the high fever. It might have been an allergy to something unknown. It also may have been some new virus or a new Ohio River variation of an old virus. Her white count was almost nil. It also could have been some very nasty kind of influenza or something poisonous to Jo we've never encountered before."

"But we didn't catch it," Joe said.

Buckner shook his head. "I was surprised."

I asked him other questions privately. He escorted me to the hospital lab and stood by silently as I asked more questions of the technicians there.

What did the tests done in the hospital show?

White blood cells depleted plus other indications of a massive illness.

What was the cause?

Unknown.

Were specimens sent on to labs?

Yes.

Had anything concerning Jo been removed from the hospital lab at that time?

Not discovered.

Who'd sent out Jo's specimens?

No one remembered personally doing it, but half a dozen people could have. One person who'd worked in the lab had left and

9

no one knew where she'd gone. She'd just not come to work one day and then had never returned.

Doc Buckner said grimly: "A lot of what we sent out to other labs at that time seems to have vanished. Not only Jo's specimens, but also some specimens taken from other patients."

I tried to stay cheerful for my son.

Even as I smiled for him I found my own heart was breaking. Sometimes I would silently cry, but only when Joe couldn't see or hear me. I saved the tears for dark nights and my solitary pillow.

I loved her. It seemed to me, now that she was lost and fallen, that I'd always loved her.

Love continued.

Christmas came and passed without notice.

Near the end of December I moved Jo home and hired round-the-clock nurses. That didn't last long. Soon after we got back in the house a person or persons unknown added to our misery by firing shots from a high-powered rifle through our living room windows.

The news about those shots spread quickly through Bington's nursing world. Our alarmed nursing staff resigned and no new nurses seemed available.

We'd had problems before. There was a someone who liked to drive silently up the street where our house stood alone and then drive into the yard. Whoever it was left behind deep ruts. The contractor told me he'd smooth them all out when full spring came. There were trees in our yard and some of the ruts were between the trees. I'd thought on what I'd do if the rutter returned next year. I'd break pop bottles and hide them in the ruts, cutting edges up.

Someone also arrived silently one night and hooked onto my mailbox with a chain and tried to pull it down. The post that held the mailbox was steel and it was anchored in many yards of concrete.

I found I owned, the morning after hearing a loud, wrenching noise, a rear bumper, painted black, and some pieces from what Sheriff Jumper said was a Ford pickup truck.

The place we eventually discovered for Jo was a combined nursing home and assisted living center, A to Z, hundreds of patients, scores of nurses and attendants, busy as a hive. We told them about the gunshots. They asked us to smuggle Jo there secretly, but they seemed unworried once she was there.

We transferred her in the middle of the night four days after the shooter fired the rifle shots into our house.

I bugged Doc Buckner constantly about the disease and that was when things became truly odd. I asked and asked again the embarrassing questions about mailed specimens and about what other specimens on other patients had vanished.

When the hospital checked, no out-of-town lab would admit receiving our specimens, not even the Centers for Disease Control in Atlanta. Lab technicians whispered to me vaguely about the other missing mail and gone-astray specimens and about the young lady who'd worked there and maybe done it for spite. That young lady had vanished, not even asking for references.

"A pretty, young African-American girl," the lab nurse said. "Her name was Amy Ringer."

"Why would she have done it?"

"Maybe someone said something wrong to her and she just decided to take the incoming mail and vanish. She seemed a very sensitive girl."

Nothing turned up. Nothing arrived or was returned in the hospital's mail.

I'm admittedly paranoid. I have reasons to be that way.

I soon decided that some cunning psycho had tried to kill Jo. Or maybe, instead of trying to cause her death, he/she/they had hoped to leave her as she now was, lost, alone, and fallen, captive in an institution filled with the halt and lame, the crazies, and the dying.

Or maybe I was meant to be the victim and something had gone wrong.

I went back to the bench without great enthusiasm. I tried bench cases and jury trials. I went to the office each day and put in my hours.

I sentenced people to prison when I believed I should send them there, and let them go on probation when that seemed right.

And aging Judge Robak, knight of the night, in love with my Jo, watched and waited. I sniffed the air of Bington, revenge in mind, looking for any faint track that might remain out there for me to discover.

I had many enemies.

2

ABOUT FIVE MONTHS after Jo became ill I sat in a wing chair behind the bench, wearing the only black robe I ever planned to own. Most times I didn't wear a judge's robe, but instead wore a dark business suit or a muted sport coat.

The robe had been a gift from the lawyers of the Bington and Mojeff County bar given to me on the day I was sworn in as judge. I'd been robed in great ceremony with several hundred witnesses present.

Now, Robak, you're a judge.

Donning a robe doesn't make a person a good judge. It only makes the false wearer (I many times felt both false and stupid) another clown masquerading as a judge. I thought it likely that the world had more inadequate clowns than competent judges.

The only time I always wore the robe was in juvenile hearings. Kids needed it and it gave me at least a chance they'd listen to me.

On this morning the case pending before me for more pretrial would also benefit from the robe, shined black shoes, and a completely serious demeanor. I wore all those. I had, early on, assumed my very best frown.

I thought about my Jo and that kept the frown more real. Her nurse had gotten her fresh and clean before I'd arrived for the morning visit. I'd sat next to Jo and remembered earlier, far better times.

Jo had been propped high in bed, staring straight ahead at the single small window and watching the sunlight that entered her room.

She'd smiled at the window while I'd told her what was to happen today and what had happened yesterday in court. The smile was probably because she liked the sunny window and had once greatly loved the world that lay beyond it.

Sometimes I thought she understood bits of what I said, but only tiny pieces.

After a while she'd lost interest in all my judicial nonsense and turned away from me, closing her eyes. I'd watched her and wished my one and only wish for perhaps the hundred thousandth time. That wish was that I could remove what was wrong from her, inject it into myself in fair exchange, please God, and make her well again.

Sometimes when I visited her tiny room I thought she was angry with me and I would try to figure out a reason. I'd always return to the fact that I was well and she was not.

Life isn't fair.

I remembered that someone else had used exactly those words to me in a recent letter. That someone was Damion Darius Wolfer, a man a bit over my age, an oversized, strong man much used to getting his own way. I'd never formally met Wolfer or listened to him speak outside of court, but I'd heard his testimony and seen him, day after day, in court. Most days he'd sat in clean work clothes, but on his son's sentencing day, now five years back, he'd worn a dark brown robe and carried an eight-foot-long wooden staff, perhaps to imitate and be contemptuous of me, my black robe, and my damnable gavel.

On the day he'd worn his robe and carried his staff into the courtroom I'd sentenced his son to death. This was after a trial in which the son had been found guilty by a petit jury of the bloody murders of two preteen girls.

Damion Darius Wolfer's letter had first proclaimed forcefully that life wasn't fair and then asked me to substitute him on death row for his son. He'd written he was surely as guilty as his son if I truly believed his son had killed the two victims. He'd raised his son and wrote he was therefore responsible for him. He'd asked me to come talk to him, man to man, about his offer or allow him to come talk to me in private outside of the courthouse. It seemed a serious letter.

Would I, please?

No. The law doesn't work that way.

The courtroom was uncomfortably hot around me, but I'd taught myself not to publicly notice. Three autocratic county commissioners (whom I'd privately nicknamed Larry, Curly, and Moe) ignored all my temperature complaints. Earlier, after the board's indignant refusal to even listen to me about problems, I'd successfully mandated them to install expensive metal weapons detectors and also station deputy sheriffs at both ends of my courtroom hall.

That had angered them, especially after they'd discovered that Mojeff County also had to pay my mandate attorney's fees along with their own.

I thought one day soon I might send a deputy sheriff down to fetch me those three commissioners on one of their meeting days. I'd have the deputy escort them to the rear of my courtroom, and then order them to sit in the pewlike hardwood seats and do the county's business for a full, hot day, only half an hour off for lunch. They'd find out better on that day the reason why this building we inhabited together was called a "court" house.

But I'd let such await the outcome of the May primary and I'd wait also for a meeting day that fell on a steamy heated day during Bington's coming spring-summer.

Keep your head down for now, Robak.

I again gave the perspiring lawyer in front of the bench my attention.

The Louisville *Courier-Journal* had described today's case in their learned pages as: "One of the largest civil-damage controversies ever heard in Indiana's state courts." Then they had added, "being heard by freshman Circuit Judge Donald Robak of Mojeff County." They could have added: "Who once killed a man during a trial in the same courtroom where he now presides."

For reasons unknown they'd left the killing out of their news story.

Freshman Robak. Killer Robak. Now near the end of my first term, and facing opposition in the upcoming primary. Also burdened with a sick-sick wife who lived apart from me in a kind of nursing home.

It was mid-April in Bington, a fine time for all to be alive. Outside it was fresh Indiana spring. Winter had been ice, sleet, freezing rain, and blizzard snows. We'd not seen much bare ground for a couple of months. Now, beyond the courtroom windows, trees showed fat leaf buds and I could see coveys of sunwarmed squirrels playing their unruly games of tree tag while robins stood guard.

I'd told Jo about the squirrels and robins and she'd stared, smiled, and tried her seldom-used vocabulary out on me.

"Gump. Ched. Indow." A smile and hands that shook in constant movement.

Outside there were already both wild and tame flowers, violets, windproof buttercups, lovely daffodils, and tall tulips. Sometime soon, when the flowers grew more thickly, I'd ask the courthouse gardener to cut me a bouquet. I'd then take the flowers to my Jo. Even if she ignored them the smell and color would fill her bleak, one-window room and make her good company.

In a few shadowed courthouse yard areas there remained clumps of dirty snow. The wind had gentled and warmed in the last week and the warm sun had melted most of the deep piles to water. Soon it would be golfing weather and I could disgrace myself anew in a fresh season if I could spare the time for such foolishness and away from Jo.

I loved Bington in the springtime more than in any other season. It was an old town for this part of the country and the downtown buildings and homes along and above the ancient river were lovely. Jo's being sick had darkened time for me, but still I couldn't totally ignore the bright sun and the changing of the seasons. We humans seem to be perennials who come back to life each spring. With the world awakening once more my hopes were renewed that Jo would improve with the weather and that she would soon grow miraculously better. Her doctor, Hugo S. Buckner, believed it could happen. Doc was an incredible optimist who also believed in visions created in his mind by double gin martinis with extra olives taken orally and often at the bar of the downtown Moose.

He prescribed such medications only for himself and forbade them to me.

Bailiff Wade "Preacher" Smyth entered the back door of the courtroom silently. I saw him sniffing the air and inspecting the dark part of the ceiling.

My courtroom had acquired a wet smell as the weather moderated. Up high the musty ceiling was dark enough to devour all but the most direct light. Courthouse workers, janitors, and even office holders had whispered to me that the roof was leaking onto my ceiling again. They told me the leaks were from winter ice and snow damage to the old roof. Some of them grinned smugly and said I ought to do something about it.

Each time they'd warned me I'd sent another certified letter to my pals, the three commissioners.

There had already been blowing spring rains. The Ohio River appeared likely to rise as it did most years and flood its shores. My river operated on its own time schedule and asked no legal advice.

The courtroom ceiling would likely sometime play out its role.

Preacher, a practical scientist, had named the discolored ceiling area the Black Hole of Bington. He was of the opinion that one day soon it would bulge open, spew hidden water, and then, in getting its breath back, suck up the courthouse, the sheriff's office, most of the surrounding town of Bington, and hopefully all three county commissioners.

The head janitor had warned me gloomily, after an inspection, that some plaster definitely would fall, maybe more of it than in all previous spring/summers. He'd also told me he'd seen returning birds building nests in the cupola and attic under the stopped clocks that peered blindly north, south, east, and west.

By summer's end those birds could turn my courtroom into an aviary.

"It's pretty damn wet up there, you know," he'd commented. "And I swear I done like you told me and informed the commissioners several times about it, Jedge."

"What'd they say?" I'd asked curiously, knowing he'd not tell all because the commissioners were the ones who'd hired and paid him.

"One of them said cuss words, but he ain't from your party, Jedge. Your official letters sure pisses them guys off." He'd grinned at me. "None of them commissioners is from your party. Neither am I, but I likes you okay. I can't vote for you in the primary, but I promise I'll help you if you need a extra vote come this fall." He looked around carefully, perhaps afraid that some political hack from his party was listening and making notes about such treachery.

I'd nodded.

Now I waited and watched.

Preacher claimed that he could foretell when something bad was about to happen. He'd guessed a few days back that the coming Black Hole disaster wouldn't occur for a while. I was loath to argue with him because he was a gifted man. No one argued with Preacher now that he'd quit drinking. In truth only a few had argued when he'd been a heavy-hitter alcoholic.

"She might collapse about the first jury trial of the spring, Judge," Preacher predicted. "Best hope for your sake that such is

18

after the primary because you'll get your ass blamed for the damage by the commissioners if it's preprimary. That's in spite of all your letters. They'll lose them."

"I made copies."

"Best lock them up in a secret place."

"I will do that and then I will damn well publish them," I said.

The hearing and arguments continued in front of me unabated. No one had noticed my mental absence.

I now mostly liked being circuit judge, having gotten used to it. I particularly liked its regular pay and its medical insurance that provided care for Jo. Some days I didn't care for the tedium and that was when I remembered when I'd been an adventurous trial practitioner, doing lots of criminal cases, defending clients wrongfully accused. I'd claimed openly I didn't take the cases of the guilty and the then prosecutor had smiled, his mouth looking like an open knife, and replied he damn well didn't file cases against those who were innocent.

Jo had been well.

I was now five years, three months, and a couple of weeks into judicial office. Next month there would be a primary election. My friends and former legal partners liked to tell me I faced only "token opposition," a likable young lawyer with a white-toothed smile improbably named Lance Jason Tacker. He was two years in Bington, barely out of law school, perhaps trying to get some name recognition. Some of the young girls who worked in the courthouse had described him to me as either hot or cute. Some had breathed hard while talking.

That young man was running earnestly, knocking on doors, seeking my job. Like me he wasn't Bington-born. Such was encouraging.

Some days I believed my friends when they said he was only token opposition. But nights, sleeping alone and cold on half of Jo and my jointly owned king-sized bed, I didn't.

* ★ ★

"The lawyers on the other side of this hugely important case have all but ignored your discovery orders, Your Honor," Anthony Pellingham complained to me severely. He'd come riding in his Jaguar ("Buy American" sticker on the back bumper) to the hinterlands of Bington from his hundred-member Indianapolis firm. He was a tall, persuasive man, a good lawyer, and I'd heard an even better club tennis player. Today he was angry enough for both of us at the heinous violations of the rules of procedure committed by his opposition.

His five associates, three women and two men, who had taken up all the space at two south-side counsel tables, nodded. One of the ladies tapped a fist silently against the counsel table for added emphasis.

My belief is that attorneys think they can snow a judge better by having more lawyers on their side of the courtroom than the wrongheaded, stupid, smaller bunch across from them. Or perhaps lawyers are like women at a cocktail party who seem only to be able to use ladies' room conveniences if they proceed there in talkative coveys.

In the spectator section of the courtroom half a dozen of Pellingham's clients, all owners of large dollars' worth of stock in Macing Drugs, shook their heads and whispered among themselves encouragingly.

Sic 'em for us, Judge.

At another counsel table on the north side of the courtroom there was a smaller squad of lawyers, just four of them, and only one of them female. They were chiefed by one of the Bington area's leading trial lawyers, Eugene Smithham. That group shook their heads piously and waited their turn at bat.

Behind that group sat their three aristocratic Bington-born-and-bred clients, two salt-and-pepper-haired late-fortyish men named Albert and Beauregard Macing and their stunning, early-fortyish, three-times-engaged, three-times-unengaged sister named Libra Phoebe "Libbie" Macing. She carried an umbrella that was as black as my robe and her own dark heart. She lifted it threateningly at appropriate moments. She also watched me unblinkingly. I was now, most of the time, a bug to her.

The three owned large, large, large dollars' worth of Macing Drugs, enough of a holding among the three of them to at least claim Macing Drug Company stock control.

On their jointly owned and occupied farm estate the Macings raised Arabian horses and lots of late-night party hell, some of it political in nature in this election year.

Twenty-plus years back, for a fine, adventurous time, Libbie Macing had owned me, but only for eleven months, ten days, and six and a half hours. That had happened when she took leave from her job at Macing Drugs to finish up her doctorate in chemistry at the university and also get a side degree in business administration. She was now the president of Macing, but she and her two brothers ran it together.

My parting with Libbie had not been completely amicable. We had not spoken much to each other since, only a snarl or two. Plus I knew, thanks to caller ID, that she was the identifiable one of the night ladies who sometimes called me and breathed intimately into my phone.

I thought she might now be remembering good times past as she watched me through her pretty, gem-encrusted glasses. Sometimes she would study me and then whisper things to her brothers and all would smile companionably.

She was on my list of Jo suspects, but twenty years and three engagements to other men is a long time to carry a romantic grudge. Besides, I thought she'd want to hurt me and not Jo.

The two women had even become kind of friends. Jo had told me, more than once, that they got along well when they played golf or bridge.

I knew the Macing threesome lived luxuriously in their fenced and guarded mansion. The estate around it was bluegrass, dotted with palatial horse barns filled with Arabian horses. Jo and I had visited the estate a time or two for joint Bington Chamber of Commerce and Macing Drugs annual parties.

It was estimated by the newspapers that the Macings were worth several billion dollars.

I'd informed all counsel of such visits. I'd even described the massive crowd. I'd not mentioned the rumors about wealth because that much wealth was beyond belief. I'd confessed my dating of Libbie.

Jo had been told long ago about Libbie and me. Libbie was pre-Jo and there'd been no Libbie since Jo and I had begun dating and had later married. Jo sometimes had mentioned Libbie to me nastily when she was angry, but only to use her name, knowing there was no real scab to pick.

The Macing lawsuit was about control. At a corporate meeting almost six years back the complainants charged that the election of the board of directors had been illegal and that all actions taken since then by the illegal board were therefore also illegal. By its then rewritten corporate articles Macing only elected directors once every six years despite a conflicting phrase in the original articles of incorporation and perhaps in violation of the Indiana state statutes.

There was still a bit more time to go before there'd be a new corporate election.

The plaintiffs contended that elections must be held every year, not every six years, although the directors could have longer staggered terms. In addition they claimed that the board member Macing trio in charge were keeping dividends low in order to drive down the price of the stock so they could snatch up the stock of minority stockholders illegally. The complaint also alleged other ways that the Macings operated illegally, seventeen pages of fire and brimstone.

I remembered when I'd arrived in Bington a long time back that Macing Drugs had then been a sleepy, quarter-billion-dollar company, a medium-sized frog in the Bington pond. That was before a bright Macing research chemist had chanced upon Corwinsil Plus for cancer. After that halcyon time a squad of other bright chemists had found various additional nostrums, mostly for cancer, and Corwinsil had faded into disuse after ten billion dollars or so in sales.

Macing's four lawyers had answered some of the complainant's interrogatories and filed objections to the rest. That was the center of today's fuss. I knew all this from a reading of the pertinent parts of my thick case file.

I wasn't a lazy judge, but I was sometimes a confused one, particularly in complicated civil cases.

This was a hotly contested civil case. I guessed that the plaintiffs were trying to obtain some settlement that would benefit them.

A local reporter I knew by both sight and the friendly exchange of mutual insults in local coffee and scotch houses sat scribbling, covering for the local paper and likely also stringing for the Louisville and/or Indianapolis newspapers. He saw me looking out at him and winked companionably.

My right knee knocked against my hideout weapon under the bench.

That made me remember that I had troubles other than the Macing case, the upcoming primary, and the angry relatives and friends of two murderous gentlemen up on death row at Michigan City.

Under the bench, because of the one actual attack on my home and several dozen anonymous mail and telephone threats, I now kept a single-shot, truncated Winchester 840 twelve-gauge shotgun. The gun was only an inch or so over the federal length limit. Such shortness allowed it to fit snugly under the bench out of sight of all but me. Earlier, before court convened, I'd practiced drawing it out of its secret place and then sliding it back.

Quick Draw Robak, scourge of the southern Indiana courts.

I'd unloaded the shotgun for my practice time, but now it was again loaded with a double-aught buckshot shell with reloads in a near drawer. I'd tried out the shotgun a few times on the police range and it had kicked harder than a losing client. It had then removed all in its path with spreading deadly slugs.

23

Pellingham paused, turned, and sneered at the opposition. "What these people are doing is criminal in nature, Your Honor. This court must sanction them for it."

Pellingham's clients arose in unison like cheerleaders at an opposing team's fumble.

"Your Honor!" Smithham cried, seemingly outraged.

Clients on both sides of the courtroom glared at one another.

I thought about offering my shotgun to the highest bidder. It seemed a good idea. I could make a lot of money to help pay the substantial, uninsured parts of Jo's doctor and nursing bills.

But we were doing okay financially. There was enough money. Over and above what I was paid by the state and county, Jo had inherited money from a deceased uncle.

I banged the gavel. I seldom used it, but it seemed specially crafted for the damnable Macing case.

The opposing sides had their clients attend every hearing, perhaps hoping to exert pressure on candidate me.

I remembered more history: Macing Drugs had been founded in Bington about a hundred years back. Early on it had made alcohol-based cough medicines, headache powders, and pills for ladies suffering from monthly maladies. It had earned the early Macings a living, then much more than that.

The two original Macing founders had died after siring large, contentious families. Members of those families had married and had numerous children. There had been divorces and stockholder fights before, plus more marriages and children. There were now Macings out in the world who were doctors, lawyers, merchants, bankrupts, and dope dealers.

Many a Macing labored in the local plant.

As the business had grown new blood had been coaxed in. Stock had been given to bright newcomers as job and work incentives by the free-acting and rich company. Now many locals and nonlocals owned Macing stock. The total number of issued shares had been one of the questions asked by the plaintiffs of the defendants and had been answered indirectly by a copy of a report showing how much money had been paid out in dividends, both totally and per share.

The stock traded only over the counter. I'd heard fantastic prices quoted as bid and ask. There seemed to be none available except when a stockholder died without issue.

My file contained a dozen depositions complaining that dividends were unreasonably low and a dozen more insisting dividends were generous.

I'd heard gossip that a megabig pharmaceutical company, or maybe more than one megabig, desired to absorb the Macing company. All hush-hush and not a part of the civil case I was hearing—yet.

"Here's what I hope to have happen, gentlemen," I said. "I'm now setting this case for trial before the court next Tuesday. That's a two-day period both sides already had scheduled for more pretrial. Instead of pretrial we'll start trial instead. I will decide all motions still pending on that day and set sanctions if need be. I've signed many a discovery order in this matter and held a dozen hearings, pretrials and the like. Down the months and years not a lot has happened except heat without light. It makes me wonder whether anything will ever happen. Both sides have declined arbitration, which appears to this court as a logical way for this case to reach fair settlement or decision. Both sides have also waived a jury so I realize that I must make sense of this in a bench trial late or soon. So we'll start a trial next week and see how far we can go."

"I have other matters set in various courts in the days immediately after next Tuesday," Smithham said ominously. "Some of such settings are in the federal courts."

"As do I," Pellingham said, nodding up at me coldly. He'd not tried to challenge me as judge in the Macing case when I'd assumed the bench. Now he could be regretting it. So, perhaps, could local lawyer Smithham. He was a first-class legal brain who made most of his money by being constantly angry on behalf of his clients in court and out.

Early on, had either side filed anything that hinted at possible prejudice, I'd have recused myself. I did know a lot of gossip about Bington's biggest employer. And Libbie and I had been combative, open lovers twenty-plus years ago, the talk of Bington until we'd split. No matter what happened I was going to be called unfair.

Several times when I'd been a one-term member of the Indiana general assembly I'd had my vote openly solicited by Libbie's brothers along with hints whispered that I'd be well rewarded if I did as I was asked/ordered.

I'd never qualified for the rewards even when Libbie personally asked for such favors and happily gave her own incentives up front.

In fact I'd done nothing in my dealings with the Macings to harm my reputation for never doing as I was told.

I remembered that a few weeks before Jo had gotten sick we'd gone to yet another of the huge annual Halloween parties at the Macing mansion, a lavish party thrown jointly by the Bington Chamber of Commerce and Macing Drugs. I'd called other local and area judges before going. All were attending and I knew that going to a Macing community party wasn't going to influence any decision of mine.

I said now, "Both parties scheduled more motions plus additional pretrial for next week. I'm hoping that if we work late and hard both days I can decide all pending motions and then hear some evidence. Other evidence can be submitted by deposition or at a future agreed trial date. In other words I plan to dispose of this case this year."

I waited. No one said anything.

"Isn't it a question of numbers, of who owns and legally voted the most stock in the election?" I asked curiously.

"Plus fairness, equity, and outright illegality," Pellingham added. "Notices of various corporate meetings were often sent late to minority shareholders. Many owners of Macing stock were never informed of meetings even after this suit was filed. Plus the facts and statutory and case law strongly suggest that the election was rigged."

Smithham answered tartly: "Your votes, if all were cast for your board candidates, would not have changed any prior election outcome or win for you in any new one. The Macing family, the two brothers and one sister, own and control more shares than all the rest of the stock owners, many of whom are Macing relatives."

"So you proclaim." Pellingham answered. "We don't believe that. We do believe they've issued a flood of stock and stock options illegally to themselves."

"Would you want to try it on that basis alone, Mr. Pellingham? That we could do next week."

"Of course not."

The two lawyers gave each other ready-to-fight looks. I thought it was possible they'd repair somewhere and drink coffee and gently converse to see what could be done to settle the case when they left the courtroom. I'd heard they were good friends.

"I think both of us must protest this unseemly haste," Pellingham said.

"I agree, but it's the only thing we do agree about with the plaintiffs," Smithham said. "We don't even agree that they have a right to bring this particular action or, for that matter, any action at all. We've filed motions to dismiss that bring such questions before this court."

"I realize these things," I said. "We're on the record and both your protests are therefore duly noted and will be taken into account," I continued. "We'll rethink things next week, nine-thirty A.M. Tuesday. Come, gentlemen. Surely a yea or nay decision in this case can't be completely distasteful. The loser and perhaps the winner can then hie the case on to the eagerly waiting state appellate courts."

Pellingham looked pensive. Smithham glanced down at his counsel table, his face unreadable.

I knew Pellingham mostly by reputation, but I knew Smithham personally. I hadn't forced them to trial because I believed that either lawyer was delaying things to milk the case for fees. Some lawyers will, some won't. These two lawyers weren't de-layers for the benefit of billable hours. They were both good, honest lawyers, as such things go.

There was likely some unknown (to me) reason why both sides didn't yet want their day in court. I didn't know what that reason was, but there had to be one. Maybe a new election of directors was brewing. Maybe there was already secret talk of settlement. Maybe both sides were waiting to see if someone huge would buy out Macing Drugs and make them all either megarich or megaricher.

I would ask Jo to solve the problem for me tomorrow morning and she would, as always, give her advice by staring at my face, then the walls and ceiling, and saying the words I couldn't un-derstand. Plus she would smile her fine smile at me.

3

THE WORD SPREAD that the Macing hearing, expected to take at least all morning and probably much of the afternoon, had finished for the day. That meant Judge Robak was available.

I went though a pile of legal files on my desk and signed things. I also ordered in a cardboardwich for lunch from an old but enterprising restaurant on Main Street, which delivered.

My aging, sweet-and-sour court reporter, Evelyn Haas, a long-time courthouse veteran and a noted enemy of law-book salesmen and dilatory lawyers, ran things from her office outside my office. Now and then she'd limp inside my office, nod, and announce lawyers singly or in crowds. The limp came from a stroke four years back which had crippled her body more than she'd admit, but had left her bright and acid mind untouched.

Some members of area bars irreverently called her "Miss Kiss My Haas." Once, years back, I'd been one of those lazy, semi-secret name callers.

By the time administrative turmoil slowed, much of it being cases set, continued, or now agreed, it was past two in the afternoon.

My lady prosecutor was waiting. Two prisoners were brought over from the jail and I did initial hearings on them, more or less begging them to hire a lawyer or let me appoint one.

When that was done I listened to a hot dissolution, the alternate trial setting for the day. Both husband and wife wanted everything, including custody of a fourteen-year-old redheaded only child named Chuck. The recriminations, tears, and testimony were quickly completed because I insisted on only no-fault evidence and refused to hear testimony about who was the biggest bastard/thief/villain/vow-breaker unless such evidence touched on the spending of family funds on nonfamily purposes.

I repaired to chambers at half past three and there listened to Chuck explain to only me that he wanted to live with his mother after the final dissolution of marriage, but wanted to visit his dad on alternate weekends. He'd reached the age where he could pick his custodial parent unless there was good reason for the court (me) not to accept his choice.

Chuck was heavily freckled, nervous, and good-sized for his age. He was several years younger than my only peerless offspring. Son Joe, since a month-ago birthday, was going on seventeen.

I don't invite opposing lawyers into chambers when I talk to dissolution kids about matters concerning custody. That's because I like children's logic about who should control them better than I like the arguments of the lawyers. Lawyers are paid by their clients to huff and puff. They don't need to make light, merely heat.

"He's sneaky mean, but he's not bad. I get along with him okay," the boy told me, describing his father. "Like he told me kind of in secret yesterday that if I happened to testify that I wanted to be in his custody he'd buy me a Schwinn ten-speed bike this weekend and a train set soon plus a pellet gun next Christmas. I'd sure like to have them things. Schwinns are true cool."

I nodded in agreement. Son Joe was now more into compact discs, cool cars, and proud, pretty high school girls approaching womanhood than bikes, pellet guns, and electric trains, but there'd been a time when trains, bikes, and pellet guns had wowed him.

"Cool" was the exact word he'd then used to describe them. Now sophomore ladies and the mysterious, older, and more curved junior and senior girls plus listening to music were about the coolest things in his life.

All these ran second only to his dream of soon owning a truly hot/cool car now that he'd turned sixteen. He could drive and soon would hold a license rather than a beginner's permit. Just now that was all on hold because he wasn't living in Bington with me.

"You can inform your father that you told me you wanted him to have custody if you want to do that," I offered. "I won't fink on you."

"No, sir. He'd yell it to my mother next time they got mad at each other and then she'd cry."

"Would she believe him?"

Chuck turned his head away, not knowing, but also not smiling. I could tell he was leery of adult me and my easy offer, unsure of what would happen if he fooled about with the awful truth.

"Do either of your parents ever physically punish you?" It was a question I always casually asked. Sometimes answering it would begin confession time for a child and I'd hear things that would tell me where the child *must* be placed. There are secret ogres and insane partners who inhabit marriages and somehow hide bad secrets from an unseeing world.

I wasn't against all family physical punishment, but I was opposed to some of the vicious ways punishment was at times administered.

"No. But sometimes he talks and threatens Mom and the men she goes out with."

"How does he threaten them?"

"He says he's going to beat those guys up and spank Mom on her pizza-fat butt." The idea of the latter actually happening made him smile and shake his head.

"Does your mother ask you about what your father says to you when you're with him?"

He nodded, willing to spill more beans in that area. "She keeps after me until I have to tell her things my dad says to me. Except I don't tell her all of it."

"That's good. You're all right now staying with your mother?"

"Sure."

"And you get enough to eat both places and things like that?"

"Exactly."

"Does your mother leave you by yourself when she goes out at night?"

"Sometimes she does, but it's okay. I'm over fourteen, Judge. Before she made Dad move out of the house they'd both leave me by myself and tell me I was being trusted to stay out of trouble. Left alone I play basketball or do whatever's going on with friends in the neighborhood until it gets dark. Then I do homework and turn on the computer and surf when the studying's done. I can cook pretty good." He grinned likably. "Better than Pop and maybe better than Mom. Nights alone don't bother me much anymore."

I nodded. I remembered six years back when my wife had left me for a time and contemplated completing a filed dissolution. It had been hard on son Joe who'd loved us both in spite of our joint, mutual stupidities. In that time she'd managed to stay out from under interested men and I'd managed to stay away from interested women.

We'd reconciled. We'd compromised. Then we'd become enthusiastic about it.

Many children of divorce become ring smart. They learn to use their divorcing parents. The husband-versus-wife war becomes a place where a child can win a few battles of his/her own and take possession of some high ground.

I wrote out my home telephone number on the back of my business card. "Take this and put it away somewhere where you can find it, Chuck. If things go bad, one way or the other, call this number. It's my office. If there's no answer then leave a message. If you lose the card both my home number and office numbers are listed in the telephone book. Call the office during daytime, my home number at night. I likely won't answer, but I'll get back to you." I spelled out my name for him despite the fact it was on the card. "Call and say to whoever answers or to the recording machine that your name is Red Chuck."

"Red Chuck?"

"It's kind of a secret code. Then leave a message. I'll get your message and we'll talk some more. Don't tell anyone else about this, not your father, not your mother. Okay?"

"I guess."

"I'm not going to decide your father and mother's dissolution case for a while. We'll give them a little more time to work things out. If you want them together do what you can."

He nodded, liking the secrecy. Like most kids, he'd eventually tell both parents what I'd said. Some parents, when they learned what I had said to their offspring, became irritated and tried to reach me at the courthouse, which they found difficult because of the good Evelyn Haas. Most eventually called their lawyers and raised hell at the place where they'd paid their money.

A few moments later I invited the lawyers representing Red Chuck's parents into chambers and solemnly took the case under advisement. Both of them shook their heads.

"Okay, Your Honor," one lawyer said resignedly. "But I bet this pair won't work out even the time of day. These folks hate each other with more passion than high school lovers love each other. Both have recently taken significant others on board in their sex lives."

"Surely you jest," I said. "Why, that's both immoral and illegal."

Both lawyers laughed and nodded. I noted one more time that Judge Robak was a wiser and funnier man than lawyer Robak had ever been. I also saw once more that lawyers aren't interested in a judge who's Solomon, but in one who decides cases quickly and who's reasonably predictable. I seldom held a case under advisement long. They knew that.

I tried to be predictable. I dislike divorces-dissolutions. They've grown to be the easy way out for too many couples who'd be better off solving their problems through discourse rather than intercourse with new, temporarily exciting partners. Most couples trade down. One judge before me said it was the eternal quest for the better 'ole and/or larger staff.

But I admit not all marriages are put together in heaven.

The local bar had kept close watch after Jo became ill and waited to see if I'd change. Some thought I'd sour and become surly and smartass. Others thought I'd fall behind and put off things that aided the bar's financial survival. Some believed I'd drink and chase women.

Most now agreed I was doing okay even if I was, occasionally, a little crazy. I laughed. They therefore laughed.

It was my world. They only wanted to live in it.

Outside my office, as the lawyers departed, I could hear Evelyn Haas talking to a persistent law-book salesman who'd tried to wait her out and catch me at rest in order to assault me with his sales list. I'd earlier heard her telling him coldly there would be no time for me to see him on this day. It was now four o'clock and a sign in the hall announced we closed down at four.

"There's a lawyer's book committee. They report to the judge," she told the salesman in nasal tones. "See them."

"Have a good day, Miss Haas," the salesman called to her from the hall, almost missing the *h* in her last name.

"Thank you," she said, her voice cold as a January creek. "But I have other plans."

I now loved Evelyn dearly. She'd worked for Judge Harner and for the also deceased, legendary Judge Steinmetz, who'd once been my law partner after he was off the bench. At times during those years, I'd not been her ardent fan, but I was now. She knew more law than I'd ever know, but she wasn't pushy about it. The worst outward thing she did was wince openly when I announced a bum decision in which she failed to concur.

She also loved and worried about my wife, her friend and bridge-game sister. She visited Jo, being one of the few who knew where both wife Jo and son, Joe, now resided.

34

I'd made up my mind that if she tried to retire I would talk Preacher into marrying her.

And so it went for the rest of Thursday's judicial day. We eventually did close, but there were still things to do, orders and judgments unsigned that must be examined and then duly signed. I sat first for a few moments of quiet time, ignoring duties. I examined again what I could see of the brand-new Hoosier spring outside my third-floor window. The sun was out and people were walking outside without coats. Store owners and employees broomed their sidewalks, taking advantage of the warmth. The bank temperature sign read 62.

I knew it would likely grow cold again. Usually it did so just in time to ruin the annual peach crop across the Ohio River in Kentucky.

There were no placard-toting protesters outside the courthouse on this day. Protesters came on schedules of their own. The most persistent were those against the death penalty. Sometimes there'd be other angry or curious people interested in whatever was happening in my court or in Judge Fred F. Fred's busy superior court downstairs.

I guessed the weather was too fine for protesters today.

From another angle I could see the front wall of the courthouse yard. Many of the sitters there were old friends or acquaintances. There were several I didn't recognize. One looked high fortyish and was dressed in clean jeans and a bright jacket. He was looking up at my window.

Maybe a watcher.

There were people who came to my court and made notes about all I did. Groupers. Members of anti–drunk driving clubs, MADD and SADD, mostly good people, a few of them half-crazed by family loss. I was also sometimes visited by those interested in husband's rights and grandparent's rights.

Keeping count.

It was the kind of temperate day that Jo and I had once used for long walks. But Jo hadn't walked without help since her illness. She might never walk unaided again.

Thinking about Jo made me become, without shame, wet eyed. I liked to tell friends that I'd cried all my tears about Jo, but I hadn't. Not by a barrel. I didn't cry enough to make myself completely unhappy about the world. I spread the tears out and tried for happy, fun times in between.

I tried again to figure out what someone or someones had caused Jo's illness. That would help solve the mystery of how they'd managed it. I had no real evidence to mull over, but still I raged inwardly and plotted against the presumed guilty. I'd once told the circuit prosecuting attorney about my suspicions. She and I got along well enough, despite her belonging to the opposite political party.

She'd made a few notes and then smiled at me.

"Judge, you must realize you have no real evidence. In fact, you can't even make a guess about who done it if anyone did."

"Please have your people look for evidence," I'd said gently.

"Sure," she'd said.

We'd dismissed each other, our relationship still cordial.

She was good at her job. I had no right to bug her, but instead must bug myself.

I took a few phone calls. One was from a Floydsburg lawyer who asked me to reconfirm I'd be along to his town tomorrow, Friday afternoon, for an agreed hearing.

I promised him again I'd be there.

Floydsburg was the city where I'd sentenced Damion Darius Wolfer's son to death, but the case for tomorrow had nothing to do with that murder.

Eventually, near five, we locked the office doors and I went home.

It was not a casual ride. A deputy sheriff in an unmarked car rode in front of me and a local police officer, also in an unmarked car, drove behind. I'd had multiple threats, some of them possibly coming from several militant and crazed groups of local and area freedom-first citizen patriots, others from antideath-penalty zealots. I wasn't exactly afraid, but I tried to be careful.

I'd sentenced young Wolfer, double child killer, to death. I'd also sentenced another defendant to death and the antideath folks liked to carry signs showing me looking down at the bright red blood dripping off both my hands.

I also had other enemies, some in prison, some not. Several times I'd made an educated guess about the total number of known enemies, some left over from my past legal life, and some from my more recent judicial one. I'd gotten past twenty with ease.

There was a man I'd sent to prison for fifty years after he was jury-convicted of killing his wife. He was now out and free to travel and plan after a governor's Christmas pardon I'd frowned publicly on.

The governor and I were not friends. I'd not much liked him before his act of pardon. I liked him less now.

That piece of released dogshit hated me. He also had family money. But law officers, checking, said he'd moved to Michigan, and that he remained there.

Still, he was a clever man. Anyone angry and clever can plan to kill.

I recalled for the nth time that Judge Harner, who'd been circuit judge before me, had received threats. He'd ignored them and one day he'd died, shot to death while sitting behind his bench trying a routine dissolution-of-marriage case.

Harner was now more than five years in his grave. At the time he'd been killed I'd been present in his courtroom and had taken a single bullet in the gut from the angry, militant citizen killer, a large, lumpy redneck who'd violently disagreed with Indiana's dissolution-of-marriage laws.

The shooter was also dead. I'd whacked him to death with a heavy counsel chair as he was in the act of shooting me because I was his wife's attorney.

I remembered that day well, never with sorrow for the deceased assailant, but always with regret for Harner, a first-class judge who should still be sitting behind the bench where I now sat.

Medically I was recovered, but there were patriot citizens who'd like it if I wasn't.

I was careful and went armed. Deputy sheriffs guarded my stairwells. They sat at opposite ends of the hall ordering those who arrived by elevator and stairs through new, state-of-the-art weapons detectors. If anything hot was going on in the courtroom the west deputy would lock his entrance door and come into the courtroom, hitching his gun belt, frowning out at the crowd and smiling up at me. He and I sometimes fished together and he liked me.

The county commissioners made public fun of the detectors in this election year. They cited the heavy price the county had paid for the detectors and added to their list of grievances the salaries of the deputies who manned the checkpoints.

I hoped they were't getting results from their jibes.

I'd been shot. Harner had been shot and killed. Larry, Curly, and Moe hadn't.

County commissioners seldom make all their constituents happy. There's just not enough asphalt to pave and routinely re-surface every gravel road unless your home county has a gambling boat. I wondered if one day someone armed and angry about lack of asphalt would visit the commissioners' meeting. Such was something to think on happily.

I had my full-sized shotgun propped against the front passenger seat on my way home. I was driving my old, dependable Ford. The gun was a twelve-gauge pump. I'd been taught the rudiments of firing it and had practiced with it on a dozen occasions.

I went armed with shotguns because a local office holder, first-term Sheriff Jumper Jimp, had informed the various area police departments involved that I couldn't hit an elephant in the ass with a revolver when close enough to feed peanuts to such animal.

"Might as well arm him with a bent umbrella as give him a handgun," he'd stated caustically. "The most likely person he'd shoot would be himself."

No one attacked us on this lovely spring day.

A couple of times someone waved to me from the sidewalk or from a passing car. Hopefully they didn't notice my armed escort.

I waved back, smiling and nodding, remembering my upcoming primary.

I'd sold Jo's Olds. If she recovered and relearned how to drive I'd buy her a brand-new car, whatever she wanted.

I knew my worn Ford and liked it. It was dependable.

A car was parked in my drive. It was a fifteen-year-old brown Chevrolet which sometimes ran and most times didn't. It belonged to my friend Morris M. Mellish, a minister of the gospel, who was temporarily staying with me. His second church, which Jo and I had attended, had burned two years back, making him churchless again. Sometimes he held Sunday services in my oversized living room. Sometimes, when he could find one available, he used borrowed churches.

The blinds on the picture window were closed. Such meant that the good Reverend Mo wasn't at my home. Were he present then the blinds would be open.

Mo preached here and there in southeastern Indiana. Sometimes people of various colors came for him and he rode in cars with them, looking at church sites, preaching when asked or allowed, doing weddings and funerals, comforting those who needed it, and praying for the dying. He seldom left me a note, but if he was coming back to my house after dark he'd call in before arriving.

I stood for a time in my front yard while the officers checked things over inside the house. They unlocked my front security door and then entered.

The sky was blue, the sun was warm, and I could look down at the muddy Ohio River. The world smelled both sweetly and sourly of spring and new life, of that which now lived and of that which had recently died.

There were flower and weed smells all intermixed with the pungent smell of a skunk who'd bombed away in some not too distant area.

Two vapor trails made a large **X** in the sky above. It looked as if giants were playing tic-tac-toe up in the high blue. I was allowed to see only a part of the game board.

The skunk had been a strong one.

I watched a towboat move in slow, stately fashion upriver, going somewhere.

My Jo had loved her river view and had looked forward last year to how it would appear in spring. Thinking about her brought again a strong sense of loss and longing. I missed her more than I'd ever missed anyone.

I missed her so much and remembered her so well that I had remained celibate.

After she'd become sick someone had killed her kitten when it strayed from near the house. The killer had shot the tiny kitten with a green feathered arrow. I still had the arrow. Someone had also poisoned most of the squirrels that inhabited our trees and the rabbits that lived in my yard and its bushes.

On the street across from our house, down a few lots, a large, new residence was being framed. Empty lots in the rest of the subdivision shared a thousand-plus trees. The lots were estate-sized tracts, two to three acres each in size, costing many dollars. Building had been nonexistent during the frozen winter, but would likely resume now. The area was called "Heiter Hills," but downtown it was nicknamed "High Dollar Hills."

I thought about Robert Frost and the snowy woods of winter he'd known that I'd never know.

I did know my town and my neighborhood.

I liked bits of poetry these days, and saved a few memorized lines for special times when I handed down a tough decision. I'd found that dead poets owned words (known also to Preacher, my bailiff) that I could blatantly steal and yet remain unpunished.

I knew a judge in northern Indiana who took many pills and drinks trying to ease constant arthritic pain. His wife was five years dead of cancer, and his only child, a nineteen-year-old daughter, had been killed by a drunk driver who lived just four blocks from the judge.

Once, when he'd been with me on the town in Indianapolis, he'd told me that he still had to resist walking those four short blocks, knocking on the drunk driver's door, and then shotgunning the bastard's brains down his hall.

That judge often read his decisions in open court. He got along pretty well because he was, like the judges who'd preceded me on the local bench, good at the business even if he now drank too much and at the wrong times. Even when he was drinking he sometimes went to the local MADD meetings and was treated warmly and gently there.

Some of us called him the "taxi judge," because he would not drink and drive. I agreed with him that such was a splendid idea.

Joe, my son, was elsewhere for this day/week/month/year. He'd departed under my orders and with my blessings soon after the unknown someone had shot into our home back in January. On weekends, making dead sure I wasn't followed, I sometimes flew to Chicago to see him.

A couple of times he'd come home and we'd secretly visited his mother.

The Bington policeman, whose name was Bob, and the deputy sheriff, whose name was also Bob, continued looking around inside my house until they were certain it was empty.

I then stood in the entrance hall while they did a quick search of the nearby grounds.

The broken picture window and blinds had been repaired and replaced months ago. Inside there remained scars where three steel-jacketed slugs had struck parts of the living room and ricocheted about, missing me narrowly. I'd hired someone to fix everything, but he'd not come yet. Or perhaps he'd not come because he was afraid of getting shot at.

Jo and Joe had also been in the house at the time of the attack. Jo had been upstairs in her bed being watched by a nurse on a scheduled shift. Jo's lights were off and she lay sleeping heavily.

Our son had been watching pro basketball on television in his partly darkened room.

41

I'd been downstairs in the light, but behind living room shades. I'd been lucky one more time, using up another of my cat lives. Not many left now.

Deputy Sheriff Bob nodded at me politely when the officers were satisfied with prowling the house.

He said laconically, "Two cars will be by in the morning about eightish, Judge. Please wait inside your front door for them. Make sure your inner doors are bolted and the outer security doors are locked. We'll patrol this way during the night as usual. So will the city boys. Someone comes sneaking in, we'll be on your intruder like huntin' dogs on a fat, dumb coon."

"Thanks, Bob."

He gave me a look. He was one of the several deputies who was running against his sheriff boss Jumper Jimp in the upcoming primary.

"My dad wants to talk to you personal about me and Jumper," he said. "I told him I'd ask you. Would it be okay if he calls you sometime soon?"

I knew what his dad wanted. I'd likely get my vote solicited for Deputy Bob.

"Sure. Any time. I'll tell the court reporter to put Billy Bob through even if I'm on the bench in trial."

He nodded. I liked his father and this young man seemed okay, smarter than many. But Jumper was a crazy super sheriff and was my choice for the full Indiana two-term limit.

I waited until the sounds of the police cars had faded and then called son Joe and we talked for a time. He was staying with his mother's sister in Chicago. She owned a huge condo overlooking Lake Michigan. I had no great use for that pretty, easy lady, but so far things had worked out. She had a lot of pro athlete friends in high places.

Joe liked sports and liked his aunt. She was, he said, *cool.* I hoped and prayed he was still too young for her to make a pass.

Joe informed me he was ready and willing to come back home and chance things.

"Things are hectic here," he said. "My auntie always has some-one around."

"Give it a little more time," I said. "I'll maybe, if I can, fly up end of next week and stay till Monday morning. We'll talk more about it then. Sheriff Jimp says he's fairly sure it was just some redneck who snuck up close and fired shots trying to scare us."

"How about Mom's kitten and the rabbits and squirrels?"

"I know. Someone doesn't like me or us. Remember that I've also still got the Reverend Mo Mellish staying here at times in the spare bedroom. I want to help him when and where I can. Do you remember his second church burned down two years ago? It was over near Madisonville."

"I remember," Joe said. "I like Mo. I just miss being home. Tell me some more about Mom even if you've told me it before."

"She's about the same. Recently she seems more alert and I think she's trying to say new things, but I can't yet decipher what comes out. She's not incontinent anymore, though."

He knew what "incontinent" meant. He'd witnessed his mother being incontinent and it had made him cry.

"That's great," he said. I'd told him several times before, but he didn't remind me of that. Good news is easily retold and re-heard.

After we ran out of conversation for this night I used the microwave and warmed me up some fabulous frozen Swedish meatballs. I drank a cold V8.

There had been a time in my life when I'd have had several martinis and/or scotches before, during, and after dinner, but not now. My stomach no longer burned when I poured one or two water-diluted scotches into it, but it still couldn't abide my once-beloved martinis or scotch on the rocks.

Doc Buckner, had several times advised me my smart stomach was trying to tell stupid me something. He said such a stomach had already had its life's supply of gin and dry vermouth over ice and that it also knew too much scotch wasn't good for it.

43

I remembered the exact day, time, and place Dr. Buckner had last told me that tale: two months back in the downtown Moose bar. He'd then placidly ordered himself another double martini on the rocks, extra olives, please.

I turned off most of the inside lights and then turned on my outside yard lights. It made patrolling police nervous when they saw no outside lights as they journeyed past in their cruisers eating doughnuts and drinking hot coffee.

Now and then someone shot at the lights, but not often anymore. There were too many peace and police officers around.

A couple of times I'd made an arrangement with the officers and purposely left those outside lights off, hoping a watcher would think dull Judge Robak had forgotten.

I'd then ventured out into the yard and prowled my solitary neighborhood.

I hoped that one day, late or soon, the shooter or shooters who'd fired into my house and killed Jo's kitten and poisoned the friendly rabbits and squirrels would return for another try. I liked the idea that I might be outside waiting, watching, and armed if he/she/they came again.

Yeah.

I lay in bed and again punished the unknowns who'd harmed my Jo. I couldn't see faces for certain, but the punishment I meted out was both illegal and unconstitutional.

Living alone made plotting against enemies, known or unknown, easy.

Sleep came and I slept for a part of the night.

I endured a recurrent dream wherein young Elgin Wolfer, who'd raped, tortured, and murdered two young girls, ages now forever to be eleven and twelve, reached his final day.

In the dream I was present for the event because the defendant had challenged me in both newspapers and mail to watch him die.

There were candlelight marchers outside the prison walls. They seemed mostly to be beady-eyed, fat ladies wearing tennis shoes and carrying umbrellas.

They'd cursed me when I was seen and then burned me in effigy in a prison-gate bonfire.

In my dream I sat next to Sweetboy Wolfer and took both a lethal injection and the now outlawed electrical jolt and we gurgled out in heat and smoke together.

Dead.

The Reverend Mo Mellish did not call that night.

4

I REMEMBERED THE execution nightmare when I awoke near dawn. It was a repeater I'd endured in various forms. I shuffled it away into a secret compartment in my brain and left it for another night.

Some nights that nightmare was worse. Those were the nights when I had to inject the lethal dose.

The law was that someone sentenced to death would die by lethal injection. Sweetboy Wolfer was years away from death. He'd lost his first appeal, but there were numerous other avenues for delay available.

A retired appellate judge who now specialized in criminal appeals once told me at a judicial seminar that twelve to fifteen years between sentencing date and execution date was the norm, but there were times the cases ran considerably longer. He'd smiled as he talked, perhaps thinking about all those billable legal hours. He was a vigorous sixty-five-year-old and proud that his father, also a jurist, had lived to be over ninety. He was now drawing his retirement and billing his hours.

I wasn't impressed. Appeals have become a game. State bars give lengthy seminars on the rules of delay. I'd heard they were well attended in my state and other states.

Wolfer wasn't a personal worry. He was locked up at Michigan City.

The intruder who'd done target practice on Jo's and my home ran free. So did the person, maybe the same person, who'd arrowed Jo's kitten and poisoned the rabbits and squirrels which had ventured close to our doors so that Jo could feed them.

It could be one of Wolfer's relatives, but it also could be others.

I glanced at the clock. It was just after six in the A.M. and still gray outside.

Time to run.

I put on worn running shoes, sweatpants, and a flannel shirt. I visited the kitchen, got a tangerine for Jo and pocketed it. Carrying my shotgun, I exited the house at the back door after locking both doors behind me. I then ran through the nearby woods.

It was about 45 degrees outside, nippy, but not bad. And it was spring.

I sprinted to the gravel-and-mud back road I'd run on many times before. That road wound past an old, abandoned sawmill and finally terminated at another back road which then exited a mile away onto an asphalt county highway.

The sawmill road was overgrown with old and new vegetation. Vehicles couldn't use it anymore.

In growing light I maneuvered my way around and through potholes and patches of undergrowth. I felt pebbles through the shoe soles, but my feet were tough from running. My direction today and every day was away from the river and north from Bington.

I'd started running again as soon as Jo was out of the hospital.

My local law officers liked to tell me that running was chancy for me, but I hoped at times someone would attack me when I was running. Maybe, if I lived through an attack and the attacker did also, I'd find out more.

Wildflowers, bushes, and trees were in blossom. There was forsythia and redbud shining in the dawn. Early-generation dandelions grew in patches. Birds trilled their ancient melodies seeking springtime romance.

I was past the sawmill before something I'd seen sent me back for a second look. I circled the ruined building, never stopping my leg motions, and saw what had set off the inner alarm. A person or persons unseen by me had built and later extinguished a small fire near the rear of the building. There was a circle of rocks and charred bits of burned wood inside those rocks. There were also small droppings of fresh earth fairly near to the fire, but I could see no signs of excavation, no spade marks, nothing.

All this was new. I'd run past the same place the day before and there had been nothing.

Someone had built a fire near the sawmill in the last twenty-four hours. Someone had dug in the earth somewhere else and then transported a bit of the dirt to here.

The sawmill wasn't on my land, but it adjoined it.

I looked inside the mill, but there was nothing to see I'd not seen before. Old logs and boards, a wall that tilted sideways with age. I entered and inspected, but found nothing.

It still wasn't bright outside, but I could make out most details.

If someone was watching me and/or my house the sawmill would be a good place for an observation post.

I held my fingers close above the dead fire and then touched the rocks and charred wood. Were they still faintly warm?

My imagination insisted they were, but my cold fingers had no true opinion.

Watch and wait. Be careful running this morning and on future mornings. It seemed likely that the Wolfers now watched me.

I was carrying the shotgun and I was growing tired of games where it was impossible for me to be an active player. I wished someone was watching and that I would see him before he saw me.

I ran another mile down the county highway. I passed the cemetery where Judges Harner, Steinmetz, and other dead friends including my original partner, Senator Adams, now rested. I nodded toward their stones.

I called softly to one and all: "Keep a warm place for me by the fire."

During the run I saw and heard nothing more that alarmed me. Soon after passing the graveyard I came to my destination. It was called Green Home. It was where Jo was now a resident. I waited in the woods until I grew certain that no one had followed behind.

I relaxed, but only a little.

I was fit and aware again and I liked the feeling. I weighed one sixty rather than one ninety. The stomach wound bothered me a little if I drank too much scotch and also unexpectedly at other times, but it was now mostly an old, healed wound that warned me of weather changes.

I was now in my early fifties, getting long in tooth, but I was still alert and ready.

I walked through a huge, but almost empty parking lot and entered Green Home, Jo's nursing and assisted-living home. I locked the shotgun in a closet using a key the head nurse had provided me. I followed her orders on the shotgun. The staff didn't like for anyone to see me walking through the Green Home halls armed.

No one manned the desk because it was still too early for administrative staff to arrive. There was an in and out sheet and I scribbled my name on it.

An eightyish lady sat in the front great room next to a false fire glowing in a false fireplace. She saw me and nodded sociably and I waved to her. She had severe Alzheimer's, so overpowering that she never knew which way to turn when she left her room. She looked around the great room from her motorized wheelchair. She called out, "Ruth, Ruth."

The little white dog she called was many months dead. She still called its name over and over and searched for it down the long, ill-smelling halls because it was a thing she still remembered.

Yesterday when I'd arrived the great room had been crowded with oldsters. A patient had died during the night from a heart attack or stroke and the nursing home survivors sat huddled together. I'd thought they were taking strength from one another, some talking, some not, but all aided by the warmth and life around them.

I walked the halls to Jo's room. It took several minutes because the building was large and complex, with corridors north, south, east, and west. There were raised and sunken areas in the concrete floors left behind by an imaginative, incompetent contractor who'd hastily carpeted over his mistakes. Some of the doors were already ajar and in a few of the rooms people listened to early-morning television: news and cartoons. Here and there along the hall people slept or sat awake in wheelchairs.

Some people lay supine on their room beds. Some made noise, some lay silently.

The hallways smelled. When I was being blunt I admitted to myself that the whole home smelled like feces, a polite word for shit.

At the door next to Jo's a lady lay on her bed, her face almost covered by her sheets. She called out: "Die, die, die, die," over and over. Her eyes, when uncovered, seemed to watch the door, but she never gave sign of seeing me. Her voice was soft and wanting.

I tapped on Jo's door. A pretty, late-twentyish nurse opened it and smiled up at me. Her name was Gertrude and she liked being called Trudy.

"Hi, Miss Trudy. How's my lady this morning?"

"I saw you running up the road. You're in great shape for a man your age, Judge. Jo's awake and she saw you also. She seems fine."

Jo lay in a hospital bed. She was propped up both by pillows and the angle of the bed setting. She watched me at her door and surveyed the rest of her room world all at one time. Now and then she would stare out her window. Whatever imaginary place and time she now existed in wasn't completely unhappy for her. Her smile was as it had always been. It lit up the room and made a man my age's heart beat almost too fast.

I thought, for just a moment, that she was trying to speak to me, but nothing came from her mouth except guttural sounds that reddened her face with frustration. We'd found that her personal war with such frustration raised her blood pressure, but not dangerously.

Doc Buckner called the condition aphasia.

Trudy smiled at both of us. I thought she was friendlier with me than most of the tenants' relatives because, against all odds, I came every morning, plus many times in the evening, to visit my lost wife.

"I'll go get her some breakfast," she said. "Would you want me to bring you anything?"

"Juice and coffee and maybe some dry toast, if you will."

I was charged for what I ate. Jo had inherited money, but I was trying without complete success not to dip into it.

While Trudy was gone I showed Jo the tangerine I'd brought her. She nodded eagerly. I gave it to her and she expertly peeled it. She ate the results in small, neat bites without offering any segment to me. She knew the tangerine was for her and not me. She loved fresh fruit. Sometimes I brought her apples and pears and even grapefruit.

When she was done I disposed of the peels in a wastebasket.

I put my mouth near her ear.

"I love you."

Her brown eyes sparkled. Perhaps it was because of warm breath in her ear or maybe she remembered the words from the world she'd lived in with me, lost, and now seemingly reluctant to be rediscovered. Sometimes when I touched her she would respond by touching me, sometimes even smilingly groping me with warm, trembling hands, perhaps remembering that part of love from past times.

Her face, when she groped me, was as innocent as that of a bright five-year-old.

Most people with her problems and symptoms showed it in their eyes, but not Jo. Her brown eyes were like a teenager's at a prom party. If all memory and language were gone behind those eyes then something warm and fine had replaced that which had been lost or stolen.

When she'd first returned to consciousness she'd had problems eating, trying to eat everything, even the napkins, knives, and forks, but now her table manners were as polite and correct as a sorority homecoming queen's.

Later, after breakfast, I lifted and placed Jo in her folding wheelchair, tied her feet to the stirrups, and took her for a ride. She could walk with me aiding her, but I thought she liked riding in the chair better. I tried to make all decisions based on what I thought might please her.

I remained in love with both Jo and the ghost of Jo. In my mind I knew it likely would be that way for my lifetime. Sometimes I wondered idly and without any intention at all what it would be like to end the two of us in a neat murder/suicide, as ailing lovers sometimes do, but there was son Joe to consider. He'd likely spend the rest of his life trying to figure out why I'd taken his mother's life and then my own. And such might ruin his own life. The things we do to ourselves have more consequences than we think they have.

The halls of the building were wide and the rooms along them were inhabited by ancient, lame, and sick patients, people with Alzheimer's and Parkinson's, people who'd had small or large strokes. Some patients had congested or diseased hearts, others cancer or diabetes. Many of them were thin and wasted, but some were grossly obese.

Patients lived and died within the walls of the home. Some kept their doors open and sat vacantly, teeth vanished, mouths open gasping for breath as they slept or waited, awake, for whatever dreaded beast it was that approached.

Others hid themselves behind locked doors.

The dark, deadly being eventually found all.

I would get to know a face and then that face would vanish into fog and darkness, found again only in a newspaper obituary, never to be seen alive again.

I didn't like to walk the halls at night because sometimes I thought I saw the vanished faces of friends I'd lost.

I knew I was getting old. I had no right to Jo or to anyone as young as this year's spring, but it was morning now and at least I saw none of the death-vanished faces.

I passed attendants. They nodded at Jo and smiled in friendly fashion at me.

Jo was lovely and drew a crowd of oldsters. Although she'd not spoken (other than gibberish) since her sickness she seemed perpetually poised to speak understandable words.

The Green Home people, including some bright doctors and nurses, plus assisted-living and nursing-home patients, slowed our passage. They reached out and touched Jo's fragile hands and talked to her. Many hoped they could help make her well or believed that she'd help make them well.

I'd heard them whispering in the great room with its ever-burning electric fire.

"She's an angel from heaven, you know. Sent down to watch and report on all of us. A last chance for us. Sweet Jesus, sweet Jo."

Jo answered them today with her small vocabulary of words without meaning. Sometimes her eyes seemed to sadden when she touched a frayed and dark-veined hand.

I would superstitiously read approaching illness or death in her sadness.

She would shake her head at me to let me know it was time to move on.

The place smelled a little better now that there was activity, but it still smelled mostly like various grades and types of feces.

When our expedition was finished we returned. Back in the room I lifted and arranged Jo onto her bed and patted her into comfort. Trudy watched. She worked for me and for a few other patient families, making sure that Jo was well cared for by the Green Home attendants, giving the pills attendants who were not nurses couldn't give, all part of a corporate company of nurses involved in a lucrative, needed business.

I didn't begrudge the pay I gave Trudy's employers. I was grateful for the expert help.

"The therapists will be here later," Trudy said. "Anything you want me to tell them for you today?"

"Just that I think they're doing a fine job." I shook my head. My wife had been exercised into semifitness. "Jo nods at everyone. She holds out her hand so the old ones can touch it. And they do touch her as if it has special meaning to them."

"I know. She's one of a kind. I think her pretty eyes see and understand more than we think she does. Somehow I think she's content being here in her own special world. She's not ready to step out yet, but she does see and feel the bad and good things around her."

"I hope it's that way. I hope she's happy. She smiles so much."

"Believe me when I tell you she's improving in numerous ways," the nurse said confidently. "For example, you know she's no longer incontinent. She lets me know when it's peepee or poopoo time. I get her something or help her into her bathroom. Something inside her brain has relearned continency. She likes to be clean and smell good. If she's relearned that I'll bet she'll learn a whole lot more. She's also just fabulous with her table manners."

I nodded. Trudy had told me the incontinent story half a dozen times and the story about using knife, fork, and spoon even more times than that.

Jo couldn't speak understandably and couldn't walk by herself. She had to be cared for in many ways and she had moderate but not continual tremors in both arms and legs. Doc Buckner thought that what she now had was a result of the crippling inner heat that had boiled part of her brain. Her condition resembled Parkinson's disease more than Alzheimer's. But no drug for Parkinson's or Alzheimer's seemed to help her, no Sinemet, Eldepryl, or Aricept. We'd tried them all and a dozen more.

Something evil and still secret had raised her temperature to the edge of death, then vanished. Now all her vital signs were normal.

Some of her good female friends, knowing of her plight and therefore of mine, had called and subtly or boldly offered me their help in whatever problems I had. Sometimes I thought I recognized a voice, most times not. I had caller ID, but only one person ever called me without blocking it or using a pay phone. That person was Macing Drug's Libbie Macing, who liked to breathe hard and then laugh and hang up when I called her by name. It was a bitter, vanished romance. Once it had been like a conflagration, but now it was only an old, burned-out kitchen match.

I held hands with Jo for another while. She seemed to enjoy it. She appeared not to have aged in the past half year, but instead grown younger.

And I, like Shakespeare in plays and sonnets, warred with time for love of Jo. Where and when she lost something I engrafted her anew so that she was always more beautiful than she had been the day before.

I stayed minutes overlong at Green Home and then ran back home.

I dressed in a dark suit for my legal day, remembering I had to do special judging out of the county in the late afternoon. Some judges carry robes to their special judgings, but I always wore suits or sport coats. There was a judge to the south of me who bundled his robe into a neat package and then rode a Harley-Davidson on special judge journeys. He was a fine judge and I liked him a lot.

I was in my office a little after eight. A few moments after I arrived I performed a marriage. Evelyn Haas and a deputy sheriff from the hall were the witnesses. The happy couple had been waiting outside and then inside the courthouse since before seven that morning.

"The clerk could have married you," I informed them, glad they'd waited. I didn't recognize either of them or the names on their license.

The bride shook her head. "We didn't want the clerk to marry us. We wanted you."

The husband nodded. "You tried to get us to stay married when you granted us a divorce three and a half years ago. We thought if we got you to remarry us maybe it'd stick better this second time for us."

"Thanks for waiting, then." It was good to start the judicial day with a remarriage.

I shook all hands and declined to charge for the ceremony, but then I never charged for marriages.

At eight-thirty I met with Preacher before formally beginning court. Meeting together was something we often did. He liked to keep me up on area news and gossip and I liked being kept up, mostly because I'm a nosy bastard interested in all the world and particularly my Bington part of it.

I also had no wife to keep me informed about what she'd heard at bridge, golf, or in the beauty shop.

I was fortunate to have Smyth as my bailiff and we both realized it. For one thing he owned a doctorate from Indiana University in psychology and had written three well-received books on alcoholism. He was, in his own field, famous. Sometimes he traveled to colleges to make speeches or to be on learned panels.

Better than that, he knew almost everyone in and around Bington plus a double dozen professors at the big state university which spread its spider web over the entire northeast end of Bington.

Preacher told his friends he was still retired and that this new job working for me was simply a final hobby.

He'd been, off and on, for maybe a total of twenty to thirty years, Bington's leading practicing alcoholic, although there'd always been stiff opposition from a couple of locals and a group of overly wet professors who lectured, wrote, and imbibed brilliantly in and around the university.

He liked to tell a story now, saying he'd used himself as the main subject for his published alcoholism treatises.

There was some truth in such statement, but he'd also studied many other alcoholics. At one point I'd thought I was among those he'd studied. All that was before Jo. It was also long before I'd been shot while trying a dissolution in circuit court and then elected judge of that same court.

He'd finally come full sober.

One possible reason was worry about the approaching, inevitable darkness, not wanting to face the dreaded specter drunk.

In my early years in Bington I'd known a fine judge who'd lived to be a hundred years old. He was a horse-racing enthusiast, a Churchill Downs fanatic, but he'd stopped going to the races at about age eighty-five despite being both spry and still interested.

He'd explained to me when I'd inquired: "I could drop dead down there, Don. What would it look like with that *Courier-Journal* saying a former Bington circuit judge had dropped dead at the Churchill racetrack? And you know they'd surely print it that way."

Preacher was akin to my centenarian judge. Preacher didn't care where or when he died, but he now seemed determined to die sober.

His health was tricky and I'd seen him take tiny pills when his face seemed gray with pain. I believed they were nitroglycerine.

He walked slowly and ate sparingly. He hid his thin, wiry body inside dark suits and wore conservative ties instead of the bright clothes he'd once favored when he'd reigned as the high chief drinker of Mojeff County.

Preacher lived alone. Wife three, the final and most alcohol-tolerant of his spouses, had died a couple of years back from a consuming cancer that had burned the flesh from her fat bones at a rate faster than max speed of a juvenile offender's heavy Chevy.

One good reason Preacher had quit drinking was likely to care for wife three.

He'd then stayed dry after she'd passed on.

When I inquired of him now and then about romance and lady friends he'd inform me solemnly there were still a few out there with the warms for his aged, bottled-in-bond body, but he only called them if something came up. He stated he was not much of a Viagra man and that his erections came naturally, but seldom. He said that he only wanted most of his erections to rise far enough so that he did not urinate on his courthouse Florsheims.

Laying Viagra joke lines on a victim like me, his boss in name only, helped keep his declining days cheery.

I believed his social life was nil. He slept early, late, and often, napping quietly in the corner of one of the wooden, pewlike benches at the rear of the courtroom or finding more comfort in an easy chair in the law library.

At times, when Jo was healthy, I'd invited him to dinner so he could take a small vacation from his funereal, historic home downtown and the classical music he habitually played there. Wife three had been addicted to that kind of music and Preacher had been awed by it.

To Jo, Preacher was the funniest man in our Bington and university world. She'd enjoyed his words even when he spouted total nonsense. She'd put up with his dirty poetry and even would listen and nod agreement when he insisted that the world was, of a certainty, flat.

My son liked fishing with him. Joe claimed that Preacher knew more than anyone else in Mojeff County about the fine art of seeking wily creek and pond fish. Joe told me that Preacher sometimes spoke about me as if I were the son he'd never had.

And to me, was Preacher the father I'd lost when young?

Preacher had lots of "talking friends." Such was useful. Area information was exchanged for other information, quid pro quo.

He knew who was sick and might die and who was well for now. At election times he knew who would file for office and who, among the contesting candidates, would win. He knew who, holding office, would steal and who would remain reasonably honest.

When I'd first met Preacher he was in real estate and near rich from it. He was a natural salesman, land contract in one pocket, well-thumbed Bible in another, with room somewhere in his bright clothes for a refillable half-pint of Jack Daniel's. He'd been married then to his second wife, a short, heroically bosomed Christian lady of about a hundred and eighty pounds. She likely had her own suspicions that his minty breath wasn't the result of a lifetime addiction to Scope, but she was so impressed by his quick-witted comments on the world of Satan in southern Indiana that she forwent intensive investigation.

Eventually she'd caught him after he'd had a Saturday hole in one at the country club. The locker-room celebration afterward had made him list on both sides. Friends, including myself, had assisted him onto his front porch and then rung the bell four or five times to announce his hole in one.

She'd come and cursed both him, the hole in one, and his porch helpers. Her words had burned us like those from a hungover witch. She'd then filed for a divorce.

Disconsolate when enjoined from talking to her, Preacher had gone completely off the track and again spent many a day in jail or at the state farm. He'd also done time in drying-out programs at the area state mental hospitals.

It was as if he'd decided to again reveal to the Bington world that, yes, he was a devout, practicing drunk, damn all your eyes.

When wife three, she being the one who'd "saved" him back into moderation, had sickened and needed his care, he'd heard her call.

All other things remained the same after drink was banished and wife three died. He still had a personal Jesus he ordered about in commanding tones; he still had amazing people smarts and an absurd sense of humor. He could quote miles of filthy, funny, and classical poetry (some of the last I stole from him for courtroom use). He could keep any crowd, except perhaps a covey of preachers gathered for the funeral of a fellow parson, in constant laughter. He could quote Kipling, Khayyam, and Shakespeare, plus (better known in southern Indiana) JackAss Billy, Hard Peter Upjohn, and Little Benny Kissass, remembering full, foul poems flawlessly.

He remained an admitted alcoholic, but one who was in remission, thank you for your inquiry.

He was proud of the cessation and I and others were also both proud and amazed.

Somehow a liter or so of humor took a step away from him as time passed and he now seldom quoted from porno poems or old *Joe Miller's Joke Book*, preferring the classics.

I believed I would have hired him as bailiff even if he'd still occasionally been into booze. He was that interesting and I liked him that much. The watching of all things in Bington's world fascinated him.

I knew he was sporadically working now on a final book. This one was about the horrors of sobriety.

He was my longtime friend. I'd gone his bond more than once when I had no reason to pony up from a thin wallet. I'd also paid his drunkard's fines. I'd argued persuasively and most times winningly with angry petit judges intent on sending him off again for drying out at the state hospital or sentencing him to a few hard months of state-farm time to "l'arn" him not to be both drunk and a public nuisance.

I'd done my lawyer's job by recalling his worth and adding up his values in hearings before Bington city judges and justices of the peace. I'd joked, cajoled, and at times lied in his praise. I'd made absurd promises in both his name and mine.

A few times when I'd acted as his benefactor I'd done it because he knew almost all that was going on in Bington and I'd needed to know what he knew for what I laughingly called my practice.

Most times I'd merely done it for him and for me.

I'd helped him also because I'd vaguely, but not fully, realized his personal agony. I'd known that he feared the state hospital and its mind-confusing shock treatments handed out like popcorn treats by arrogant doctors.

When sent north to the state penal farm and its well-remembered sunny potato and bean patches, he'd sweated and dug on guard command, a familiar face returning to familiar punishment. He'd been terrorized in both institutions by vicious guards and/or attendants. He'd both hated and feared the ones who'd abused him, but never with enough fear to stop his self-immersion in booze.

I now smiled in secret at the fact that many in Bington believed I was his patsy. I didn't regret being politically despised because I'd personally chosen him for the cushy job as court bailiff instead of giving it to some good party member who (it was whispered) deserved it more. I'd selected him because he was, when all was added and subtracted, a good man, brighter and better than most, myself included.

He sat now on the other side of my big desk, watching me. He was sipping scalding, stolen/borrowed county clerk's coffee through oversized false teeth, his most prominent feature.

The old county courthouse in the early morning was as quiet as a bankrupt mortuary. My third-floor chambers smelled of Preacher's strong coffee, dirt, rust, sour food, wet ceilings, plus the usual restroom smells. The worst of the odors wafted up from the filthy public toilets in the basement and joined forces upstairs with the bad smells from our own executive johns, and those for juries, office holders, and staff.

Traffic, as I glimpsed out my window, was starting to grow. The nineteenth-century Bington downtown business buildings shone in the sun. A few squirrels and one lonely rabbit plotted together against the day on the courthouse lawn.

I tried to count things in bloom but lost track in their bright profusion. Soon, to join the others, there would be grand growths of cultivated flowers in the tended patches bordering the court-house walls. The courthouse head custodian had a fine green thumb.

"You had two calls this morning," Preacher began. "I wrote them down."

He searched through his pockets and found the phone note.

"Reverend Mo Mellish said he'll be back to your house to-night about seven o'clock. He's your African-American friend from over in Madisonville, ain't he? The one who keeps having his churches burned?"

"You know who he is."

"I've seen him with you once or twice. He's an odd-looking man."

"I've also seen you engaged in conversation with him. He likes your looks, too. If you were a little taller you could borrow one of his black suits."

"I've got him beat by a good six inches," Preacher replied, stung.

"Where?"

That brought a tiny smile of wit approval, and then a nod. "Things are cool about you out in the county, Donny," Preacher went on, looking wise.

"You mean for the primary election?" I asked, alarmed.

"Not that. I don't hear much election stuff about your race. All the talk's about who'll win the primary for sheriff. Jumper's had his first term and enough don't like him so there's, count 'em, twelve stalwarts who long to be his replacement, six of those worthies being his own sworn deputies, *et tu times three, Brute.*"

"How about quoting me the odds on honest Judge Robak in the primary?" I insisted.

"Quit worrying. You're a sure winner. Pretty sure anyways. That's a nice young man running against you. Polite, when he stopped by my house recently. Said I was taller than he remembered." He smiled and nodded to himself, unwilling to allay my fears. "Lots of the good people of Mojeff County might want to vote for a handsome, polite young man like Lance Tacker for judge."

"Then what things are cool?"

"People out there in the county say you're too damn mean, and too crazy, to get yourself killed or beat in any election. They tell other crazies and conspirators that both badasses and the good people of Bington have been after you most of your adult life and you're still around while lots of the ones who was hot after you either ain't livin' or ain't livin' happily." He shook his head. "They say fooling with you results in seven times seven years of bad luck. You're a legend in your own crime time."

I nodded, not really interested. He saw it and dug further: "Raybin McFee, chief nutball minister out at the Church of the Redeemer and New Saints, is now telling his church people to go to other counties to file their divorces."

"Okay by me."

"He tells his flock it's a major sin to file a divorce case in your court seein' as how you never give custody of kids to the parent who stays with his Redeemer church. Can people living here and wanting divorces file in other counties?"

"Sure. You can file an agreed dissolution in any county of the state."

He shook his head in surprise.

"Did you tell someone that it couldn't be done?"

"Yeah, but I'll straighten it out. You said 'agreed'?"

"That's right."

"Most folks hassling in their divorces can't agree on the sun rising. I do hear McFee's sticking his long nose into marriages just as soon as he hears a hint of family trouble," Preacher said. "Some of his people, the true militants, have moved away from him and gone on down to another group of crazies known as the Wolfer Farm Militia in Floyd County."

"I've heard about that and I say good for them," I said, yawning. I noted the name Wolfer was the same as the last name of the one I'd sent to death row, but then I already knew about that relationship.

I said, "McFee's got a church school that's always bugged me. None of his teachers are qualified to teach anything beyond McFee's Old Testament Bible beliefs, plus repeat his hate for blacks, Jews, Catholics, and most Protestants. McFee believes heavily in Satan, but not in anything good."

"Give the man credit, Judge. He has fourteen disciples/apostles. That's two more than Jesus had. All of them heavenly helpers hate your guts. Some carry guns and knives. They'll never be done hating you. McFee won't, either. Once his church had a thousand members and an armed militia waiting impatiently for him to prophesy a Second Coming and declare holy war on area sinners, such mainly being African Americans and members of all other temples and churches. Now it don't have a third that many members and the best of his militia has moved to Floyd County on him. I even hear it said McFee'll likely shut the church school down next fall. You're the most of why his trouble's happened."

"I didn't do a thing."

"True, but you talked to people who did."

I nodded. What Preacher said was true. I had talked and talked and talked.

"So what you're saying is maybe, just maybe, no one will come sneaking around to shoot into my house again?"

"Can't guarantee that. I can't get anyone worth a quarter to even guess who done the job on your house. I ask and people smile. But it ain't the kind of smile that means they know something."

"How about a guess from expert you?" I asked.

"If I could make one with any chance of it being close to right, I'd do it just because I know how that shooting bugs you what with Jo laying almost dead in the house then. I think it could be like Sheriff Jumper believes—that it was just some peckerwood passing by, a redneck who don't like you, one who had his rifle in his pickup back window, and who took the chance on a couple of quick night shots."

It was a thing I'd long conjectured on. Jumper Jimp's statement, which I'd already listened to, made a lot of sense to me.

Still . . .

Preacher looked down out of my window. He leaned back in his chair and I knew there was something new, something he'd saved.

"What are you holding in reserve this morning, Preacher?" I asked.

He took a deep breath. "Did you know that one of them Macing people you had in court yesterday morning, one of the two crazy, big-moneyed, cough mediciners, got himself shot at and mostly missed last night?"

"No! Which one?" I was surprised.

"Deputy told me it was the youngest brother, Beauregard. They look alike to me as two peepees in a chamber pot. Both of them are runnin' after our local cash trader ladies plus hauling down drug pussy by company limousine from up in Naptown."

64

"You're jealous."

"Not hardly," he said, stung. "You know I'm high class. Too high class for pussy you have to pay for with some of their inside-the-plant designer drugs."

"Have they got designer drugs?"

"Lots say so. They got their own private lab and both them boys and their sister mess around experimenting in it."

"Tell me what happened."

"I got told Beau was standing inside the hall of the mansion the three of them live in out on their high-fenced estate and someone shot at him from outside. Didn't hit him, but stone from one of the big hall columns stung him and damaged a painting of one of them fancy million-dollar Arabian horses. Macing's got full-time hired guards out there, a squad of them guarding the walls and fences. There's also coveys of guard dogs plus motion lights strung all over."

"Did they catch the shooter?"

"Whoever done the shooting got clean away. Sheriff's been out there looking into it along with half a squad of state cops. He's having to deal with an angry trio of rich-fart Macings plus a bunch of red-faced guards. I'll bet Jimp's as nervous as an old maid watching an X-rated movie with her shades up. I hear Macings have spoken to Jimp about taking over security at the Macing plant and at their farm if he loses this election, primary or fall, which he ain't likely to do. So he's hard into finding out who did the shooting."

I thought about it and got more interested. "Take some time away today and see what else you can find out. And maybe whisper to High Sheriff Jumper Jimp I'd like him to compare whatever slugs they find out there with the ones they dug out of my house walls."

"Can do."

I nodded. "Tell him to come over and see me Monday morning if he can't come to our poker game Saturday night. Some of his primary opposition is after me for support."

"You won't do it?"

"No way."

"The only thing's similar is that this shooter also missed his target and got clean away."

"Agreed. But it'll be interesting to know whether the shots fired came out of the same gun. And you said earlier I had two calls. Who was the other caller?"

"Earl Hardiman. He sounded like he was drinking again. He wanted you to stop past his trailer Sunday." He nodded. "Bet he wants to borrow money again."

5

I DROVE TO Floydsburg late in the afternoon to do my special judging there. An unmarked sheriff's car followed behind me.

At times, if things were complicated for the local peace and police officers, I'd have my former law partner, ex–football player Sam King, or my double-tough, gay lawyer friend, Kevin Smalley, travel with or behind me. They both claimed to be dead shots, pistol and rifle.

On this Friday in April there were plenty of officers available.

The drive was an easy one, forty miles or so, moving a bit over the speed limit on good roads. We drove through the small towns of Old London and New London, each too small to erect more than speed-warning signs.

A county councilman I knew ran the Shell station in New London. He waved to me, recognizing my car or knowing the deputy sheriff who followed. Sometimes I stopped there and filled the tank, but today there was plenty of gas.

I counted the telephone-pole primary-election posters in Mo-jeff County. Most were for sheriff candidates. There were hundreds of sheriff posters. One was for a name I couldn't even remember hearing or reading about as one of the sheriff's candidates.

I believed Jumper Jimp would win his primary and I had real reason to feel that way. I'd made a personal polling trip out to the sitter's wall that surrounded the courthouse. Most of the daytime wine drinkers out there were touting Jumper. That was good enough for me.

I wondered how much money all the sheriff candidates were spending for signs, bumper stickers, etc. It had to be lots of dollars.

While driving I also puzzled on why a man in his right mind would run for sheriff. Year after year many do run. Sometimes they pauper themselves in the purchase of posters, radio and television time, and newspaper advertising and get only a few votes.

I'd put up no political signs. My opponent Lance Tacker had. His were polite, merely inviting votes.

If he lost he knew he still had to practice before me if he stayed in Bington. My attitude toward him wouldn't change, but he'd never believe it and most likely he'd move on if he lost.

I arrived unscathed in Floydsburg.

I liked Floydsburg. It was a town where I was both hero and villain. In that it resembled Bington.

I drove to the Floyd County Justice Building. Floydsburg's courthouse was newer than most Indiana courthouses. That was because someone had burned its mostly wooden predecessor to the ground in the late 1940s. The replacement was part limestone, part brick. Floydsburg folks claimed it would be harder to burn, but not impossible. It boasted sturdy concrete benches in the yard and a low brick wall in front, a sitter's wall like my courthouse wall in Mojeff County. Sitter's walls allow loafers to watch area evil and complain in the open air about the bad, crooked world.

The Floyd County circuit judge was an old and ailing friend. I also knew both of the county superior court judges from the days when the three of us had scrambled to survive in private practice.

Now we were all judges; hoorah.

In Floydsburg I was known mainly because I'd presided over the month-long murder trial of Elgin Wolfer years back. My picture had been in the Floydsburg *Future* newspaper so many times then that I'd thought about subscribing.

When young Wolfer (sometimes called "Wolf" Wolfer, as were his brothers, and more times "Sweetboy" Wolfer) had been found guilty of murder the jury had hung during the punishment phase on the death penalty. I'd then sentenced Wolfer to death myself. That sentencing had followed a rally in the courthouse yard. Armed Wolfers and Wolfer friends and allies had built a large bonfire in the courthouse yard and listened to hours of stirring speeches.

The speeches, what I'd heard of them, and the militant crowd, hadn't done anything to change my mind.

Among the Floyd County judges and police that sentencing had made me a hero. Those officials felt that the jury had hung on the death penalty because some or most of the jurors feared reprisals from Wolfer's gun-carrying, dangerous relatives.

Within Wolfer's large family my sentence had made me a marked and hated man.

I remembered Sweetboy Wolfer had screamed furiously up at me and my "Goddamn cheatin' world" after I'd sentenced him to die and explained to him the many reasons for invoking the death penalty.

At the same time he was yelling the deputy sheriffs who were guarding him were smiling. They kept him close in his seat, strong, mean, and helpless.

"I'm innocent, damn your black-robed ass," Wolfer had yelled at me, crying big tears in frustration. "There ain't no real evidence. You'll not make this crazy verdict or your bloody sentence stick, you fuckin' empty-headed judge."

So far it had stuck.

His huge, stern father, his bent, vacant-eyed, Grecian-faced mother, who some claimed was either mentally retarded or insane, four reputedly deadly Wolf Wolfer brothers, and three vulpine, pretty sisters plus their lucky, sexually tired-looking mates had stood beyond the courtroom rail like soldiers under orders. They'd watched me all the way out of the courtroom and courthouse when I'd departed, their eyes filled with enough rage to cook me in my own juices. They'd not followed behind me that night because I'd been escorted by sheriff's deputies, many of them, but I thought open insurrection had been a near thing.

Their handsome, bachelor twenty-seven-year-old had been sentenced to death by a mean, hard-nosed, obviously prejudiced jackass/judge from another county.

Why? How could I do that? They'd probably heard, when I was picked as special judge from a panel of three, that I was known to be a judge who generally disliked the death penalty.

I did feel that way, but there were reasons I'd pronounced that death sentence on young Wolfer. I knew from the presentence papers for one thing that Wolfer, at age sixteen, had killed every animal he could secretly catch in a dozen-block area of Floydsburg. He'd been clever about doing it. For example he'd not hunted animals in his own immediate neighborhood. He'd also done his deadly work in the dark of night.

Later he'd talked too much, taunting owners about their dead pets, trying to get them to fight him or one of his brothers. He was, at sixteen, as quick and powerful as most men. His brothers were already formidable men.

For that offense he'd been sent to a juvenile home. Soon he was released and back on the streets. I'd later heard the swiftness of his release might have been because the home supervisors were afraid he, or others for him, would burn the juvenile home.

At age seventeen he'd been charged as an adult with raping and killing a thirteen-year-old newspaper carrier, picking a boy who didn't carry the Wolfer route, finishing him off after three-plus days of inventive, mostly sexual tortures in a wooded area near Floydsburg. I believed he was then trying to learn more about his chosen trade of death. He'd been suspected because he was absent from school on the day set as the time of death and because of his previous misadventures with dogs, cats, and the rest of the animal world.

At first, when questioned, he'd smiled his sweet smile, acted horrified, stoutly denied all, and therefore hadn't been a prime suspect. Once again he'd talked too much, made vague boasts, and been convicted mostly on his own words in a jury trial.

The case had been reversed on appeal because there was not enough credible evidence in the record to convict. What Sweetboy had said concerning the dead boy could have been picked up by anyone reading the angry stories in area newspapers.

At twenty he'd been found guilty of using a pocketknife on one of his several girlfriends (he seemed to be bisexual), carving his initials widely on her buttocks and breasts after she'd let some gentler, secret lover penetrate her prettys. He'd gotten a two-year sentence, done most of it, and stayed out of trouble for a time after his release.

The girl who'd testified against him had disappeared by Sweetboy's release day. She'd not been seen or heard of for a long time. Many believed she was dead.

I believed it also.

Six years later, he'd trapped and killed two young females, ages eleven and twelve. Death for the two girl children had occurred only after a long, hideous time of pain. That same period of time had likely provided hours of frolic and fun for Sweetboy.

Major parts of the dismembered bodies had been found in the woods no more than a mile from where the newspaper boy's body had been discovered. Some minor parts of the bodies have never been found.

I acquired a belief, while listening to the trial evidence, that Wolfer likely had read and taught himself much from the large body of literature concerning Jack the Ripper. I thought both he and his hero Jack had mutilated and then stolen bits from victim's bodies. Lawmen liked to speculate on whether Wolfer had eaten the missing parts crudely cut away or saved them in a hiding place so that they could be secretly admired down his future years.

Sometimes members of Wolfer's family hung around the Floyd courthouse lying in wait for me, but I saw no one on this day after I parked in the lot. My deputy waited in his car, watching me enter the building, then guarding my car.

71

I left my shotgun leaning against the dashboard on the passenger side of my Ford. I locked all the car doors.

I took the elevator up and found the courtroom where I'd set my special-judge case for hearing. The lawyers gathered therein waited patiently. I entered the outer offices of the circuit judge.

From his office the circuit judge saw me enter and waved me inside his chambers.

His name was Max Fromm. He'd been the circuit judge of Floyd County for thirty-four years and he now was eighty-one years old. He sat in his swivel desk chair, his skeletal hands clenched tightly over the chair arms.

Holding on.

It appeared he'd lost more weight since I'd last seen him.

Fromm's bright, sunken eyes inspected me for flaws. The eyes were more alive than the other parts of him. They still watched the wicked world alertly.

"I was waiting to catch you because I want to discuss several important things with you, Judge Robak," he said. "It'll need a bit of your precious time. But do go on into the courtroom first. Miss Minnie's already in there and my local bar boys will need you to listen, nod like you know something legal, and then affix your signature onto some papers. You can write your name, can't you?"

I nodded. "Most of the time, august sir."

Special judges, when a case has been worked out, are dear friends to the attorneys who've painfully achieved agreement, usually without complete trust on either side.

All was smiles on this late afternoon inside the courtroom. I added my own smile to the mix. I listened to a smidge of evidence for the record, agreed with the lawyers and their clients that what was transpiring was all for the best, and then signed their order.

Miss Minnie nodded up to me when all was done.

She whispered: "Maxie, him don't weigh enough to keep from blowing away in these April winds. Him still makes it to the courthouse every day, but I swear I don't know how him does it."

She was a fine, aging lady who owned lifelong, minor speech impediments, but who took perfect shorthand and could type like a Gatling gun.

"Did anyone ever find out what it is that's got him?"

She shook her head. "I guess it ain't the cancer. The town and the bar still mostly bet it's cancer, but Maxie him swears to me secret like that it ain't. Come on now. He'll be waiting and him don't have much patience."

I followed and we entered Judge Max Fromm's office.

"Everything go okay?" He asked the question of Miss Minnie, not me. I had, after all, only been on the bench for a piddling five years.

She nodded and retreated quickly out his door. He watched her leave.

"Sit," he growled to me.

I sat. "How you doing?"

"Better than I look like I'm doing. I had a meal last night, a full bowl of clear soup, six crackers, and half a bowl of Jell-O. Stayed down and I didn't bleed a drop."

"What is it that's wrong?" I asked him for perhaps the twentieth time.

"Nothing for an old slug-in-the-gut like you to worry about. I'll maybe be back in fighting shape come the end of summer." He nodded at me. "And if it's not to be that way I've done about everything there is to do in this wicked world except the final dying part. Besides, I'm not in big trouble. You're the guy in big trouble."

"Tell me the why of that?"

"Because I believe Sweetboy and his loving family have recently decided they need you dead. Watching and listening tells me that such is the truth. Besides, Wolfers are my not too distant relatives. Blood knows and tells. Now and then one of my relatives who lives on the Wolfer farm will sneak in here and tell me what's going down."

"I carry a twelve-gauge in my car and there's a deputy in another car following me."

"If Sweetboy's family army gets you in the right place on or off the highway you won't get much of a chance to use your damn shotgun. Think on it, Don. Sweetboy's been sitting up there in his cell close to the poison door for a considerable time. He's been making plans while listening to guys gurgling and choking on their lethal cocktails. They've executed two or three since he's been there. He's heard all the jailhouse advice about what to do before the executioner knocks."

"So?"

"He knows things about you and your people good because he's had his family asking questions and watching you and yours close. He's likely discussed things with that family and particularly with Pappy Damion Darius, nickname being Double Damn. Pappy visits him up in Michigan City whenever it's allowed. He also knows the law on dead judges because his fat-ass lawyer cousin has told him exactly how such legal happenings work. It therefore is known that if you get killed someone else will inherit his case as judge and he'd have a slim, new chance."

I shrugged. "That's how it would go. We both know that."

"So the Wolfers would now like you dead. It's as simple as that."

"Pass the word that I'm unwilling. I could recuse myself, but I'd have to give a reason and the only reason I have would be fright."

Fromm fell silent. I could see his chest rise and fall and I could also smell him. I'd smelled an odor resembling Fromm's in Jo's hospital room when she was sick.

"Tell me what's wrong with you," I said, changing the subject. "I won't tell anyone else."

I'd asked before and never gotten a direct answer, but this time he nodded.

"I've got an ulcer or two inside me that are bigger than both of us," he said. "If they got born we'd likely christen them and discard me. God knows where the things came from. I've had the problem for years and nothing has helped it. They keep getting bigger and worse. I've had four operations and was up at Mayo's for a month of Sundays. I should have died along the way, but I didn't because I'm a tough bird and not like you and your new generation of judges. Now it looks like there's a brand-new drug that's just right for me. You're not to tell anyone anything about this new medicine." He shook his head, his eyes suddenly gone happy. "I'm hoping to start eating lunch soon with various lawyers. I'll be taking along my court reporter, sweet Miss Minnie so she can watch my plate lunch shows. I'm going to try eating more than the lawyers do. That's after I sneak a dose of my new medicine. It's going to drive them all nuts the way I eat. I'm going to try to get fat. And if this new stuff don't work the docs say I'll likely be dead in six months or less."

I nodded. "If it works then your lawyer enemies here and elsewhere will have many a heart attack."

He shook his head gleefully. "Come down and go to lunch with me one day soon."

"Okay." I nodded and waited, knowing there was more.

"Let's get back to being serious about you and forget me for now. Lean back in your chair and relax. After a time, when it gets further on toward dark, I'm going to take you and your deputy for a car ride. There's a big place I want you to see, one you've not likely seen before."

"Whose place is that?"

"It's a farm that ain't a real farm. It's a nightmare place for you to worry on. You've probably heard that some of your old Bington enemies are in the army there. I know you looked over all the stuff in the probation officer's sentencing recommendation and that you sat through a long trial and sentencing, full of crazy family fireworks and scared jurors until you let the jury weasel off the hook when they said they were hung. You didn't even send them back to the jury room to try some more. Not you. Tough judge. You watched the bonfires and guns and still had enough guts to sentence Sweetboy Wolfer to death. I agree that piece of shit deserves the sentence even if he is a blood cousin to me."

75

"Then why do I need to bother looking at anything else?"

Fromm grinned, his face almost as thin and fleshless as a death's-head. "His daddy wants him out of the death prison and he says if I can help he'll promise me to keep a close eye on Sweetboy and never let him leave the family farm again."

"He came to see you on that?"

Fromm nodded. "Came right in here bold as a horse bettor at Churchill's legal track. Sat right where you're sitting."

"I'd not even hold a hearing should they file anything."

Fromm grinned more widely. "I know that. I just want you to listen to things I know about Daddy Double Damn and his family and friends. Then we'll take our drive. Listen and look good because what I tell you and what you see might one day save your miserable ass. I'm going to drive you to this fine farm where they want you under the ground like a rapist wants his pussy scared."

We talked for a long time. Nothing much was new to me except that the Wolfer clan had moved to the farm I was to be shown. And from what Preacher had said, many of the Mojeff Redeemer army had joined them.

When Fromm was done talking I leaned back in my chair and thought a while.

Fromm said: "Your car or mine?"

On the way outside the courthouse I saw someone had crudely spray-painted a sign above the front double doors: Execute Shit-bird Robak.

The paint was not yet dry.

Someone had been watching and waiting and had seen me arrive at the courthouse. Then he'd rushed for his spray paint-can.

"I guess the Wolfers know I'm in their neighborhood," I said.

Fromm nodded and said: "I'll have the paint scrubbed off first of the week, Shitbird."

6

WE DROVE FROMM'S almost-new Buick. My Mojeff County deputy sheriff decided to follow behind in his unmarked car rather than ride with us.

"It'll work better if you judges should get in trouble," he said stolidly.

Fromm nodded. "That's us, trouble all over the place, Deputy. Let's proceed."

The judge was a fast driver. He first drove out the Interstate for maybe ten miles and then turned east at an exit onto a well-maintained two-lane state road. Traffic along the state road was light. We passed an airport that had both a grass and a concrete runway.

I'd lived in Bington for many years, but had never seen or heard about this airport in our adjoining county. Later we traveled west down a numbered country road. We finally took a gravel-and-dirt road, one of numerous such roads we crossed. It was unmarked and unnumbered as far as I could tell. It was in such decrepit shape I wished it on my Mojeff commissioners Larry, Curly, and Moe.

Fromm's car bucked along hitting potholes head-on like a rowboat fighting waves on a stormy Ohio River. The aged driver paid no heed to such road problems. He ran down his driver's window all the way and my window a foot by using control buttons. He hummed and whistled off-key as he drove.

I smelled again the freshness of spring through the open car windows.

On the left we came abruptly to an eight-foot metal fence with bayonet wire running along triangle tops. That added three feet to the fence height. The fence seemed in fair condition. It was shiny bright in places, rust brown in others, but sturdy everywhere. Signs inside announced that the fence was sometimes electrified and also stated there were dangerous guard dogs running free. Many inner signs warned about various forms of trespassing. No Hunting. No Fishing. No Parking Within Twenty Feet of Fence.

A repeater sign read: "No Trespassing. Enter this property at your own peril. This is the privately owned land of free patriot Americans. Business affairs and invitational entry only accepted at Main Gate."

An arrow pointed. The main gate was ahead.

All the signs had crossed axes on them. I remembered that some of the Wolfers had carried axes with their signs when they'd rallied and paraded in the courthouse yard. That was just before I'd sent their beloved relative Sweetboy on north to Michigan City to await execution.

"What are the crossed axes for?" I asked.

"It's a family emblem kind of thing," Fromm answered. "Lots of the younger Wolfers carry small axes or hatchets on their belts. The men and some of the unmarried women sometimes carry full-sized double-edged axes. Tribal weaponry-worship stuff. Sometimes they have an open-house party: looking for new followers. Rock bands and the like. And they also have games with axes for those guests to watch."

On the unfenced side of the road at my right there were trees, most of them small. I saw no houses and no wild or domesticated animals. There were no cultivated fields on either side. Not a single car passed us. I also saw no birds except for a lone vulture which rose from its pickings at the edge of the dirt road. It flapped up over our roof, narrowly missing Fromm's windshield.

I had thought such carrion eaters only flew by day and it was full dark by now.

As we drove the moon did a disappearing act and the night became darker.

I saw a lone man in jeans and a dark jacket standing in a copse of trees in thicker woods on the unfenced side. Our lights caught him as he watched Fromm's car and talked earnestly into a cell phone. He was armed with a headsman's axe. It was four or five feet long. Its bright double blade rested on the ground. A long bow hung over the man's shoulder and a quiver of arrows was within easy reach on the other shoulder.

He stood by some small water or oil tanks. The tanks weren't big, but there were many of them crowded together, held upright in metal racks.

I thought this guard sensed my eyes on him. He set his axe aside, notched an arrow quickly and shot it in the air in our general direction. It hit a tree near the road and stuck there. The feathered end looked to be green in color like the arrow that had killed Jo's kitten. He took the axe up again.

"And here comes a chopper to chop off your head."

That line came from an old poem or story that once had frightened me as a baby-child. Sometimes I still heard that ancient scary verse in nightmares that brought me up and wide awake.

I had a desire to have Fromm stop the car while I investigated the arrow.

I didn't do it.

Some of the land behind the fenced side had been cleared so that there was perhaps a hundred feet of empty space from the outer fence to wooded ground. Now and then as we drove on I could see parts of overlong buildings in the woods. The buildings seemed too big to be called chicken houses. I imagined I heard chickens, but when I leaned my head out the window I could hear nothing but road noise and the singing wind.

Ground cover on both sides of the road was a sparse mixture of green and brown, some of it dying, not as much alive. I noticed something peculiar. There were no flowering trees or shrubs at all. There were also no flowers to be seen by Fromm's lights except thousands of hardy dandelions.

The soil where the land was bare was a tannish brown. Poor land.

"What do the occupants of these lands grow here, Judge? There aren't any flowers except dandelions."

"I don't know what they raise for cash other than millions of eggs, Judge Don. Some say all the other things they raise inside are lots of hell about the shape of this poor world, especially the Washington, D.C., and Indianapolis parts of it. They despise all government and they openly proclaim it whenever and wherever there's a chance to shout and show off their hate slogans." He looked out his window. "This isn't good farm land and never was even before the government took it for a military base fifty or sixty years ago. Maybe a hard worker with lots of fertilizer and a strong back could grow a few soybeans and some jackass corn. The Wolfers and family, from stories I'm told, have spread tens of thousands of dollars' worth of cow- and pigshit plus commercial fertilizer on this land and still aren't sending anything to market but eggs."

"And the Wolfers live here by choice and not chance?" I asked, wanting to understand.

"The Wolfer family owns or leases every acre of this land, both the owned and fenced part and the leased woods on the other side of this road. I'd guess there's maybe five to seven thousand acres in owned land behind the high fence," Fromm said. "This place and a lot more of the land around it used to be a military training base. That two-hundred-thousand-acre army base was shut down by the Feeps ten years after Vietnam. The whole huge base got sold and the Wolfers bought this cheap, empty chunk of it and leased more from the original buyers. Once more, I believe the only thing that makes them money are the chickens. They keep chickens inside big coops and they harvest and sell a hell of a lot of eggs."

"What's a Feep?"

"It's a local nickname for any federal government official. A lot of folks around Floyd County use the name, usually with contempt. It stands for any and all federal agencies in the plural and particularly the area-enforcement agents in the singular."

"That many thousands of acres is a lot of land to use for an egg farm." I said. "By my memory murderer Elgin Sweetboy Wolfer lived in town at crime and trial time five years back. Why, then, am I looking at so much after-the-crime acquired land?"

"What you're seeing is where almost all of the Wolfer family and followers have moved over the past few years. I think they did it for tax reasons. Papa Damion Darius, old Double Damn, mother, brothers and sisters, and cousins live here. The Wolfers had many tax and legal troubles in town. They couldn't get federal, state, or local governments to believe that the whole family were ministers of the gospel and that all their property therefore was exempt from taxation. Then the state of Indiana filed a condemnation action against various Wolfers, kin, and friends on farmland owned along the interstate, better land that doesn't adjoin this place. The Feeps later filed a bunch of tax liens because no self-respecting Wolfer or kin ever paid taxes. A lot of the property involved got sold at auction. There are still some appeals pending, but the Wolfers haven't won any of the cases."

"So property tax caused the Wolfers to move out here?"

"I'll guess it did," he said. "There's a lawsuit pending against various area judges, including me. We're all defended by the attorney general in Indianapolis. Every time a new judge dismisses the case the Wolfers and kin file a fresh suit and add the dismissing judge as a new party defendant. Do you know Ed Amesworthy?"

"I know who he is. He doesn't practice much in my court. The superior court judge at home, whom he does occasionally practice in front of, calls him 'Mr. Pus Gut.' A fat man."

"I agree with that nickname. Around Floydsburg he's referred to by many as 'Fat Ass Ed.' Amesworthy's a cousin to the Wolfers.

He's also a mouthy crackpot of a lawyer, but he's not a stupid one. He lives out here on this farm-fort. He didn't file the first or any of the later refiled cases against all the judges which, once more, includes me; but my guess is he's the one who prepared the papers. Other family members then filed the cases *pro se.* They attempted each filing to file as paupers, but no judge around this area will allow them to do that now. Without a judge's order the complainants have to pay filing costs and that bugs them. My county clerk says she's been roundly cussed out about the filing fees more than once."

"But they do pay the fees and file their cases?"

"Oh, yes. I don't think even the Wolfers expect much to happen out of their repeater antijudge lawsuit, but it does keep the sandpaper effect going so that the judicial system's warily aware of them. I believe the family's about given up agitating on the town scene since they moved out here. Living on the farm lets them pick better spots to cause problems and maybe better places to bury them."

"A heavily fenced egg and dandelion farm," I said, no longer that curious about it. "Complete with occasional rock concerts and axe contests," I added.

"These fenced acres are guarded day and night. Men and women inside hold semimilitary maneuvers sometimes, usually where such can be seen by their neighbors. They shoot their guns at targets. Sometimes they parade near the gate swinging their axes. They act tough and dress to kill. As a mob they have force, but as individuals they're nothing. I've been told by people who claim to have been watchers that some of the men can throw the axes pretty good, though."

"They throw them?"

"Yeah. Think about it."

I did think about it. A fearsome weapon.

"Whose name is the place titled in?" I then asked.

"It's not in a Wolfer's name, that's for damn sure. It's held in the name of some unknown guy named Harry Jones. Now and then someone sues Harry Jones, but he's hard to serve because there are half a dozen guys on the farm who'll say they're named Harry Jones. The problem's none of the dozen admits being Harry Jones, the owner."

"We both know there are ways to obtain service on people who try to avoid process."

"Sure. Lawyers do what they have to do and achieve service of sorts. After that lawyers appear out of the woods for Jones and for the Wolfers. Delays then begin. Eventually answers are filed along with motions for change of venue. It's hard to get the Wolfers into court. Some extremely diligent lawyers have managed, have then gotten judgments, and are now in various appeal stages."

"How about visitors? Do they let visitors inside?"

"At times. Mostly it's kids that come for the concerts. Callers, including law officers, must go to the single gate we'll soon see. If they trespass they risk a fight. An officer with a search warrant or a summons has to go to the main gate. The house is called, and the officer with the papers usually will be admitted alone. Sometimes such officers aren't admitted at all, at least not for a long time. And no papers are accepted from blacks, yellows, known Jews or Catholics, and so on. Nor are kids who appear to have impure blood under Wolfer rules allowed inside for the rock-around-the-clock shit."

"Do officers of whatever faith and color with a search warrant or summons in hand just stand around and wait that sort of silly nonsense out?"

"So far they have. A person trying to enter without passing gate inspection likely would get his butt shot off. The Wolfers supposedly have people with sniper rifles out of sight and in sight all around inside their fence," Fromm said. "And, after Waco, Ruby Ridge, and other television bad-news places, the feds have grown leery concerning agitations and confrontations. Our local officers have adopted a similar viewpoint. The feds have some people watching the farm, but there aren't many just now."

"How many?"

"Only one that I know of," he said.

"Could I talk to this federal watcher?"

"Ask your sheriff or mine. I'll bet that Feep would love to talk to you."

"If I were running things for a state bust I might just send lots of people with guns along to make sure a search warrant was immediately honored."

"People would then likely get shot and you'd have a news problem," Fromm said soberly. "Newspapers no longer have automatic love for officers or others entering places like the Wolfer farm where the residents want to be left alone. So order up something like that *after* you qualify for retirement, Don. One reason I'm showing you this crazy place is because I know your reputation as a curious and sudden man. You were that way when you were in the criminal practice, and from what I hear and know I believe you might one day, as a private citizen, accept the dare of the fence and guards and decide to look things over inside. I'm showing and telling you what the problems are so you won't let your stubborn curiosity make you try to go inside this damn fence, even if invited. In fact, it would be safer for you if you never returned here again."

"Is there a better reason than what you've already said? I mean, what with me being a rock fan."

He nodded. "I believe there have been times when people who did get inside the fences have been killed in cold blood. My belief is strong. Some area people and likely some curious strangers have disappeared."

"Murdering a trespasser would be a bad thing to do," I said. "Could bring on search warrants aplenty and a lot of heat."

"It would only bring heat if someone witnessed it and thereafter filed a report. A body would have to be found. Those inside the fence claim they are free men and that no one has the right to enter upon their land without invitation or valid search warrant. They are not friendly to the curious."

"And people may already have died?"

"I think so, but can't prove a thing. I also can't be one of the searchers armed with a warrant because I'm not a police officer.

State troopers have investigated parts of these fenced grounds on several occasions. No one's been arrested, but there's a lot of land inside to hide things. A couple of large creeks end up draining into the Ohio River. They get wide as they run through Wolfer land. In flood time the creek waters sometimes will run twenty feet deep and a hundred yards wide in places. Drop a dead body into the flood and its next stop would be the bottom of Big Muddy, the Ohio River."

I nodded, thinking on that.

Fromm looked at me and then away, perhaps not liking what he read on my face. "I believe the Wolfers would and could kill you or anyone else without fear of being caught if they found or got you inside their fence."

"Because I'm the bad judge who gave the death penalty to a member of the Wolfer family?"

"Partly that. What you did in sentencing the youngest son has wounded them deeply. I believe no jury in my county would have dared do it. I was surprised when you had guts enough to pass that death sentence. You had to damn well see and feel the menace emanating from all those whackos around the courthouse with their axes and guns. I was also surprised when the jury of locals convicted Sweetboy. More than just the conviction and sentencing the Wolfer family and some other so-called free men patriots living inside this farm feel they can make their own rules. They boast openly that the death of someone in the family using Indiana laws and Indiana justice they despise isn't going to happen. A couple of the people on your jury have died suspiciously. Others have moved away."

"But eventually Sweetboy Wolfer will die."

"Legally you're correct. Right now I suspect they're eyeing us with binoculars from inside." He smiled without humor. "I'll wager they've already written down your deputy's license plate number." He shook his head. "They'll guess later you were here with that deputy and that I showed you the way. They already have my license plate number in their files and it's likely they also have every Floyd County citizen's license number. They may courteously or, more likely, discourteously ask me the reason I drove you past their egg fortress. I will then baldly lie and tell them you up and ordered me to show you their place. You did do that, didn't you?"

"Of course. Tell them I threatened your poor, wasted body if you didn't show me exactly where the crazy Wolfers lived. And tell them that I also got a letter from the senior Wolfer inviting me down for a talk and so I drove past to look things over before visiting. Then tell them, if you want, that after looking the place over I told you I've decided not to appear at their gate for any Wolfer family hospitality."

Fromm nodded solemnly. "So Double Damn, cunning bastard that he is, did ask you to come visit. I wasn't sure he would. Well, please don't hurt me now that I've done what you ordered, strong, young Judge Robak." He said it carefully, not smiling at all. Instead he made his voice sound childish. "One more question for you: Did you meet Double Damn in the course of the trial?"

"In a way. You've likely already heard the story from your court people, but I'll tell it again. On the day of the sentencing the senior Wolfer came to court wearing a brown robe with a hood covering most of his head. He sat in the front of your courtroom, arms folded, watching me. He carried a thick wooden staff about seven feet long. He's maybe six four, and likely weighs three hundred plus. I didn't start things until I told him he'd have to remove the hood and turn over his staff to a deputy."

Fromm's old lizard eyes sparkled. "I heard about it, but proceed."

"He refused to do either so I had your deputies remove him from the courtroom. That brought some booing and foot stamping, especially when he tried to resist. I had lots of special deputies you'd assigned to the court for judgment day so I then ordered the entire courtroom cleared. Sweetboy's lawyers made all this a part of their outraged appeal, but it didn't do them a bit of good upstate."

"There was more to it than that, wasn't there?"

"Not a lot. I later let all of them, including Double Damn, come back in for the sentencing on their promise of no noise, no problems. Then I sentenced that pretty strongboy to death in front of a courtroom full of his relatives and friends."

"Was D.D. still in his robe and carrying his staff?"

"No. That was part of the deal. I'd seen and heard the senior Wolfer testifying at the trial and sentencing hearing. At those times he wore a suit and tie. You and I both know he's big and wears a thick black and grey beard. He also looks through tinted glasses day and night. It's hard to read his eyes, but I do believe he was angry. His letter to me was gentle. He said he'd gladly take his son's place on death row. His life in trade for the boy's."

"Double D's mean as a water moccasin, Don. One time he got into a petty argument with an oversized local farmer who had a reputation of his own for meanness. They were sitting and discussing politics or something on my courthouse wall. Damion Darius beat the farmer half to death, hitting him without warning, then hitting him again and again. He later got off with a fifty-dollar fine."

"Happens sometimes."

"Sure it does."

"Part of the system. The farmer could have filed a civil suit against him."

"Not and likely remained healthy. Now D.D. and his allies want you down home on their farm, Don. They want to fit you ten feet deep in a hole, so far down so you'll never be found. They've likely already dug your grave someplace out in their cornfields close to the chicken-shit piles."

"How about a deep dive for me into the Ohio if the weather's right, what with this being April and possible flood time?" I asked.

Fromm nodded. He slowed the Buick to a crawl as we drew near the main gate. There were many lights, some on poles, some hooked on the fence. The entrance looked like a military post gate in an occupied, hostile country. Sam Browne–belted men with rifles watched from a cement-block guardhouse. One of them exited a door and ran quickly, rifle held at port arms, to the left side of the gate. He put the rifle to his shoulder, sighted our car in, then watched us drive slowly down the rutted road.

I could see his lips moving, either talking to himself or to his mates at the fence.

I thought he was saying, "Pow, pow, pow."

Cowboys and Indians. Me and Judge Fromm, Indians.

The night air at the gate smelled different. There was an odor of diesel oil and hot engines overlaying a sour smell. I believed most of the sourness emanated from a million chickens existing together in enclosed worlds, living, dying, laying egg after egg.

On a high post over the drive that entered Wolfer land there was a large sign decorated with sets of crossed axes. It read: "Entry by Invitation Only. Next Rock Party May 1. Axe Exhibition." A high flagpole held only one flag. I looked and saw it was like an old Revolutionary War flag with a coiled snake and words that read, "Don't Tread on Me."

Inside, below the sign, there was a large garage of sorts. In a driveway in front of the garage there was an oversized four-by-four truck painted black. It bore a big white Arabic numeral on the door: 23. My bet was the truck had been bought at some large army surplus sale. Behind the first garage there were more small garages, each big enough to hold cars or pickup trucks. I saw no cars in the open. Where I could see truck doors each door was painted with a 23.

"What's 'twenty-three' mean?"

Fromm shrugged and speeded up. I could see he was shivering a little.

Eventually the fence along the road turned inward near the bottom of a hill. We drove to the hilltop and Fromm pulled over to the side and shut off the motor.

"My sheriff also wonders what the twenty-three means. Most or all of the truck doors bear it." Fromm said. "After Oklahoma City he worries about them maybe using the trucks to bomb our courthouse. So he stops the trucks now and then and checks them over politely. I think the Feeps worry also and so he sends them

88

a list of what he finds. So far that's not much, mostly zilch."

"How many trucks?"

"Lots of trucks. Most, but not all, are small pickups. Like I just said, my sheriff and other law officers stop the trucks every time they run five miles over the speed limit. They've searched them a dozen times. There's never a thing but grinning drivers. I think what the Wolfers want is for all of us to believe they're building bombs and their main plan is to revisit a small-town Oklahoma City called Floydsburg."

"Or maybe blow away Bington, home of bad Judge Robak. Tell me more."

"Look back away from the lights of the single gate and to the right of the trees. That's the house. People who live around here call the place Wolfer Castle if they're feeling polite or Wolfer's Anal Retreat if they're not."

I looked.

There was a rambling stone building with a thick brick wall all around it. The stone house was huge. The brick wall around it was maybe six feet high and had twenty-foot-high battlements at each of its four corners. Outside the wall there were more garages for vehicles.

As I watched and listened someone fired an automatic weapon and someone else answered with rifle or pistol fire in return.

"Does everyone inside drive a pickup truck?"

Fromm nodded. "I guess. Makes for a good parade when they come to downtown Floydsburg or drive over to Louisville or up to Indy to protest something. Many of the trucks are diesels and make plenty of noise after they tinker with them."

"Do they also make a lot of noise in their war games?"

"Sometimes. There's a deputy sheriff who lives nearby. He says they set off little bombs just for the fun of it. It's July Fourth stuff, but the bombs sound powerful enough to blow up a house."

I looked around some more. Once away from the lights of the big gate my eyes had grown accustomed to the dark. I saw a name on the mailbox and a dirt road leading from the county road to a place unseen inside a wire fence.

Ann Sembly.

I'd once known and represented a lady called Ann Sembly.

Police officers and Bington city officials had called her the cat lady and charged her with maintaining a nuisance because she kept a dozen or so cats in her house and on her property. I'd represented her and gotten her off even after the then prosecutor and his cat-hater pals in Bington proved she owned too many cats for area ordinances.

I thought cats were okay. I liked them far more than I'd liked the damn-fool prosecutor of those days wasting time with cats when the high school and university were awash with drugs.

Assuming it was the same Ann Sembly I recalled she'd not cared much for me, but she'd had little use for any human after her late-night arrest and jail lodging. She didn't like the prosecutor, the judge, or the police and she also hated the citizens who lived near her and packed the city courtroom for her lynching.

Hang the old bitch and shoot her damned cats.

Ann Sembly claimed in testimony during her trial that she could understand cats.

She stated to the city judge that she liked talking to them because they made more sense than humans, particularly lawyer humans. The city judge had been troubled by what was happening in his courtroom between the prosecutor and the defiant lady. He'd solemnly taken her case under advisement. He'd then never decided it. He was a Bible-carrying man and she was a widow, and he kept muttering to the prosecutor when prodded on the case: "Honor a widow."

"Is Ann Sembly, who apparently lives over there down the dirt road, the same one who once lived in Mojeff County?"

"I don't know. She keeps a lot of pussycats."

I nodded. "She's the same person, then."

"What do you think of the fort?" Fromm asked.

"I'd not been going to stop in for high tea even before seeing the place and I certainly won't be stopping at all now," I said. I thought some more on it, sitting silently in the Buick front seat with Fromm watching me carefully.

"Have you ever heard anything about the Wolfers being into church burnings?"

"I've never heard it, but I guess they'd set fire to anything they hate and they hate many things, most churches included. Some Wolfer followers go up Sundays to visit that big crazy church in your county."

"Yeah."

I thought on the shape of things: In my lifetime I've met with many people who believe their natural rights transcend all other rights. I've no use for such dumbheads.

What we now have in this crazed twenty-first-century U.S. of A. are flawed individual freedoms that extend until someone puts fist to someone else's face. When a defendant in a criminal case tries to use some added extension of his or her "freedom rights" as a defense after having committed a wrongful act I, as judge now and as lawyer before, give that defendant only what the law says he must have.

I'd once sat as judge in the criminal case of a man who'd burned a bakery near his home because he said he didn't like the smell of baking bread and that such smell lessened his property values. He'd argued with the baker concerning the odor, then threatened him, and finally carried out his threat. He'd come to court and wanted to introduce evidence about smells and temporary insanity. I'd not allowed the evidence to be admitted.

He'd been convicted of felony arson and was still doing his time, smelling offensive prison smells daily and writing me letters bitching about them. He also made copies of each letter and sent them to members of the state supreme court.

Maybe he believed he was wearing all of us down, but it wasn't so.

I no longer opened most of my own probable hate mail. I give letters with no return address to Evelyn Haas. Sometimes on dull days I could hear her opening my mail and chortling happily in her office.

She'd read and then file-mark the letter and put it in the large file where she'd kept other such letters down the years. At intervals my sheriff, Jumper Jimp, would come and look over the file. Or, if it seemed something I should see, then it would be shown to me.

I'd also tried a murderer who killed because he didn't like a neighbor's looks, religion, and observed sexual mores. He knew the sexual stuff intimately from window-peeping. That killer had many friends who held his religious views. He'd wanted to call all those friends to testify in his behalf.

I'd not allowed into evidence any of his proffered hate evidence.

The defendant's lawyer had made offers to prove. He'd then taken a confident appeal and lost it.

There are many things wrong with this era's courts, but to tolerate racist jackshit isn't one of them.

I'd sentenced that defendant to death and he now awaited execution. I'd heard through the prison-guard grapevine that he and Sweetboy had discussed me warmly and poisonously a few times.

What I do believe: The world is full of bullies and badasses, people without redeeming qualities, people who live to enjoy hating the rest of us.

I've no use for them. They read my frowns and my overrulings and hate me on first sight or quickly thereafter.

There is another thing which troubles me even more than badasses and bullies. That's people who use money and influence to buy themselves the verdicts they want.

Later, with me drinking hot, stale coffee and Judge Fromm sipping cool but not cold water because cold water bothered him, we sat again in his office. The interior halls of the courthouse were dark with only small floor lights to show the way to the exits. We were like shadows conspiring together.

Outside the courthouse powerful arc lights brightly lit the yard. Soon the nights would grow summer warm and the arc lights would draw ten thousand moths to flutter and commit suicide each night. Now, in April, the lights were clear of insects.

"We hire guards who patrol our courthouse yard at night," Judge Fromm said, seeing what I was seeing out his window. "We started it last year because a juvenile tried to set fire to our courthouse again. An arrogant sixteen-year-old kid set some rubbish piles next to the building on fire after I took his driver's license."

We nodded at each other.

Punish all the rest, but don't dare punish my kids or me.

Someday soon I believe we'll have to live in armed enclaves. There'll be a short limit on the time we spend fooling with the dangerous folk. There won't be enough food or enough clean water for all.

Maybe when that time comes there'll be about as many bads as there are goods. Maybe I'll be one of the bads.

I might. I don't believe everything authority tells me.

I'd brought my deputy inside and he also drank stale courthouse coffee. He sat in an outer room, waiting patiently for me to finish my time with Fromm so I could drive back to Mojeff County. He could follow, then be off duty.

"Life's tough on us poor old judges," I said to Fromm.

He smiled. "That's so, but people like you enjoy having assholes hate you. Please have enough sense to keep your Wolfer-wanted butt away from that farm. They won't give up trying to get you there. Eventually, they'll try some kind of force and you'll be lucky if they don't succeed. They might stop your car on a public road and load you into your own trunk and drive you on to fabled Wolferland. They might even raid your courthouse or catch you when you're running in skinny-dipping clothes down a back road to visit your wife."

"How do you know I run to visit her?"

"Same way they'll likely know. I asked."

"I'll watch carefully."

He shook his head, unsure of me.

I said: "Remember, Honorable Judge Fromm, benefactor to me when I was a poor, practicing lawyer, that I'm now a judge like you. I'm not as smart as you are, but I seldom do any investigating. There's a single exception. I'm trying to find out who did a poison number on my wife. I'll look into that until I find what I need. But I won't come back down here to spy on the Wolfer clan. I won't enter their fort-farm. I'll leave such things to your law officers and the Feeps."

"I know nothing about your wife other than what I heard secondhand. I'll ask you to tell your Mojeff County law officers about the letter from Wolfer and then say to a full assembly of them that you're never willingly going to visit Wolfer Fort."

"I'll do that. And I'll also tell you now so that if I vanish you can testify as to what I said. That's if the Wolfers get me in there and bury me on the back four thousand."

"I hope to God you're telling me the truth. I know someone shot into your house. I know Evelyn, your fine and friendly court reporter, and my pal for thirty years, says you have many local troubles. Some of your problems up there in beautiful Bington may have been caused by Wolfers. They could be your house shooters. They could also be burners of churches. Nevertheless, if there are legal things for you to do concerning Sweetboy you must do them strictly from the bench here in my county court-house with a court reporter, a bailiff, and about three dozen sher-iff's deputies present. Don't agree to any private meetings any other place with the Wolfers or their counsel."

"Anything else?"

"When you're coming here for such a hearing then you might have your sheriff notify my sheriff."

I was willing and so I nodded. "Tell me more about the Wolfer family. Are tax people still after them?"

"Sure. Once you get caught trying to cheat the tax gatherers never let up on you. Plus there's a deficit balance due on old judgments. I asked several federal officials why they don't just come and take possession of the fort. I've not heard a reasonable answer."

"What else?"

"There's other good stuff, sex and kinky kiddy behavior that drive the Wolfer neighbors and my never happy, tough sheriff wild."

"How's that?"

"*A* lives with *B* out on the farm, but *B* also lives with *C*. And so on. Use the whole alphabet, mix it up, then let the letters all screw away like alphabet worms. Some of those males and the females who endure the screwing may not yet be able to grow much crotch hair. Lots, young and old, do things in the open they ought do only in private. It's usually not enough to arrest them and they do it on their own property. Some of the women shave below and so you also can't tell how old *A* and *B* are. Now and then a bunch of the fort kids come nudish near the gate and inflict corporal punishment on each other with sticks and whips in some kind of rough game that makes both sexes scream in pain and laugh wildly when they lay on a good one. Some who appear to be kids don't wear clothes at all on special days. The family seniors sometimes wear robes like Damion Darius Wolfer wore to your court on his son's judgment day. Many carry their big axes with them into town. They also bother the neighbors and my sheriff's deputies, trying to set us up."

"Do you know if this Wolfer group is part of some national free citizen's group?"

"I don't know. It's not likely. Feep people watch them, but not close, like I already said."

"So they stay inside waiting and hiding behind their electrified fence, eat mostly corn, eggs, and chickens. They fool around and whip each other. They run around close to bare-assed and do all this within sight of their neighbors so as to both frighten and scandalize the area folks? Plus loud rock concerts?"

"Exactly."

"Is part of it religious?"

"I'll answer again that such is not likely. They use the name of God only when it benefits them."

"Who are the neighbors?"

"The area around the Wolfers used to be mostly Amish, but when the government took the land over for an army base all those years ago such destroyed the neighborhood. The church was abandoned. A lot of the Amish moved on, but a few stayed. Some who stayed gave up the old ways and some didn't. A few of the close neighbors used to be or now are Amish. Good people. Hardworking and friendly."

"And those people are the ones who get upset?"

"They are some of the upset. The Wolfers ignore all complaints. The family male seniors are the ones who run things and I'm told they take the best of the girls and women for their own personal screwing. They believe that they're completely free, that they can make their own laws, and aren't subject to any other laws while they're on their own land."

"I see."

"Where'd all of this free-citizen patriot horseshit come from, Don? You got any ideas?" Fromm asked forlornly.

"I've thought some on it, but I have no real answers, Judge. Maybe too many Feeps, as you've nicknamed them. Add too many nuts, plus judges like us who allow those nuts overmuch freedom. The old mental hospitals are mostly emptied and we live in a world where everything can be treated and cured by pills from the Macing Drug Company and its many trillion-dollar competitors. Commit someone to an asylum and pretty soon someone else with authority will let them out."

Fromm said, "Lots of people think free men are a good answer these days. I hear you have your own free-men militant churches up in Mojeff County."

"Well, not exactly. We have Reverend Raybin McFee and his fourteen disciples. The movement up there's weaker than it once was, but it's one of the reasons I keep deputies up in my courtroom hall checking for guns. I've heard that some of McFee's Armageddon army have moved into your Wolfer Fort."

"That's true. I'm told McFee visits now and then, partaking of the extra women. Good idea checking people for guns," Fromm said. "I've had a gun-check system for maybe ten years. I'm still alive and still meaner than shit."

7

WHEN I ARRIVED home in Bington there was a limousine parked in my drive under Joe's basketball hoop, just behind Mo Mellish's aging brown Chevy. I recognized the limo. I'd seen it a number of times. I knew many facts about it. It was armored, had special tires, and a supercharged motor. A previous limo, twenty years back, had been equipped with a lot of the same extras.

The burly male driver looked to be in his late twenties and wore a chauffeur's cap. I didn't know him. He was reading something by the light of the inside car illumination. It appeared to be a brightly colored comic book. He paid no attention to me or to the deputy sheriff who followed me into my drive.

The deputy sheriff got out of his car.

"You want me to check the limo driver and maybe also check inside your house, Judge?" the big deputy asked hopefully. "I'd like to roust the limo driver around some. I've seen his bad ass a couple of times before."

"Where?"

"Local bars. Moose, Eagles, and Elks open dances. He's a troublemaker. Drinks too much and gets into fights. I'd like it more than a little if he wants to play his games with me. He needs his damned butt kicked and I'm the man for the job."

Twenty to thirty years back the deputy might have been speaking about a younger me.

"Not tonight, Deputy. I know who owns the limo. It belongs to the Macings," I said. "I'm not afraid of the Macing female although all sane men should be. I still can take care of troubles when they're female and smaller than me." I shook my head. "Somehow she got herself inside my house without a fight."

"Yeah," the deputy said. He rolled his eyes a little. "I was at the Macing estate yesterday night just after someone fired a shot into their Arabian-horse-palace home. She's a real tall handsome lady and she was angry at the sheriff." He smiled and something that might be hope returned to his eyes. "I've heard it said that you're not friendly with her or her brothers. Maybe she's already done something bad inside your house, Judge. I really ought to have a quick look so as to be a possible witness if you need one."

"No. Someone inside opened the door for her and I know who did the opening. Everything is okay."

He continued to look doubtful.

"Go home. Get some sleep. And thanks for the first-class escort job, Deputy."

"Okay, Judge," he said. "I hope I don't ever have to go on a raid into that high-fenced place we drove past. I never seen such shit."

I waited until the deputy's car was all the way out of the drive and I could see his taillights receding down the muddy subdivision street.

Libbie Macing was a living Bington legend. She was a woman with tons of money who lived with her never-married brothers inside the family's guarded and gated estate. I'd seen her in court the day before, but we'd mostly ignored each other for what was now more than twenty years, even though I knew I remained a part of her local legend.

When I'd first known her it was said that half the men in Bington fantasized often about what might happen in the limousine's back seat. Such fantasies had never come true for me when she was my lady. Other fantasies had occurred and recurred,

98

but we were always discreet in the back seat of the limo with a driver up front who reported to her brothers.

She was my business and not a deputy sheriff's. Thinking on that warmed things inside me a little. The sex had been great, loud, wild, and adventurous, but I remembered that the very worst sex I'd had in those days had also been wonderful.

The blinds on the picture window were open. Mo was back.

I entered my front door. An unlocked security door stood ajar.

The chauffeur continued to ignore shotgun-armed me although he had to have noticed me. I locked the security door and silently slipped my shotgun into a hall closet.

Elizabeth "Libbie" Macing was curled up catlike on my couch. She'd turned on the television and was watching an evening soap opera in which all the heroes and heroines were married to wrong spouses. Most of the cast were into self-help to alleviate such sexual problems.

I'd renamed the soap *Worms Castle* after watching it a few times. I no longer watched it often as I could usually predict the action.

Libbie was showing a lot of lower leg and also a bit of nearby-to-upper leg. She was five feet eleven and I remembered there'd been a time when she'd liked to put on heels so she could look me in the eye and sometimes high heels so she could look down on me.

She was also brilliant, with a mind that clicked and whirled and was in charge.

"Make yourself at home," I said.

"I always do. I remember there was a time in our past life when you thought such to be one of my few good habits." Her voice was low and husky. It was a voice that had caused tremors to run through me twenty years back when I was thirtyish. I found it still did.

I reminded myself that I was a married man and that looking and remembering backward twenty years wasn't something I ought to do.

"How'd you get in?" I asked.

"Your butler opened the door for me."

I smiled inside and wondered what Mo Mellish would think about being called a butler. He was surely someplace close, listening carefully, viewing this new twist in my life with interest.

Libbie was dressed in shades of red, a bright red, long-sleeved cashmere sweater to warm her body against the spring evening cool and a muted red and green plaid skirt, very short. Her long legs ran down for about a mile from skirt bottom to dark maroon slippers. In the glimpse I'd had I wasn't sure if she was wearing panties and I found myself interested in discovering the truth. She was capable of anything.

She looked lovely. I knew she was now in her early forties, but she looked at least ten years younger and was both slender and full-breasted. She'd always owned the gift of being able to wear anything and look both good and sexy. She still had the knack. There was money, lots of money, to buy her clothes and pay her help. There were people to exercise her, people to fix her diet dishes, people to drive her limo, people to do her every bidding.

And those people, if they were smart, did just what she told them to do.

Once when the money had already been significant I'd been certain I loved her. It was like being crazy in love with a sometimes sullen, sometimes enthusiastic porcupine.

We had fought about everything. Early on she'd won most of the fights. Late in the game she'd refused to lose any.

Then, for some reason, when it was done and I'd taken all I was going to take from her she'd sought forgiveness. I'd wisely or stupidly refused to take her back.

She was then, at twenty-three, a rich, stubborn girl/woman too proud to ever fully apologize to me or anyone. She'd never learned to say she was wrong or sorry. Her mother had died shortly after she was born and she'd grown up with an adoring father, two older brothers, nannies, nurses, private tutors, and fancy girls' schools. She was far-out intelligent, able to remember all she read, all that passed before her eyes. When I'd rarely beat her in a card game she'd sometimes tear up the deck or throw it in the waste can.

After we were done with the affair I'd met, dated, and married my Jo.

I'd given up on all negotiations with Lib before my Jo.

"Say you're sorry, Lib. Say you lied and you're sorry you did it."

"Screw you, bastard. I'm never sorry. I'll only say I love you. I've never stopped loving you."

"Could you fix me a drink?" she asked now.

"Do you need one?" I thought she might have already had a few.

"Of course. I still drink. Sometimes I drink too much, a habit you once joyously shared with me. We drank and talked and played games. I haven't given up my drinking. I know you can't drink really good stuff anymore but might you have a sniff or two of gin for your playpal Libbie?"

"I have some Seagrams. Such common gin might burn your patrician throat, Lib. I believe there even might be a bit of dry vermouth in the refrigerator. No olives or lemon peels, though. Sorry."

"I'll have to rough it, but something else I'm hoping about might make drinking gin martinis a problem. Maybe you should fix me some other kind of drink."

I waited. She was full of self-authored commentaries on life, love, and the state of things in Bington and the surrounding world. She was bright enough to run the huge drug company, CEO now in name and deed.

"Should I kiss you with my mouth open in the midst of my frontal-attack reconciliation, could not the gin cause problems inside your poor, wounded stomach?"

"I doubt we'll be doing any necking after all these years, Libbie."

She gave me a sharp-edged look. "Spoilsport. Please remember me and our times together. Remember the long days and nights

I happily gave you when we were whatever we were. The in-fighting was mean, but it was also fun. You need me now, lover Don. Someone without morals or decent manners. A lady who wants you and who has had you before. I remember how warm it was."

"Warm as a razor cut."

"That describes it quite well." She went on. "I was the one who wanted everything out in the open and damn my damn brothers even if they caught us right in the act."

"Which they tried hard to do. I remember brother Beau hired himself an extra-large private detective who followed us every-where for a time."

She shrugged. "Almost everywhere."

"I now have a wife."

She nodded her head, her eyes confident. "You have a sick, sick little wife who my informants say is lost and useless. She always will be from what I'm told. She has Alzheimer's or Par-kinson's or maybe has had a stroke."

"Your informants may be telling you wrong. Jo may one day get better. Her doctor still believes there's a slim chance. She had an illness where she had high temperature, pain, and blood pres-sure spiking high and low. That was about five months back. Were you making anything at your plant then that might cause such symptoms?"

She hesitated and then shook her head. "Nothing."

"And if they were making something like that in the plant you, as the CEO, would know of it?"

"Undoubtedly. I'm the head lady. My brothers just hang around and chase ladies of the night. I make money. All of us like it that way."

"Whatever she got almost killed her," I said. "One day I'll learn what it was and who gave it to her."

"I remember you're good at digging."

"I hope so."

"Your princess," she said, "I've been around her lots of times. I've played golf, tennis, and bridge with her. A nice little lady.

She looked to me then like nothing bothered or upset her, even you. I heard she filed for divorce once. You should have been a nice man and let her get it."

"She did file, but I soon talked her home. Some things might bother her. If I were to jump into bed with you I guarantee she'd be upset."

"Ahhh," she said, uncaring. "I'm not the kind who goes to bed and then tells. If she gets unexpectedly well I'll then fade to grey and we'll keep our secret. I'd eventually like to have you back, but just now I need only a borrow of you for this single night. You're in my thoughts these days. I come to court and see you up on your bench looking like an English lord. You make me burn from my knees to my navel."

I doubted her statement about fading away and I thought she read the doubt in my eyes and answered accordingly.

"I did twenty-plus years back. That was when you found and married her. I could again. We're older and more settled now. I'm a responsible executive lady, forty plus. If you let me come back and it jelled for us and your Jo died, I might even try to stomach your legal friends in a coming life. My memories and dreams of you are still warm. I stand here waiting and shivering, caught in an old trap by the sight and sound of you up close. You haven't changed that much. People say you run and keep in shape. I also keep in shape, believe me. I've an exercise room at the farm. We could go there, lock it off from the rest of the house, and exercise to hell and gone together. One night or even an hour or two might cure me for a time. Please take me back for tonight. I finally and fully apologize."

"What you need's a cold shower," I said, examining her, the blood inside me running warmer than waves in an equatorial sea. Her hands shook and there was a tic near her mouth. Old memories made me suspect a few drinks taken to cure a hangover or perhaps recreational drugs acquired or tailor-made with her flasks and Bunsen burner at Macing Drugs.

She nodded at me. "You still look the same, you still smell the same. You've still got your hair and it isn't even grey."

"It's prematurely black."

She laughed, but not at my words. "I think it's bitterly funny that you're the one man of my former men I now have to have, the one man I can imagine myself being with in the dark of night and waking up with in the morning."

"Bull. You dated a hundred men and got engaged to three."

She took four or five steps toward me and stood a few inches away, her breath burning my face, her well-remembered body smell almost overwhelming me. She was wearing flats tonight and her lips were two inches below mine. "It's true. We fought about everything, but I never lied to you."

"You never had to lie. You believed I'd come back to you because you owned a lot of the money in this part of the world, even back then. You thought I'd give anything, allow you to do anything, in order to share your money and be available in your bed when and if such pleased you."

"Are you saying you never gave a damn about my money?"

I ignored that question because I hadn't disliked the idea of being a partial partner in that money. It was a personal fault I'd admitted to myself many times.

"How about the rest of your problems? Are you engaged again now, Libbie? Three engagements without a marriage is not any kind of record, but it's a damn good average for a full lifetime."

Her eyes went cold as a February creek. I'd always been half afraid of her when she was really angry. "I'm willing to bet all my money that you know I'm not involved and haven't been involved for ten years. You got married and it stuck. I got engaged, engaged, and engaged and nothing stuck."

"I've not spent time checking up on you, Libbie. The only places I've seen you in these past years have been at your estate when I went visiting there along with my wife and the rest of the local chamber of commerce peons. One night a year. Every year you and your brothers get richer until your total wealth is now ridiculous." I then added, "And then in my courtroom where you've come recently to spectate and demonstrate."

"You did notice me in court," she said triumphantly. "I bought a special umbrella to match the color of your robe."

I ignored her umbrella although mention of it almost made me smile. I thought she'd carried the umbrella not for me, but as part of her costume for the day. Her life was an act, but there was no doubt she was in total charge of it.

"I've wondered, down the years, what was wrong with serious affairs one, two, and three. And why do you keep calling me at night on the phone?"

"The men bored me. They were, every one of them, accountants at heart. They had no guts, no conversation, and never fought back. I kept making the same mistake in adding, subtracting, and trying to multiply with the bastards. And I call you on the phone to hear your voice."

"You told me several times back when we were lovers that I was boring you. Remember?"

"No. I remember telling you that most of the social things we did outside of bedtime bored me, but never did I tell you I was bored with you. If we were back together I'd not care if you stayed a judge."

"That's big of you."

"Of course it is," she answered placidly.

"I also heard you had recent trouble at your estate. Is my old pal, your brother Beau, recovering well?"

Beau was the younger Macing brother. He'd once informed me that I was unwelcome as a suitor for his beloved sister Libbie. He'd been in earnest and I'd laughed at him because I was certain that Libbie would make her own decisions and not be governed by one or both brothers.

Libbie, early on, had told me funny childhood tales about both brothers which indicated their interest in her had mainly been carnal, incestuous, and unsuccessful. Their father had finally caught on and sent them on to boarding school.

Beau's threats to me had been vague and polite because we'd been face-to-face when he made them.

I'd warned him that day that if he hired someone to help get rid of me, which is what he'd need to do, I'd catch him alone and repay him twice over.

He'd bragged about his boxing and judo trainers and said he wasn't afraid of me, but all the Macings and one Robak knew he was.

"Both my brothers are well, Don. It's said around the plant offices that my brothers plan to donate heavily to your primary opponent. They don't think you're always fair to Bington's largest industry and employer."

"I doubt that either of your brothers ever had a thought on fairness, Libbie. They both want damn all. So, probably, do you." I shook my head. "And that's the last word I'll listen to about legal problems."

"My brothers don't even know I'm here, Don. Damn it, get me a drink and then please give me a tiny bit of what I truly desire. A sweet kiss and a strong hug for starters. More. For old time's sake. Just for the damn fun of it. I want you back sometime for all time. It's my destiny and I know it. But tonight I just want something kind."

I shook my head. "Try the shower. I'm unavailable. I'm married. I love my wife. All I want from you are assurances you weren't involved in her illness. If you were I'll punish you."

"How?"

"I know you. You're deathly afraid of rats and snakes, so much so that you pay the country club the money it costs them to hire yearly exterminators."

"Please don't even talk about such things."

"It's one way to make you think."

She shook her head. She was now angry. "Of course I know nothing about your wife's problems. There's one more thing for you to think on, then. I came also to tell you about it. Your sheriff roughly compared the bullets shot into your house and the one shot into my brothers and my house. He then sent them on to the state police lab, but he's informed us the bullets came from the same gun."

That surprised me. Who would shoot at me and then shoot at a Macing or a trio of Macings almost half a year later? "Tell me more, Libbie. Maybe this has to do with my wife."

"I don't know anything else. It gives me shivers trying to figure why someone would shoot into your house and then, months later, use the same gun to shoot into ours. It also gives me the shivers to think that you suspect me of poisoning or harming your wife."

"We're shivering the same, then. What else did the good sheriff say?"

She smiled without any meaning. "Only what I'm saying now. Who would want to hurt us and also hurt you and yours? Maybe, unknown to us Macings and to you, we have a common enemy. I'm curious about that because I badly want to be your closest friend again."

"After twenty years?"

"Whenever. It doesn't have to start tonight, but I know it will happen sometime."

I mixed her a large gin martini and we had more conversation. She was beginning to lose interest in me and my world for this night. I thought she'd come on a whim and now wasn't that set on the whim.

She'd never been openly promiscuous. I'd been her only man for my year. No one else had lasted that long, not even any of the three men she'd been engaged to. I remembered the news stories.

"There may be a time in the future when I will come hunting you, Libbie," I said. "But not now, not yet. When I want."

She sighed. "By that time I could have a new someone sniffing around the bait, hunting for what's left in the Libbie reserve tank. What there's left is maybe worth a nickel or a dime. I might even finally find a man I'll have to treat right like you from now on. Timing is everything in this life. I'm getting on in years, Don. I'm goddamn into my forties. I'm into the change. I grow cold and then I burn. The blush is gone and all that's left is a vacant rose garden where you previously plucked all the damn flowers.

I don't think I'll be calling you again for a while. Not till I'm dead sure we're forever. No more thinking, remembering, and burning. Make love to me tonight, Don."

"Not tonight. You don't want it to happen and I'd not ever let it happen here in Jo's house."

"I say I do want it. And we can go and do it anywhere you want. I suggested my exercise room, but anyplace will do."

"No. I hope things work out for you. We had fun even if you hated every friend I had back then. Why do you hate lawyers, judges, doctors, accountants, professors, and the rest of the intelligent world?"

"I hate all men who did long years studying so they could act smarter than me. While they were doing that I first went to a women's college, sent by my father. There I learned to write bad poetry, drink gin, smoke pot, and fake a few orgasms until I met you and enjoyed real ones. I hate watching men add up in their silly heads what's in my purse, while they're thinking about how far they can go because my breathing rate went up after a kiss. I hate them when they talk important court cases, nasty diseases, and computer ailments. I fucking hate being bored and argued with when I'm always right."

"You went back to school yourself while we dated. People say you're not only a very good research chemist, but a far smarter administrator than your brothers ever were."

"I'm okay, but running that huge plant is a lonely business."

"How about my wife? Could she have got hold of something, some crazy drug, that came out of your plant?"

"Impossible."

"Why impossible?"

She shook her head, saying no more, maybe not having more to say. I thought my questions had upset her.

She cried some tears, but her crying had never reached me before and didn't on this night.

I walked her back to her car.

The chauffeur's eyes watched me all the way back. I could tell from his actions that he knew Libbie was unhappy. He got out of the driver's seat and walked around the car.

He opened the rear car door for her, roughly pushing me aside.

He said, hands clenched: "If you've hurt my lady you'll pay for it through the nose."

To the best of my recollection I'd never seen him before.

I said: "You're on my property, bud, so act nice. The name's Robak."

His hands unclenched. "I thought you looked familiar. She just told me how to get here. I apologize for my anger. I like her."

I nodded. "Don't we all."

He bowed and patted her a little in the process of seating her.

He was a large man and I figured he likely would win a fight between us. Besides, I had no intention of fighting.

He smiled at her, but not at me. I thought he might be pleased that her clothes looked unruffled even if her eyes held tears.

"Would you step on out of the way now, Judge? I want to turn my lady's car around."

"All right."

She didn't look at me again through her window, but the chauffeur nodded at me through his.

I believed he might have high hopes of ruffling her clothes himself.

I saluted the rear end of the departing limo.

"Luck."

I waited and watched until after the car had vanished from sight.

8

I'D KNOWN MO Mellish was somewhere inside the house. The living room blind was open and a man Libbie had thought to be a butler had opened the front door for her.

Only Mo, son Joe, plus the police and sheriff had keys to the security doors.

I walked to the kitchen, remembering Mo's affection for that big and comfortable room. After a childhood where hunger happened often he liked rooms that were associated with food.

I found him. He sat at the kitchen table. The room was dark and he was sipping a Diet Pepsi poured over ice cubes. His hands gleamed in the half-darkness like dark velvet gloves. He'd taken off his shoes and his feet were white stockinged.

He smiled at me and said softly, "Best not turn on the kitchen light yet, Judge."

"Whatever you say."

I'd known him and we'd been friends for about six years. He was an African American with skin so black it shone in dim light as deep purple. He stood only about two inches over five feet tall and his head, above a massive body, was small. He'd told me once that the black and Hispanic kids in his dangerous western Louisville neighborhood had nicknamed him Runthead when he was growing up. He'd added that a few brave friends still did call him by that name when he returned to the Louisville streets for a visit. I'd never been invited to join the Runthead brotherhood. Still, we were friends.

I knew some things about him from shared question-and-answer sessions, but my knowledge of him was less complete than his of me. Once he'd been a combination strongman and kids' clown in a circus that had toured the country performing in both large and small cities. Another time he'd worked as a paralegal for Indianapolis lawyers who then and now advertised for accident clients in Indianapolis and its television outskirts. When I'd first met him he'd run a trailer court in Madisonville, twenty miles from Bington.

I thought he'd probably liked doing all those jobs, but the overwhelming desire to preach his version of the Gospel had now settled him into southern Indiana. He'd been half a preacher when we'd met at his trailer court. Now he was almost all preacher.

I had no knowledge about his education, but I knew he was bright.

He was also driven by demons and substantially less so by saints.

My bailiff Preacher, who'd met Mo, agreed with me that Mo was intelligent. He'd added that he and Mo did not read, remember, or preach from the same Bible.

Mo had read and now remembered his versions of Bible stories where sins drew harsh and quick punishment. He believed in a judgment Bible.

Preacher owned a God that forgave, a God that obeyed his orders.

Mo's God exacted vengeance.

Preacher's granted prayers.

I had no true deity of my own. I'd prayed long and desperately when Jo fell sick. When she'd remained sick I'd slowed my prayers, disappointed in a Being who didn't hear me and didn't help her.

I prayed for Jo now only when I was taking part in Mo's church service.

I planned my own punishment against those who'd hurt Jo.

Mo's health was good, better than when I'd first met him. He'd described himself to me then as a man whose heart was insufficient. His present health was improved because he'd had successful open-heart surgery two years back after someone set fire to his second church. That church, like his first one, had burned to the ground. A year after the second fire the land had curiously been sold to the Macing Drug Company. A huge drug-storage warehouse had been erected on the land where Mo's church had once stood.

I'd checked that out, but it seemed only happenstance. Was Macing Drugs going to set fire to a run-down church so that they could, a year later, build a warehouse?

Not likely.

After that second fire I'd had Doc Buckner send Mo to a very good heart surgeon in Louisville. Soon after the referral Mo had received open-heart surgery.

He now weighed about thirty pounds less than he'd weighed back when his first church had been burned by a Madisonville crazy I believed was now deceased. The loss of weight did not make Mo appear thin. In fact he seemed now to be very strong, mostly muscle and bone, with long arms and short legs, the body immensely powerful, all topped by his undersized, cartoon head with the eyes that observed and measured all.

He ran with me sometimes in the mornings. After a mile plus he'd usually slow to a walk. He'd turn back. He'd breathe hard at the turning, but his running now covered far more distance than it had in its beginning.

"I was listening to you folks sparring sex out there in the living room," he said. "I thought that pretty lady was sure as squirt going to steal your poor, misused virginity." He shook his head. "Do you know that that lady sometimes comes and sits by herself in a car, some kind of bright red convertible, and watches your home through binoculars from a few blocks away?"

I shook my head. I'd never seen Libbie watching my house. Perhaps she made her telephone calls to me from that car. "I have my virginity preserved in a liter of Dewar's White Label in the basement below us, Mo. Such keeps it safe from all but scotch addicts. The lady, being a martini person, wasn't about to topple me over this night," I said. "Besides, once I knew you were here in the house, I had no intention of giving up easy and letting you overhear my famed rutting sounds. You'd surely learn bad stuff from such. It might spoil things you've yet to learn about as you grow older and gain in virility and desire."

He lost his outward smile but his eyes sparkled. "You've a great gift, Your Onus. The ladies, black, white, and even green, look at you and smile with anticipatory joy. They look at me and break into open laughter. What makes this bad world work so well for your benefit and pleasure and not at all for mine?"

"Maybe you've just not met the right lady yet. The one your Lord meant for you."

He nodded. "I'll admit I've not had much time to search for my intended during continual bad times."

He lowered his head and stretched his white-stockinged feet restlessly. I knew his legs sometimes ached, but he never showed pain.

"Thank you for letting Libbie in. She's one of the Macings who have to do with Macing Drugs."

"I knew who she was when I opened the door for her. I also knew her earlier when I saw her watching your house from inside her red convertible. You can't live in the Bington area long and not know about the megamoneyed Macings. I looked out through the shades of your upstairs window when she arrived in her limo. It's armored, isn't it?"

"Yes."

"That's nice, it being armored and all. She likely needs the armor to protect herself from men like you, Mr. White Label. She's got right good movement in her walk. Walks like she enjoys doing it. Made me hustle right down and open the door up wide for her so I could see her walk more close up once the door was unlocked. Smells good, too."

Mo was an odd man. Somehow in turning aside Libbie Macing's offer I'd bothered him inside his head. At the same time I thought it likely I'd risen in his eyes because I'd not shuffled the willing Libbie off to my bedroom and so broken my vows to my poisoned Jo.

Win a few. Lose a few.

"Did you discover anything in your searches?" I asked.

"Are you still my lawyer?" he asked in return, his face suddenly gone serious.

"I can't be your lawyer now because I'm an elected judge and am no longer allowed to practice law. I'm now a decider. I allow the best of various courtroom lies to win. One of my former law partners or a lawyer you choose will represent you should you need counsel in any matter in which I once represented you when I was in the practice. I still have the retainer you gave me for that one problem case we discussed together six years back. I've hidden that money away in a secret place, safe even from the prying eyes of the IRS. That retainer, no matter how much you gave me once I accepted it from you, means I can't talk about what you hired me to do or what I know of it with anyone without your permission."

"And you also remain a faithful part-time member and treasurer of my burned-out churches?"

I nodded. "I'm at that full-time. Your church is now my church."

When Jo had been well we'd been fallen-away Methodists, not visiting our church except at Christmas and Easter and for an occasional funeral.

We'd listened to Mo when he preached because he was our friend. I'd liked what he said because of a realization he believed his own words.

I'd listened to him also because he said prayers for my Jo and was now helping me seek those who'd harmed her just as I was helping him try to find the person or persons who'd burned his second church.

He'd confided in me recently that he was seeking Jo's lost dreams in the night lands he traveled.

I mostly looked for Jo in my own dreams and seldom in daytime. I wanted her to be medically well, the same as she'd been before her sickness.

Mo examined me with care and I thought I had, one more time, convinced him that I was his friend and that he was safe with me. Maybe I had to do that over and over because of the two churches lost to arsonists. Part of his distrust might also be because I was white, but I didn't believe that. I knew him as a man without prejudices, even against the damnable white race.

It could also be that he was just funning me as I had done with him when he'd made his statement about love being easy for me. He was good at funning and playing small jokes on me for his own amusement.

Thinking on it, I was never sure when things were real for either Mo or Preacher when they were dealing with me.

Both believed in reincarnation. Mo remembered places while Preacher better remembered lost people.

"Set down and have yourself a drink of whatever you want, Jedge," he said, intentionally mispronoucing my title. "After all, it's your table, your ice, and your beverages."

I fixed myself a splash of scotch over ice cubes with a lot of water and then waited. It now seemed he'd relate what he'd seen and heard in his travels.

He said: "I looked many places. Today I found a piece of possibly magic land. There are no buildings on it. It's ten acres of sweet land where I can build my final church, a church that will overlook waters which run on to the Ohio. There's space enough for those who listen to me to park cars and there's even a grove of good trees. There have to be trees so I can have a picnic ground kind of final church."

I nodded.

"You understand the why of a picnic-ground kind of church, Robak?"

"Certainly," I lied. I didn't understand what he meant despite the several times he'd explained it to me. I only knew what he said and wanted was necessary to him and so it was fine with me. "Is the land in this county?"

"One county south." He shook his head, perhaps dubious about the distance.

"This time we'll build your church as fireproof as it can be built, Reverend Mo. Brick, stone, and steel. I'll want to see this spot soon."

His eyes sparkled once more. "Yes. Brick, stone, and steel. We'll go tomorrow. I had a few bad feelings when I walked it and so you must see and approve it."

"All right, tomorrow."

"I also asked many questions around Madisonville. I used both your name and mine. I asked if any stories or rumors had been heard about rifle shots into your house and firebombs into my last church. There's been time enough for both our hate stories to spread. People around Madisonville remember you on account of that fine witch woman you defended who was falsely charged with murder there six years ago. They also remember me. Some over there have heard you're now the high judge in Bington."

"Good."

"I promised cash rewards in your name. I believe most I talked to would have told me if they'd heard something."

I thought Mo might have had a small stroke or heart attack in his anguish the night his second church had burned. I knew he was different from what he'd been when we'd first met after he lost his first church.

I'd been with him at the time of the second fire and I'd talked softly to him during that long night, talked until he'd grown calm and cold as we watched the ashes cool.

"We will find them," I'd said, over and over. "We will find them." I hoped we would.

He'd not had a major attack or stroke that night, but it had perhaps been a close thing. I remembered that the great veins on his head had popped out like fishing worms from the ground after a rain. He'd breathed hard and fallen stiffly to the ground. He'd writhed and dug his fists into the earth. He'd pulled the dirt up by handfuls and poured the gathered clods over his face, dirtying himself. His hands and legs had trembled and then become stiff as boards.

I'd managed to take him away from the ruins of his church after the fire cooled. When we left a light rain was falling on the still-hot ashes. I'd taken him immediately to Doc Buckner who'd given him a shot and some pills.

As far as I knew Mo had never returned to the fire scene.

Once, when he later asked, I'd told him the Macing Drug Company had bought the church ground after the fire. In checking I found it appeared to be an arm's-length purchase, with the chemical company looking at several tracts.

After the fire night I'd talked him into seeing Doc Buckner again. I hoped he was now sound, but I was uncertain. Buckner also thought there'd been a happening the night of the fire and still detected faint signs of old heart damage when he periodically checked Mo.

Inside Mo's head from his church fires there were now visions. Good and bad dreams came when he slept, but his daytimes were more complicated than his nights. Fully awake, he could look up or down a hill or at ground and sky and see dementia things the rest of the world didn't see. Some of those things frightened him. So did some of his nightmares. Fires. Blood. Death. But sometimes there were also gentle things, small children, animals, a friendly type of brain-and-eye insanity.

He'd told me once that he'd seen Jo in one of his dream visions.

I never questioned what he told me. Part of that was because I wanted to hear his vision tales.

That didn't mean I believed all. I realized he could tell himself that he saw something and thereafter it became a fact in his mind.

Just now I thought he was seeing something as he sat smiling and nodding. Most likely he saw his new church, but maybe he saw my Jo and she was well again.

I hoped it was the latter.

The smile changed and he frowned. Perhaps he now saw a fresh grave.

Mo preached a lot about fresh graves. He preached softly about the crypt Jesus had left behind on a long-ago Easter morning. Mo told the tale as if he'd been in the crowd there watching it.

He also talked about the graves he dug in his mind for Satanic church burners.

I'd decided six years back (beyond a reasonable doubt) that Mo had cold-bloodedly killed the man who'd ordered the burning of his first church. I believed after he'd done that killing he'd then disposed of the body so that it would not be found.

When I'd told him of that belief while asking him my questions and trying to learn the full truth about the man's disappearance he'd at first laughed at me. Then later, when I showed willingness, he'd hired me to represent him in the matter, "if there ever was a problem about it."

By that time I no longer had a client who needed me and so I'd willingly taken Mo on as my new client.

I'd asked him to pay me one single bright penny as my retainer. I still had it.

I'd advised him to answer no questions and refer all questioners to me.

All this had happened when I was still a practicing lawyer. Then I became circuit judge.

Nothing new had happened in that now-forgotten matter. My old client had been released and another person was being sought by the law and would never be found. Mo had not been suspected as a killer. Or, if he had, nothing concrete had ever come of such suspicion.

I believed I knew what Mo would do if he learned for certain the name or names of those who'd burned his much-beloved second church.

I'd taken the insurance money from that second fire and later added to it the proceeds from the sale of the church land. With Mo's consent, I'd put the money into a certificate of deposit in a bank, using Mo's name. Twenty-two thousand dollars, not a lot of money, but also not a small amount. Interest payable every six months. I kept the certificate in my house desk. Mo knew where it was and sometimes he'd open the desk and take the certificate out and hold it in his hands, using it to see bright visions. When done looking he'd carefully return the CD to the desk drawer.

Mo had many admirable qualities. He could preach hellfire and damnation. Listening to him rage against sin was good for my dark soul. I admitted to both of us that I was sinful and likely wouldn't change.

Mo could also work all day at hard labor. He could laugh and cry all at the same time. He was strong. And he was, like Bailiff Preacher, my friend.

Mo had come to visit me and see Jo several times while she was well. They had taken to each other so that she would hold out her hands to him each time she saw him. Then she would hug him and kiss the top of his head.

He'd come to the hospital and had seen her lying comatose there after the doctors had decided she was no longer infectious and that she would perhaps get a bit better.

I'd also escorted him to the assisted living center when she was better and she'd done the same outstretched-hands thing there with a gentle hug and a tiny kiss, surprising me. I wasn't sure Jo knew me, but something inside her remembered and knew and believed in Mo.

He'd said to me after his first visit: "Someone caused her this hurt, Robak. I feel it. Do you feel it?"

"Yes. The question is, Who? And how? And was it the same one or the ones who shot into our home afterward? Also was it the ones who burned your second church?"

He shook his head.

I have been a lawyer and am now a circuit judge. Circuit judges wear black robes and are supposed to be dignified personages. They listen to lawyers' learned arguments, and decide cases. They're required to believe implicitly in the law.

I practiced law for a long time before I became a judge. I believed in the law then.

But I learned down the years that the law is sometimes only words on paper. I learned also that those words can be flawed.

There are people out in the smoke and shadows who want my life and want Mo's life and have already taken large parts of my Jo's life. They crouch and wait, demons in the dark. They have been out there for all of my adult life. They lie, steal, and cheat. They rape and kill. They burn churches and poison people.

They are merciless, remorseless, and timeless.

They scheme and hide and are hard to find.

Mo is a good hunter. I own some minor cleverness at it.

I have decided that where my law works I will be a willing part of it. And I am.

I decided also that sometimes my law won't work or will only work poorly. Different problems then arise.

At such times I now do the best I can. I seem to be incapable of hurting someone unless that someone directly tries hurting me or mine in my presence.

I'm therefore not able to totally defend myself and my loved ones.

The inability to coldly kill doesn't keep me from seeking, and from sometimes finding, perpetrators.

I know, from our shared past, that Mo doesn't suffer my disability.

"Did you hear anything on our other matters you can tell me now?" I asked, recovering from my own inward vision.

"Only rumors. There are no rewards for you to pay."

"Did you hear Libbie Macing saying that the same rifle that was shot into my house was used to fire one or more shots into the Macing mansion?"

"I heard. We must jointly think and talk on that tomorrow as we drive to walk my church site."

"Yes. All right. I'll want to see Jo first thing in the morning."

"Of course. One more thing. Someone is looking into your house from outside. I sat upstairs in the dark and looked out under the shade. You know I see well in the dark. There is or was a someone out there near the first road. He or she is there in the weeds, lying quiet, near the old sawmill we run past mornings."

"Is the watcher armed?"

"I saw nothing of a weapon."

"There were the remains of a cold fire when I ran this morning," I said. "Do you think the someone is still outside watching?"

He shrugged, not knowing.

"And that's the reason you told me not to turn on the light?"

"Yes."

I thought about it. Whoever was out there likely could have taken a shot at Mo when or after Mo arrived. He/she could also have shot at me when I got out of my Ford or shot at Libbie when she alighted from or returned to her limo. So I wouldn't sneak out a door of my house with my shotgun.

Or would I?

I'd been informed by the area subdivider that Boy Scouts had once used the farm as a camping ground and that I should watch out for them.

Maybe Scouts still camped. I'd never seen any.

I tried to decide.

"Easy, Robak," Mo said. "You're becoming visibly upset. For what it's worth I read no menace in the watcher."

"All right, easy. Yes, easy. We can check it in the morning. That sawmill's not on my property. If it's the someone who built the fire I saw the remnants of this morning then that person will likely return again and we can lie in wait." I stopped and then thought of something else. "There are police patrols past here all night. I could turn a prowler report in to them?"

"Yes. The best of all answers."

I did call the report in. Later we saw flashlights moving about in the darkness.

No police officer came to the door and no one called me on the phone even though I turned the ringer on.

There were some phone messages, but all were from unknowns. Someone tried to sell me a credit card. Someone else offered fine windows. I erased them.

While we watched and waited I told Mo what had happened earlier and what I'd seen and heard at the Wolfer farm and thereafter.

"So you believe these people would kill you in order to obtain another judge for this cannibal baby-killer?"

"I do."

"Then I must also. What would happen if there was a new judge?"

"Incompletely known. Likely nothing. And nothing to help the Wolfers should happen in front of me or any other judge. Sometimes a sentence of death can be commuted to life or set aside, but this case probably won't end that way."

"So the case is done?"

"The appeals will go on for years more in state and federal courts. One day five or ten years away in time they'll finish and then Sweetboy Wolfer will be executed."

"Why such a long time?"

"It's the way things are. I think the courts justify the death penalty because the defendant gets so many chances to take a hack at it."

"But at some time this man will die?"

"Right."

"You had me read the transcript. Before I read it I didn't believe in the death penalty. I think I do now." He looked away and then back. "There are worse people out there than those who burn churches."

"The people who live on the Wolfer land call themselves patriots, citizens, and free men. They train as if they will soon go to war. They're something like that church that was a problem to you in Madisonville, but these folks have a fort and not a church. I think they want the federals to war on them so they can seek public sympathy and support. But before sympathy they likely want me."

We sat silently for a time.

He finally yawned and I yawned in return and it seemed a good time to end the day.

"Tomorrow's Saturday. It'll likely be a busy day for us," I said.

He nodded and I left him there in the dark kitchen with the dregs of his drink.

"Sleep well," I said.

"Yes," he answered. He was looking into the air again.

I went upstairs and thought on the day while I got ready for bed. I conjectured about what was going on around me and what I'd do if I was a part of the Wolfer clan and wanted a sure way to do in dumb Judge Robak.

If I vanished off the earth then that made problems for all my cases, pending or decided. The Wolfers couldn't show a future judge I was dead and that a new judge must be appointed. My disappearance could muddy the waters and slow the execution process, but not the appeal process. That might seem better or worse to them than killing me in the open so that my body would be found and a new judge named.

I mentally shrugged. I'd done no research on such and didn't plan to do any. I meant to stay alive.

And what good was young Wolfer to them in a prison? They wanted him outside.

I thought on it all for a long while and then called son Joe in Chicago and talked to him. I described the Wolfer farm and answered his questions about it. I passed on Judge Fromm's warnings. We talked about precautions.

"Judge Fromm believes they've already buried people there?"

"Yes."

"And you think they might fake an emergency involving you or Mom and then try to take me by force, kidnap me in the Louisville airport or along the highway, so that you'd then have to pay them the visit they want. Then they could kill us both?"

"Yes."

"Wow," he said. "You got imagination, Pop. But they won't get me to come because only you can get me."

"Don't fly into Louisville at all from now on. If you get what seems to be an emergency call then you call the sheriff or the state police and I'll get back to you."

In the dew-wet morning Mo and I inspected the old mill. There were no new ashes. Whoever had visited and watched us had done so last night without building a fire. So not likely a Boy Scout.

We found the place where we thought the night watcher had lain in the weeds. Small bush branches were bent and broken and there remained a body-sized indentation in the grass and weeds.

Once again there were particles of earth as if someone had carried them there and then dropped and spread them uncaringly.

We examined all carefully, looking for trip wires, wary of set traps. There was nothing.

There were no cigarette butts and there was no evidence to show whether the watcher had been armed.

"Whoever was here might also be out on our running route waiting for us to come past this morning," I said. "How about we drive to Green Home this morning to see Jo?"

"Good idea," Mo said.

We returned to the house and drove my Ford. We both watched for followers, but if anyone was behind us that person was better than we were.

Trudy and then Jo smiled at both of us at Jo's door. Jo, as she had done before, held out her hands to Mo, then pulled him close and gave him a phantom kiss on the top of his head. I was momentarily jealous, but then I put it aside, glad for both of them.

He took both her hands and she smiled up at him, thin, lost, brave, and achingly beautiful. She used her store of language on him. He listened intently and then nodded at her encouragingly when she was finished.

"She's looking for a way to get to us," he said. "She'll likely find it soon."

Jo went silent and watched both of us from her bed. Her eyes were bright as new pennies.

Trudy said: "I have some more news for you, Judge Robak. Yesterday, after you left, she pointed at a walker in the hall and had me get her one. She then stood by her bed holding on to it, not sitting down for a time."

"Did she try to walk?"

"No. She seemed content to stand looking around the room. She'd stand and then she'd sit down on her bed without my help. Standing up had to tire her some, but she kept at it, up and down. She did it four or five times until she got so tired she could't get up again." She nodded her head. "You know what I think?"

"Please tell me," I said.

"I think she'll walk soon. Lots of things are going on in her head. She's like a bright one-year-old."

"And she'll also talk?" Mo suggested.

The nurse nodded uncertainly. "I hope so."

Mo's church site was situated less than a quarter of a mile from the Wolfers' fortress farm. His tract was to the south and slightly to the west of Wolfers'. We followed different back roads than I'd traveled the evening before. The church tract was on a descending hill in a place where smaller streams converged and fell together in three leaping falls to become a larger bottom stream named Big Clifty Creek. From the bottom pool below the falls Big Clifty ran on to the Ohio River, maybe a dozen miles south.

There were several small farms across the road from the church land and to its northeast. North of those farms the land was higher than the church land. The small farms abutted the huge Wolfer tract on its south. I could see a lot of the barbed fence that made up the Wolfer boundaries. One of the creeks which ran across what was the church land ran southward from the Wolfer tract, passed under the fence there, wandered on down through a smaller farm, and then under a road bridge until it spilled its waters at the church falls.

We had passed no one on the road and that was lucky. I decided that if I came again I'd muddy up my license tag so as to obscure the numbers.

From Mo's church land I could also see a part of the cat lady's place. There was a log cabin off a gravel drive. On this day a person who might be the cat lady sat in her yard intently working on something she held in her lap. Her land was uphill from Mo's tract and it kept on rising to the Wolfer northwest corner at the road. Behind her cabin the hill ended. The area was where I'd observed the Wolfer castle the night before.

I could see cats, large and small. Many cats. Now and then one or more of the cats would come to the seated lady and she would interrupt her work to pet and scratch.

There were things I couldn't visually make out in her front yard. I thought for a moment and then guessed what they were. I'd seen things like them when she'd lived in Bington and I'd successfully represented her in city court. Whirligigs. Red and green and yellow, dime-store-sized whirligigs. She'd planted them in the ground all around her yard, fans whirring. Children's whirligigs made of bright plastic.

She'd told me once that some of the cats liked to play with the whirligigs and that the whir of them and their spacing helped keep interlopers outside her property.

I thought more on Ann Sembly. Once she'd been an engineer by trade, doing supervisory office work at a nuclear plant under construction in the Bington area. Something had happened, the plant had never been completed, and now she lived with her cats. I also remembered that she'd had an engineer husband and that he'd died.

If I took the dirt road to the west of the Wolfer land it looked to be no more than a quarter of a mile up that hill to her house.

I found an old cap in my car trunk. I pulled it over my ears.

Mo sat on the back of the lot. He looked down at the falls and the deep pool below.

"You like this land?" he asked me.

"Seems perfect except for one thing."

He waited.

"The land over there enclosed in barbed wire belongs to the Wolfer family. It's the place I told you about last night." I thought for a moment. "Could we get an option for maybe a year? I'd pay for the option and we'd not have to use any of the church funds."

He nodded, liking the idea. "I'll see. This place has been on the market for a long time, Judge. Do you think that's maybe because of its neighbors?"

I nodded. "Only because of the Wolfer neighbors. The people across the road on the small places were described to me as mostly Amish farmers, friendly folks."

"I'd not want to build a church where we wouldn't get along with all our neighbors," he said.

"It's unlikely you'd be accepted by the Wolfer clan. The list of what they're against starts with color."

He shrugged.

"I want to go up to the cabin on the left of the road," I said, pointing. "I know the lady there. She takes care of cats, lots of cats."

"Cats like me and I like them," he said easily. "Do you want company?"

"Are you finished here for now?"

"Yes." He looked around and I saw he was suddenly shaking a little.

"You okay?"

"I feel suddenly as if I've been on this land before, Robak. Another life, past or future. I believe something bad has already happened here or maybe that something bad will happen here in the future."

9

WE DROVE UP the road to Ann Sembly's cat farm. A rusty gate hinge was locked with a bicycle lock. I pulled the car off the road and parked it under white and purple dogwood trees that were in full bloom. We then scrambled up and over the gate.

Back across the road on Wolfer land I could feel eyes watching us. I pulled my cap lower.

We walked up the lane, not hurrying, but not dallying. If they were watching us from across the road all they'd see was a black man and maybe a white man walking up Ann Sembly's rutted road.

That lady sat in a folding beach chair in the middle of her yard of weeds. I thought soon her yard and the surrounding acres would be overgrown with high weeds for her cats to hide and play in, but for now most of the vegetation remained short, a mixture of brown and green.

She was sewing something, turning it about on her lap. When I drew closer to her I could tell she was trying to repair a rip in an old blanket.

I'd left my shotgun in the car because I'd not wanted to be identified by a keen watcher across the road who might recall that the hated Judge Robak now constantly carried a shotgun.

Ann Sembly had a shotgun beside her. I was encouraged that she didn't reach for it when she saw us. Instead she watched Mo Mellish with wide eyes. Cats surrounded him, curling around his knobby ankles. He laughed at them, petted and scratched the heads and backs of those nearest him, and, at the same time, managed to keep from stepping on any of the cats. There must have been fifty of the animals in his love parade.

The woman smiled at him and allowed me a small remainder of the smile. She was late fortyish and not unattractive, a short, chunky woman a little over five feet tall, with straight brown hair and intelligent hazel eyes. Her clothes were old and patched. She seemed huddled inside the tatters of a calico dress.

"I've never seen them act like this with a stranger, Robak," she called. "In fact, I've never seen them act like this at all. They're usually shy with anyone unknown."

"Reverend Mo Mellish told me that he likes cats and they like him."

She watched me, suddenly suspicious. "What are you doing on my land? And with a black minister who loves and is loved by my cats? Last time I saw you, Robak, you were overcharging me for a simple matter concerning my good cats in the Bington city court. Have you perhaps been Judas hired by that crazy outfit across the road?"

"No, ma'am. I'm not hired by them and we won your case, didn't we?"

She allowed me a small smile. "Yes. We did so only because I was in the right. It certainly wasn't because of your lawyering."

I was stung a bit. "My recollection is that Bington's animal control officer and many of your fine neighbors wanted to shut your residence down as a nuisance because you had more cats than the city ordinance allowed. You did have too many cats and your yard and house stank of cat offal. You had maybe twenty cats more than the Bington ordinance allowed."

"And so? That's old news. Get to the point."

"Your cat population seems to have increased three- or four-fold since that time." I sniffed the air. "They do smell better out in the air."

In the yard a few of the cats left off adoring Mo and sought battle with nearby whirligigs, attacking the whirling parts, stopping fans momentarily, uninjured by the wind-driven, delicate blades. Other cats watched the whirligig attackers with or without interest.

Ann Sembly sighed audibly. "The population has increased. I am given to loving many cats. Those savage bastards on the fenced farm over there try to kill every cat of mine that enters their land. Now they've had some jackleg lawyer file another nuisance case against me in court a few days ago." Her eyes narrowed in thought. "I don't suppose you would want to help me out with that?"

"I'm no longer practicing law. I'm now the circuit judge in Bington. But I have some friends I can inform of your problem. One of them will come or call and then take care of it. And because you believe I overcharged you before I will pay such lawyer from my own pocket. Do you have a phone out here?"

"Yes." She searched in a purse and handed me a worn card with her name, address, and telephone number on it. There was also a drawing of a kitten. "I accept your offer to pay. Money's tight."

I pocketed the card.

"Are you all puffed up about being a judge?" she asked, watching me.

"I hope not."

Mo had drawn close and she turned back to look at him again.

She then said to me: "Why don't you go up to the cabin porch and get a couple of folding chairs for you and your friend, Judge Robak. Doing something menial for people with less money than you might be good for you. And then we can all set easy and talk a spell. Later I'll run the two of you off before it gets full dark here and I have to hide my poor self inside." She shook her head. "And know that I'm interested in your purple friend a lot more than I am you. Cats don't like everyone and I certainly don't see packs of them hanging around you."

I followed orders and humbly walked to the porch. There was a stack of folding picnic chairs. I got two of them and started back. None of the cats paid any attention to me. Some had now ended their Mellish worship, but many of them still frisked lovingly near where he stood.

"Why do cats like you?" the woman asked Mo.

"I have an agreement with them. I promise each cat all of my love."

She smiled. "They're worth our love far more than most people are worth it. Cats are smarter than dogs. They have their own society. What is it they promise you in return, Preacher?"

"Nothing except that they'll treat me as a friend. They won't love me, but will tolerate me and play with me when it's the proper time for them to do such."

She nodded. "Good answers. You can come back anytime you want and be with my cats. Leave the damned self-important judge behind if you will."

I smiled grimly and gave Mo a chair. He unfolded it and sat down next to the woman.

"You are good to care for them," Mo said to her.

"It's my mission."

"I know about missions," Mo said.

I also sat down.

Mo looked down at the eight or nine cats that had hopped into his lap. I could see Ann Sembly was intrigued by him.

"All of us here have a mutual enemy," Mo said to her, using his Sunday voice, the one that sounded when he preached.

"Are you including the cats who live with me?"

"Of course. You, me, the cats, and the judge versus all the axe people who live across your road on their barbed-wire egg farm."

The woman nodded. "Tell me what it is they've done to you and the judge and then I'll tell you what they've done to me and my cats."

Mo told her about his second church fire, my wife's illness, and my house gunfire. I listened. He made it sound as if he and I knew for certain the Wolfers had planned and committed all the crimes.

Several cats still sat on Mo's lap and a dark pair moved under my hand as it dangled off the chair arm. They used the hand to scratch their downy backs. The feeling of it was not unpleasant. I'd never been a cat person. Jo had owned a now-dead kitten; he and I had ignored each other. This pair seemed to like me.

"Did they burn your church?"

"I believe they did. They are prime suspects."

"And they want to kill the judge?"

"Yes."

She said: "They wait and watch for my cats to come on their land. At first they shot at them to scare them away. Now they shoot to kill. For a time they picked up the cats they killed and hung them on their barbed wire as a warning to me. One afternoon I took my big gun from inside the cabin and shot that part of their wire fence to hell. I recovered the bodies of my dead cats and buried them in the cat cemetery in back of my house where my rear escape tunnel exits."

"Did they bother you after you shot up their fence?"

"Half a dozen of them soon tried to drive up my lane. I think they intended to kill me and scatter my cats. They tore down my gate at midnight. I sleep light and I shoot good. I got a big gun inside the cabin. It's a Sharps fifty caliber that came down to me from a cavalry great-uncle. My husband put new works and a new barrel on it just before he died ten years back." She smiled. "Those that came for me didn't stay long. That Sharps blew their truck into pieces. Four men were carrying two when they ran back across the county road. I was shooting the Sharps low on purpose that night. I won't shoot low again."

"What happened to the shot-up truck?"

"They came under a white flag. I allowed them to tow it away."

While we were talking I was watching the land behind the high fence. There was movement there. I saw a flash of light in the trees, maybe someone watching through binoculars or maybe the sun flashing off a rifle.

"I think the people over there might be zeroing in on us," I said. "We could get picked off by a shooter with a telescopic sight."

"Now and then they shoot this way. Mostly they do it as a nuisance," Ann Sembly said. She turned to Mo: "Let's go inside so as to keep the high judge safe from harm. I can give you coffee or some cola. Or we can move back behind hilltop cover and I'll get my big gun and shoot back. I'll allow you men to use the gun if you want."

I shook my head. "No war if it can be avoided."

We went inside. There were a few new cats prowling there. Ann looked the inside cats over fondly. "These housecats think of themselves as my favorites." She pointed at a white furry one. "That one's Lady Jane. She's very prissy. Somewhere, hiding from you, is Reverend Alben. He only likes lady cats. There's a Maine coon I call Queen Victoria although he's male."

Mo nodded. "Maine coon cats are big, fine, very independent cats."

She nodded, delighted. "Yes, they are."

"Have you ever been on the Wolfer place? I mean beyond their electric fence other than when you shot it up?" I asked her.

"Sure. I've walked all the way up to where I could see the big house. I've watched the guards parading around it. Them guards are thicker than flies and dumber than creek rocks."

"Without anyone ever catching or seeing you?" I continued.

"Sure. The ones inside think that if they dress themselves in camouflage that such makes them woods smart and invisible. It doesn't. They mostly watch the front gate of the farm. They keep lots of their people up near that gate. That's where they look for action. There's a two-person patrol that walks around the fence about every two hours at night. There are other people out and about during the daytime walking along the treeline. Sometimes at night I've seen guards carrying lanterns and flashlights through the woods. Sometimes they carry folks with them, folks all tied up with ropes."

"Prisoners?" I asked.

"They might be."

"Tell me what else you've seen."

"There's dozens of big chicken houses and maybe a million chickens. The chicken houses are twenty- to thirty-foot wide and more than two hundred feet long. I've watched people take the eggs away and other people arrive and clean things. They bury the chicken shit they take out in high ground which'll likely, later on, get it into the streams that flow through their farm. They bury dead chickens in shallow holes. It stinks bad near them chicken houses. Some big chicken-sized buildings just sit there without chickens, storing things inside."

"How many times have you been on their land?"

"Maybe a couple of dozen. It's easy to evade their patrols. And all you have to do at night, once you're under or over their rusty back fence, is use a little sense. The watch patrols they send out make a ton of noise coming and going."

"Do you believe they'll try to invade your place again?" I asked.

"Maybe. I'm a semiretired engineer. I'm also one-quarter Indian. That works good for me and bad for them. I've dug some traps on dark nights to catch their vehicles. If they come over here again I'll be waiting." She shook her head. "They now want to buy me out. They sent an offer registered mail. Then they filed their lawsuit to make me think more about the offer."

"How much was the offer?"

"Maybe more than this place is worth. With a promise it'd be in cash. But I'm not about to sell. The farmers around the bend of the road on the back of the Wolfer place also have had good cash offers. They came here once, four whole families of them, and we all talked while their kids played with cats and kittens. Some of the adults saw me shoot up the Wolfer fence. They liked that. The four families say they won't sell without me telling them to sell."

Mo asked: "Could you take me onto the Wolfer place?"

"Sure. When it gets dark." She looked at me. "You want to go?"

"Best not. There's good reason for me not to go on their place just now. I made a promise I'd not go to the judge in this county. So I'll stay here and keep an eye on things."

She shrugged, perhaps not displeased. She turned back and looked Mo over.

"Can you walk okay? You seem to walk funny sometimes."

"I can both walk and run okay."

Hours later when it got dark I drove the Ford back to the highway, then on into Floydsburg. I got a bucket of Colonel Sanders and fixings. Returning, I parked my car inside the fence and close to the house. I retrieved the car's shotgun for Mo.

We ate in silence. The cats sat near us watching one another, very social.

"Dogs would be all over us wanting to share the food," I said.

"My cats don't do that. I don't feed them from the table."

"How long are you going to spend looking around over there behind the fence?"

"Maybe two or three hours?" Ann Sembly said, mostly to Mo. He nodded willingly at her.

"Sure you don't want to change your mind?" Mo asked me.

"I made this other judge a solemn promise I wouldn't go on Wolfer land. I'll maybe try to opt out of the promise sometime, but not now. If you get into trouble over there shoot the big gun and I'll start calling police and sheriffs."

"Anything you want us to look for?"

"If you get close to any of those trucks they have, see what they're carrying in the truck beds. What I'm worrying about is whether they have any fertilizer mixed with diesel oil and maybe some dynamite to set it all off."

She shook her head before Mo could reply: "Like Oklahoma City? I've checked the inside of the trucks before. Maybe they want people to worry about truck bombs, but I've not seen any so far. If I had I might have set them off."

"Do you keep dynamite?"

"Sure. I need it to blow out tree stumps, Judge."

"We'll look things over good," Mo said.

Instead of exiting out the front door they went out into the night through a tunnel in the floor.

After the two of them were gone I made sure the shades were closed tight. I found a big bookshelf and picked out a Harlan Ellison collection. I read for a while, and then put it back. The stories were great, but reading them all in a row was too much for me, maybe too much for this world or any other world.

I waited for a while, listening. Somewhere an owl hooted and somewhere, farther away, a dog barked.

I finally went to sleep sitting in my chair.

They woke me when they came back into the house.

"I bet Mo you'd be sleeping," Ann Sembly said.

Mo nodded.

Neither of them looked the worse for wear. Both seemed slightly damp and I could hear a gentle rain tapping the roof of the old cabin.

Mo pulled a chair up next to me. "It was quiet inside. We saw a few guards when we got close to the house, but almost everyone was inside because of the rain."

"Tell me all of what you saw."

"Most of the land beyond the trees is barren. The trees, when you sneak through them, look half dead, but there are lots of them. After you get into the the treeline and walk a good ways you can see the house. There was something going on up there, maybe a party of some kind. Before we got close to the house we looked things over where they have most of the chicken houses."

"Tell me about that."

"There are two dozen chicken houses and they are huge build-ings. A few of the houses have no chickens and, instead, have sacked fertilizer in them. A few have the fertilizer shoveled in loose. Piles of it. I checked the ground where they're trying to grow corn and soybeans and they hadn't used much of it yet, but it's only April."

A question skittered through my mind like water down a shower drain. "How about the trucks? Did you check any of them?"

"Yes. None of them had anything other than corn and old cobs inside the beds."

"Go on."

"In the largest of the mostly chicken-house factories, this one half again larger, there were four chains hooked up to a ceiling beam in the big inside room," Mo said. "Maybe they use chaining for discipline. The cuffs on the four chains weren't shiny and looked used. You could chain someone or several someones up, lock the door, and use the dark to punish him or her. On the off chance that Miss Ann or you or me might wind up getting chained to that beam if we keep nosing around I stuck one of my little pocket picks, one like I once gave you, up where the chains hook over the beam, at the far south chain. I also loosened the chains some, and hid a stout stick to use as a weapon in the wall. It's up high and dark, pretty much concealed by siding boards. Then I generally bollixed that whole chicken house up, pulling things loose here and there, weakening the ceiling by pulling some of its nails and the roof apart, and like that."

"I told him to," Ann Sembly said. "Looking around that par-ticular chicken and chain house gave me the willies. It did the same to Mo. He kept imagining that sometime, in another life, he was hurt bad around here." She shook her head, saw Mo wasn't looking at her, and winked broadly at me. I waited for her to make a twirling motion at her head but she didn't.

"Someone will see the damage and they'll then watch closer," I said.

Mo shook his head. "Maybe. Maybe not. If they notice they might just think that someone who lives inside their place did it to get even for something done to him or her for punishment there." He looked around Ann's main room. "What now, O Judge of great ability and renown?"

"Home."

We said goodbye to Ann Sembly, got into the Ford and drove away, headlights off. We didn't turn them on until we were far away from the Wolfer Fort.

We went back to Bington the way we'd come instead of driving past the Wolfer main gate and being observed.

Two Saturday nights a month I hold a poker game in my basement. Lawyers sign up for the simpler of the games in my office. That one's penny ante and for laughs, young lawyers eating the judge's food and drinking from a keg of his beer. It was a chance for the bar to get at the judge, being me. I had a reputation in the penny-ante poker game of being an easy mark. I did little to change it, calling when I knew I was beaten, trying to catch three-card flushes and inside straights. Chances, slim and none.

On the other monthly game night I played serious poker, dollar ante, half the pot limit. That game was also in my basement. The eight invited game players were usually the three partners in my former firm, namely Sam King, a large African American who'd once played football for Indiana U. Despite that he was extremely bright. Then there was Kevin Smalley, who was gay, but who could likely best the larger Sam King in a fight. Jake Bornstein, one of my first partners, came sometimes. He was small and good and had six kids and a lovely wife. Then there was sometimes Preacher, sometimes Mo, Sheriff Jumper Jimp, Doc Hugo Buckner, and me, all rock-hard losers.

I gave Sam King and Kevin Smalley Ann Sembley's card, and told them of her cat problems and that I'd pay for her.

Sam said: "These people who are harassing her, they don't like us African Americans?"

I nodded.

"How do they stand on gay rights?" Kevin asked.

"Don't ask, don't tell. And I'm paying the fee because she thinks I overcharged her once."

I told them some of the things I knew about the Wolfer farm and also warned them to exercise extreme care.

"Why, of cose we will, Boss Judge," Sam said. "And I won't let Kevin here pick a fight and beat up anyone." He thought for a moment. "I have a lead on the whereabouts of the person who was in charge of the mail at the hospital when your wife was a patient there."

"I need to hear about that," I said.

"And so you shall as soon as I find out enough to tell."

Jumper Jimp appeared wearing a red shirt and wool pants. He squeaked when he walked because he was wearing an oversized gun in a leather holster on a leather belt. He was a big man and he was strong, but something was obviously wrong with his body. It was bent and twisted. It had happened in his state-police days when an eighteen-wheel driver, enraged because his drug cargo had been discovered, had jumped into his huge truck, locked the doors, and rammed Jimp's cruiser four times with Jimp inside. Other officers had shot out many of the tires on the rig, but nothing had stopped the rogue driver until a trooper had jumped on the cab and fired a riot gun through the front windshield.

It was a tribute to Jimp that the tale about the truck was far down the list of stories told about him. Once, after golf, I'd viewed Jimp in the country club shower. He had so many old, healed wounds that he looked like an assembled jigsaw puzzle with a dozen pieces missing.

Jimp nodded at me, not smiling. "Someone unknown shot a thirty-thirty rifle into your house some five or six months back and then shot that same gun into the Macing mansion day before yesterday."

"So I was told by the mean and lovely female third of the Macing family."

Jumper nodded. "I didn't know you were friendly with her these days, Judge."

139

"I'll tell you and all else present just one time and one time only that we're not bed pals," I answered, biting off each word. "Have you found out anything on the Macing shooter?"

"He or she got away. Shot one time and then vacated the area. No one seems to have seen anyone or anything suspicious, although we're not done asking questions. By the time the deputies, the estate guards, and the rest fell all over each other even the ground where the shooter had sighted in was trampled."

"Someone who hates them and also hates me?"

"Could be that way," he said, nodding. "Does it mean anything to you, Judge?"

"Was Libbie Macing inside the house when the shots were fired?"

"Not more than ten feet from her brothers, Judge." He shook his head, maybe guessing at why I'd asked that question.

"Let me think on some possibilities a while," I said.

I reflected that I was a friend to Jumper because he was a good sheriff and I admired his work, yet he need not be a good friend of mine. To him I might be just another problem, a high-profile judge lots of people wanted dead or out of office.

But from what I'd heard he was strongly backing me for re-election, tying my second term to his own in his speeches and advertising.

"Mojeff County needs an effective justice system. We have one. Keep it."

Downstairs, waiting to sit down at the poker table, Jumper gave me a second nod and then drew me off into the side room where I kept a refrigerator, snacks, and drink fixings. I'd fixed up the house poker and party rooms with money paid me for my interest in my old law firm's offices. I'd done it only after I'd bought an expensive dinner ring for Jo, a ring that looked extremely fine with her brown eyes.

"I have two deputies out in your driveway watching things tonight."

I was willing. "Okay."

"And another deputy told me about the trip past the Wolfer farm, plus the lady who waited at your house when you returned. What the hell did Miss Pretty Pants want other than the obvious?"

"I'm not sure. I think she and her brothers would like me to contact them and offer to buy their support by helping them in their current problem with stockholders who've sued them. That's presently before me in court and I recently hurried the case along. Neither side seemed to like that."

"And you're not going to do anything to help the Macings?"

I remembered that they were going to hire him if he lost the election, but I answered truthfully. "No. I'll judge it honestly. I've been turning down offers to purchase me made by the Macing family for more than twenty years."

"I swear you and me are the only honest politicians left. Beyond us there's the whole damn evil world," Jumper said.

I smiled at his tone. "Someone is playing a game around this county more interesting than our card game. Maybe it's somebody who was an enemy back before I was on the bench or maybe someone I put in prison." I shook my head. "Listen hard for me. All I'm able to do so far is make bad guesses."

"Yep, I'll listen," he said. "I like you, Jedge. You'd truly rather die than give an inch." He whacked me on the back approvingly and we went out to play cards.

At a break there was a short opportunity and I talked to Preacher.

"Conjecture on a reason Libbie Macing came to see me? Other than because of my irresistible charm?"

He frowned and then shook his head. "I don't know, Judge. How long-lasting are you?"

I ignored the remark. "Is there anything going on at Macing Company or in the lives of Libbie and her brothers that you know and I don't?"

"Nothing known, but I'll check around."

I won a few and lost a few. I remembered that Jo had never approved of the stakes we played for, but had liked and approved of the men who appeared and reappeared for the monthly game.

None of the men had ever complained about the stakes. All of them, to my knowledge, could afford them.

Over the length of the evening I brought the players up on news about Jo, and related to them what I'd seen at the Wolfer farm.

When the game ended and all of my guests except Mo left I tidied up and then slept.

I dreamed about cats, a whole flowing sea of them. They were on my side and I was a full general of cats.

Going to war.

10

ON SUNDAY I took an afternoon drive by myself. I wasn't supposed to go about without police escort, but I went anyway. After a time of watching behind me in the mirror I became certain I wasn't being followed.

I had my loaded shotgun in the Ford.

The day was fine. There was abundant spring sun and lots of Sabbath drivers on the main roads. I didn't stay on those heavily traveled roads long.

The Church of the Redeemer and New Saints was about a dozen years old. It was built on a hill above a decent county road one mile off an Indiana State highway and five miles north of Bington. In wintertime the church building and its tower—a steeple with a Latin cross at the top—could easily be seen from the road below. Searchers didn't have to seek the eighteen-foot-high stone statue of Jesus, His right hand out for either a shake or a blessing. That statue marked the hill-bottom gate to the church. On this spring day with April not quite two-thirds done and with the world turning full green in Indiana, the statue helped.

Today I used Jesus and His gate only for a journey landmark because my destination wasn't the Redeemer church.

I remembered while driving my Ford that the Right Reverend Raybin McFee, called by his friend Jesus to be minister of the church, lived alone in a large house his church had built for him in gratitude. The house was about a hundred yards from his church doors.

Raybin was a strong, spirited man about my size and age who dressed and attempted to look like Abe Lincoln in Lincoln's beardless years. He was loud-voiced and unread except for his heavily thumbed and thumped Bible.

Once, before I became judge, he'd claimed in public that he was a fighting man like Old Abe and also had an invincible friend in Jesus who was on his side in all things. He'd done this while he was threatening me physically. He thought I'd made trouble around Bington for him and I had done that because he was an overbearing man who used his church mostly to avoid work and taxes. He'd sought and found me on one of Bington's wide streets. I'd stood confronted by him near the courthouse and we'd soon drawn a crowd around us as he spouted his ideas about my pedigree. I'd smiled and then grinned at his threats and given back words as good as I was getting. Such had infuriated him and he'd finally taken a roundhouse swing at me. That had worked badly. He was strong, but muscle-bound and slow. I'd scuffed him up more than a little, breaking his nose and doing a lot of dental damage.

Since then, up to this fine day, his threats against me had been made long distance. He now claimed he'd slipped and also that I'd fouled him. He proclaimed to his followers that I'd been lucky to live through the street fight.

He'd promised them that one day my time would come.

Momentarily I paused at his Jesus gate remembering the fight and liking my recollection. I thought about banging on his door and bearding him, making a personal matter out of my present problems, whacking him around for my poor Jo.

I truly had within me the intent to scuff him up once more and then tell him my time didn't appear to be up yet.

I finally drove on. Absent Jo informed me that circuit court judges just don't do things like that and that she wasn't mad at Raybin and didn't want me to be mad at him anymore, either.

I wished I wasn't a judge and had my Jo back where she could better keep me straight. She'd had more common sense when well than I'd ever have.

I slowed my car a little and looked back, tempted to silence Jo's inner voice. McFee's church was surely done with its wild services until evening. He'd likely be around the grounds and available. But I'd not come to bruise McFee on this day. The urge lessened, probably because of what Jo continued to whisper inside my head.

I stepped down on the Ford's accelerator.

I drove another mile. There I found a trailer camp with a half dozen rusty trailers sprawled among twenty poorly marked spaces.

The biggest and best of the trailers belonged to Earl Hardiman and his daughter Alma June. They'd lived in the court for a long time. They were friends of mine.

I parked my Ford nearby in the thickest patch of gravel and knocked on Hardiman's door, first softly, then loudly when no one answered.

The door eventually opened a fraction and Hardiman stared blearily out at me. He drank some.

"What the hell time is it, Judge?"

"It's mid-afternoon, slugabed," I said, fond of the last word, remembering it from a poem. Hardiman was in his early forties, but he appeared to be older than that.

Wafting out from his door I could smell the trailer interior. There was the odor of fried bacon, stale coffee, minty shaving cream, perfume, and something I thought had to be pot.

Once, a long time back, I'd defended Hardiman in a major Mojeff County murder case. I'd gotten him found mostly not guilty after a ten-day jury trial. He'd only been declared guilty on a single minor gun charge. The jury had believed my self-defense theory. My client Hardiman had admittedly shot and killed an area drug sales manager. That large and belligerent man had come armed and threatening to Hardiman's trailer door and there found his final reward from a Chief's Special .38 slug.

Earl owed the drug salesman pot money.

The jury had quickly found for us on all major counts of the indictment. With credit for jail time already served there was only half a year to go on the gun charge. A thoughtful special judge, after a sentencing hearing, had sighed and suspended even that time to the chagrin of the prosecutor. I thought the judge figured the legal system would surely see Earl again and could remind him of that suspended sentence while laying a long prison term on him next time.

The jury defeat had so perturbed the prosecutor then holding office that he'd made great newspaper and radio fuss. He'd lost in the primary of his next election year. Later on he'd moved across the river into Kentucky seeking an easier town to live and practice in than bad Bington. I'd heard it told recently that he'd gotten himself disbarred down there, but I didn't know such to be true fact.

Hardiman had several bad qualities. He not only drank but he also smoked pot, sometimes by the bagful. Like the Reverend Raybin McFee he didn't care for manual labor and he had a thousand dodges, learned in the southern Indiana school of hard knocks, to get out of such drudgeries.

He burgled and stole, but was cautious as a rabbit in a spring snowstorm when he committed his felonies.

He also sometimes legally bought and sold overpowered cars, being good with his hands on auto motors and loving fine cars. Many charter members of the local thief-and-robber group had limited trust in Earl, but they were careful and respectful of him mostly because of his beating the murder charge and also the memory of the dead drug salesman with Earl's .38 slug in him.

Earl also treated his twenty-one-year-old crippled daughter Alma June poorly, sometimes smacking softly at her, not wanting to injure her. He was always in charge of his family in his own mind and would order her about, but he was also aware of her values.

I knew she loved him and he loved her in his way. She'd come to see me when he was charged with the drug dealer's murder more than a dozen years back. She'd been eleven then, mildly spastic, spending most of her waking hours in a manual wheel-chair, half pretty in a twisted-body, huge-eyed way. She'd cried out for help and so I'd accepted Earl's case without enthusiasm or retainer. Then I'd won it when I thought I'd lose it.

I'd eventually talked the then Honorable Judge Steinmetz into hiring me as Earl's pauper counsel so the case hadn't been a complete financial loss.

Earl had two things that helped me win his murder trial. The first was that he looked good. He had the face of an overworked priest. No one could look at Hardiman without liking his looks. His movements were careful and nonthreatening and his voice was soft and even cultured at times. He smiled genially. He read a lot and remembered a little of what he read, so he seemed brighter than he actually was. I thought that the thing about his looks was more likely what had saved him from a long prison term than my stellar, table-pounding defense. The vanished prosecutor had laughed about such defense (and the jury obviously had not) in his own final argument.

One elderly juror confided in me later that she wasn't going to send such a nice-talking, handsome man to prison just because he'd shot an armed and dangerous drug king no matter what that loudmouthed prosecutor, who'd moved to Bington and hadn't been born there, told her the law was.

I'd nodded my thanks, but hadn't commented on the prose-cutor's birthplace, seeing as how I also suffered from not being born in Bington.

Earl was also loyal. In jail I'd supplied him with two or three packs of necessary Winstons a day. I'd told him bad stories about cancer and cigarettes. Having myself quit about then I'd become

Christian about proclaiming it. He'd smiled and nodded pleasantly at me, puffing away and blowing smoke at me while wishing what he had to smoke was some good Kentucky pot.

After I'd gotten him off I'd loaned or given him Bud Light money at times. I'd been his friend and pal for advice and I also served as his minister of finance in times of need. Having unexpectedly gotten him off a murder charge he felt I'd adopted him and he, in turn, then adopted me.

Therefore he was loyal to me, but only when it suited his purposes. He'd told Preacher he wanted to see me and so I was at his door on a Sunday.

He opened that door wide.

I entered and sat gingerly on a battered couch. He sat near me on a folding chair and smiled his good smile. The trailer living area was full of junky furniture, the kitchen with piled dirty dishes, and the floor with soiled clothes. Inside the smells were stronger, but it wasn't unpleasant, just smells all crowded together in too small a living space.

"Where's Alma June today?"

"She's got a new job down to King's Daughters' Hospital. She goes there weekends and sits behind a desk and is the Saturday and Sunday telephone emergency lady. They like her so much they send a van after her. Load her in, wheelchair and all." He nodded, probably thinking of Alma June because the smile remained when his words were done.

"You know she never met a stranger, Robak," he added.

That was true. Alma June had a sunny nature and she could and would talk with anyone. She was also maybe two or three times as bright as Earl would ever be. I liked her a lot. So had Jo when well.

"Preacher said you called and wanted me to come see you. What's up?"

"Well, you know who lives about a mile down my road, don't you? I hear you sure ought to know who it is."

I thought on it. "West of your trailer it would likely be the Reverend Raybin McFee with his church and parsonage house.

East it would be the fine Macing estate with all its big barns and Arabian horses."

"East would make you right as a revenuer with a sweet sense of smell," he said, nodding to me encouragingly. "Some state police and deputy sheriffs stopped past here late the other night and wanted to know if I'd seen or heard anything from up the Macing direction. Alma June was asleep in her bed and they pounded hard on the door and woke her up along with disturbing my television time. We both know Alma June needs her sleep. Peed me off the way they acted. But I was polite as a cake-and-tea erection and I told them I'd been in all evening and hadn't seen or heard a thing. Alma June backed me up. They also wanted to look around in our trailer and I gave them permission although they were already doing their looking and their messing things up by the time they asked permission."

"And so?"

"I kind of told one itty-bitty hot-titty lie. I did see some stuff when I was out doing my constitutional walk up near the Macings' big house earlier."

"What time?"

"I go out early in the evening."

"What is it you didn't tell the officers?"

He shook his head. "I need to get this straight with you first, Don. I mean what with you being the high judge and you and me being good friends. Let's say first off I didn't tell them anything because I'm a citizen these days. I'm not on parole and I'm not fresh out of the county jail and no one's looking to put me in there. I damn well don't have to say one damn word to overbearing pricks. I don't have to say anything to you, either, but we're close and so I called. You tell that to them state troopers and that sheriff, who looks crookeder than I ever will be, if you feel like you must. That's if you decide to tell them what I'm going to say to you now, which I'd just as soon you didn't do."

"Next time they might pound you if I tell them you held any crumb back."

"Wouldn't buy them a damn thing. I've been pounded a lot of times before in this life, Judge Don."

"I remember." He was tough as a half-dollar steak and we both knew it. "I won't tell them."

"Thanks. It's not that much of a deal anyway," he said. "I walk along quick and quiet, Don. I don't bother no one. Such behavior has always been my way. It was a nice night for walking. Warm for April and all. I was near the Macings' gate and one of their uniformed guard officers was also near it. I stopped and waited in the dusk with him not seeing me. Most of the Macing guards are crooks or ex-crooks but, once more, I don't look for trouble these days. I was just about ready to turn around and start back, but then I stayed doggo and listened instead. That was because I heard someone coming from inside of the fence."

"And what did you hear?"

"Not real much. There was this lady who came down the drive about then. It was the one I heard you was once sweet on and who I now hear might again be your sweetie pie."

I shook my head unbelievingly. Everyone in and around Bington seemed to know that Libbie had come to visit me at Jo and my home.

"I almost missed seeing her. She was dressed in clothes so lookalike to what the guard was wearing that I thought she was a guard replacement until I heard her voice and saw her curvy-lady figure in the gate light. She's a pretty woman and I guess the both of us wouldn't kick her out of bed, not that I'll ever get a hack at her."

I gritted my teeth and asked once more: "What did you hear?"

"She was talking to this chief guard. It listened like she was taunting and laughing at him, maybe mostly joking like. I heard her say he wasn't much good at guarding the gate. I heard her say that all the damn gate and grounds guards ought to be fired. Maybe something had gone wrong earlier."

"It had," I said. "Someone fired a rifle shot into the front door of the house."

He shook his head. "No. That shooting happened later than when I was there, Don. I walked home and the trooper and sheriffs came to my door maybe two or three hours after I got back. From the time they supplied me when they asked about someone shooting it was more than an hour later from when I was doing my listening."

"Sure?"

"Positive."

"So maybe something else had happened to make Libbie talk nasty to the guard. Did you hear what it was?" I asked.

"She said to the guard that she knew he spent all his shift time watching television and drinking beer or coffee inside the gatehouse. When he said that wasn't true she followed up by saying the only thing he knew from guard duty were baseball scores and the headlines on area sex crimes. She said he was supposed to watch also for labor agitators, but that one had drove in through the gate earlier just because he was in a shiny black Chrysler. She said the one who'd come was okay but no one was to come inside the gate to visit without a call to and from the house okaying it. She named people she especially didn't want coming inside. Your name was one of the names she used. I heard her say your name twice. 'Judge Don Robak.' That's what she said."

That surprised me, but only a little. Maybe Libbie thought I might come calling on her brothers to plead my reelection case or to read off one or both of them. Or, more likely in her mind, come calling on her. I smiled to myself thinking about that. I had no intention of making any deal with any of the Macings. I doubted they had the power to sway many votes. They liked to pretend to great political power, but they had little.

If there was labor trouble at the Macing Drug Company's several area plants I'd heard nothing about it. But then there'd been multiple labor problems at Macing in the past because the plant paid peanuts to the untrained.

I'd ask Preacher. He'd likely know.

"You said most of the guards are crooks. Tell me more about that."

"They just are. Whoever does the hiring of them isn't checking their arrest records."

"How about what the guards get paid?"

"They get good money."

"You said also that the guard Libbie was talking to was the head guard. How do you know that?"

"Because he's my cousin, Judge Don. I didn't want him catching me watching him. He's a mean son of a bitch and he's bigger than the two of us."

I thought on one more thing. "I keep seeing black pickup trucks with the number twenty-three on the doors. You know anything about that?"

He shook his head. "Not me. But, thinking on it, I believe there was a black truck on the driveway inside the Macing place that night. I didn't see any numbers."

I found that interesting.

"You know someone shot into my house about six months ago. Do you know or have you heard anything about that?"

"No."

"Or anything about the reason Jo got sick?"

"There were some rumors around when it happened, but I never heard anything worth wasting your time."

"Tell me the rumors."

"Some thought because your wife was kind of poisoned that you ought to be checking out all your enemies." He nodded. "When I heard Libbie Macing was around your place recently I thought maybe you was checking her out personal. I mean looking down at her while you was asking interesting questions."

"I'm not her lover and haven't been for about twenty years. Are there any labor problems at all around Macing Drugs that you've heard about?"

"People are always complaining because the Macings run their own damn union. I guess you can do that when you own as much shit and apple butter as they do."

I drove home and sat in my kitchen thinking some on what Earl Hardiman had told me. I'd tried to refit Libbie into Jo's puzzle before, but nothing had worked out of it. The time frame was all wrong.

I reluctantly put Libbie back into the running. All I had to do to include her was ignore the fact that we'd been enemies and not lovers for the past twenty years.

Mo was gone again. This time he'd apparently been able to get his brown car's motor running. It had vanished with him. I thought he might be out with the cats I'd dreamed of the night before.

The house was empty. I disliked emptiness. I sat there mulling over Libbie some more. She did have big-time money and she could buy lots of people to do her bidding, no matter what it was. My bet was that she'd hired the outlaw guards at her gate, not her brothers.

But why? I reread inside my head that it had been twenty years since we'd been bed pals. The relationship had then been hot, but I didn't think she'd carried a torch for a double decade, three engagements, and lots of other boyfriends. That was despite what had happened when she recently visited me. Visiting me was a part of one of her games.

I thought and rethought and finally ran empty.

I moved to the living room and settled into a comfortable chair. I put my feet up on a stool and slept through most of a professional basketball game, dreaming of Jo. The sports television station showed almost as much game time as it spent shouting strident commercials selling cheap furniture, no money down. After the game was done I watched an action movie where they killed a few dozen people and sold everything from extremely soft toilet paper to sexy clothes at commercial breaks. I liked the movie okay. I'm partial to those where underdogs win out in the end, like *Quigley Down Under,* and *The Natural,* and maybe *Top Gun.* If I can I only watch the endings.

I checked my home phone. I no longer kept the ringer on because too many calls came from the crazed and the angry. If a person called they got a message center and could leave a message, but only when a name and return telephone number was furnished. Today there was nothing of interest. I pressed numbers and made all calls vanish. I then called son Joe, but the phone rang and then his own message center came on. I reminded Joe I'd be up next weekend if things remained calm.

I went upstairs and let Barbra Streisand sing me to sleep with her perfect trumpet of a voice. Jo had loved Barbra. So did I. Sometimes Barbra sang songs that ill fitted her, but she made even those sound good.

On that Monday morning in April the day began cloudy and wet. It rained cold drops on me running home from seeing Jo, but then you can't depend on the weather in April because that changeable month seldom realizes it's a part of spring.

Jo was about the same, but she'd blown in my ear before I'd blown in hers. That was an improvement.

I thought I missed her far more than she missed me. She seemed content in her make-believe world.

Her old friends had told unbelieving me she'd been a tomboy when young. By the time I met her, and soon loved her, she'd been, at the least, an elegant and completely female ex-tomboy.

I wanted her back with me. I wanted all to be as it had once been.

I knew it wasn't going to happen.

I toweled dry in the bathroom, dressed quickly, drank my morning orange juice, and then waited for my escort. When they arrived they parked outside my door instead of tooting their horns. I went out on the porch, waved, and was informed that there was an ugly crowd waiting in the third-floor courthouse hall.

It began to rain harder as I listened. I got into Deputy Bob's vehicle instead of driving my Ford. The rain beat down hard. We had to raise our voices to hear each other.

"You've got a loud bunch of turd kickers up there, Judge. Mostly men, but there's some women. All ages. None of them, except one man, are dressed up in suits or ties. I don't know who they all are, but I believe they ain't locals," said Deputy Bob. "They got a big, fat lawyer with them. I've seen him before around our courthouse doing his business. He's sitting with them wearing a cheap suit with a well-fed tie. They've got your benches and hall walls full of sitters. They keep yelling they demand a hearing."

"What's Jumper say about it?"

Bob grimaced and I remembered again he was running against Jumper. "He's treating it redneck like he usually does. Sheriff thinks we ought to roust them out of the courthouse before they start big trouble, but he says such is your decision. They're smokin' and spittin' and just generally messing your courtroom hall up."

"Did anyone hear what they want a hearing about?"

He shrugged. "I don't know. I guess no one knows. Death penalty is usually a good guess, but they don't act like them old ladies that come around so hot against the death penalty that they dribble cheese. This bunch was making a lot of noise outside the courthouse before the doors were opened. They ain't carrying any signs."

"And so?"

"When the doors did get opened they literally ran up the stairs to the third floor and took control of your hall. The courtroom is still locked up tight. All this was before your deputy guards arrived at the courthouse. We kept the guards from going up and so no one knows for sure if any of the hall crowd are armed."

"See if Judge Fred will let me use his office on the second floor for a few moments. Then separate the oversized lawyer from the mob if you can. His name's likely Ed Amesworthy. Take him away from the others and bring him downstairs to Fred's office.

No one else. Just him. If he refuses find me and tell me. And tell the people who work for me not to go to the third floor. Rescue them off it if they're already up there."

Bob nodded. "None of them got upstairs. They all got stopped. You going to wait in the sheriff's office?"

"No. I'll be in the courthouse close to Judge Fred's chambers. Look for me in the clerk's office. When I see or hear you bringing the lawyer I'll show up also, but make sure it's okay to use Judge Fred's office before bringing Amesworthy there. Sometimes Judge Fred's got his own program going and he might not want me or my rainy-day problems."

Judge Fred had one of the two superior courts on the second floor. His full name was Frederick F. Frederick. I'd never had enough enterprise or courage to ask him what the middle initial stands for. It was a tribute to his intelligent but caustic nature that I'd also never heard about anyone else asking.

We were cordial friends without being close. Sometimes he used my courtroom and jury room for a trial, mine being much larger than his own rooms and more fitting for longer, larger trials. Sometimes I used his office when I wanted privacy or when a special judge was using my office.

F. F. F. was a first-class judge. Whatever he did was all right with me.

I entered a courthouse side door and walked up steps to the second floor. I went in the back door of the clerk's office and stole a cup of their strong, stellar coffee. I warmed my hands and throat with its savory darkness. The back rooms were filled with hundreds of shelves containing old record books dating back into the early nineteenth century.

The county clerk, having been notified I was in her offices, came back to see for sure.

"Need anything special, Judge Don?" she asked politely. We were pals and so she was smiling even though she belonged to the other political party.

"No, Gertie. Just hiding out from the crowd upstairs for a few moments."

"You got yourself a mean mob upstairs," she said. "I didn't know any of them by face except the overlarge lawyer. His name's Ed Amesworthy if you don't already know. I don't think anyone in this bunch of complainers is from our own beloved Mojeff County. Amesworth lives and practices in Floyd County."

"I'll bet a dollar you're correct."

"You can stay here as long as you want, Don." She nodded. "Even if my commissioners don't like you I do."

I smiled and blew her a kiss.

Deputy Bob soon came in the back door to the clerk's office. He saw me and nodded. "You can use Judge Fred's office and we got the fat lawyer sitting inside it waiting for you. You were right about his name. He didn't much like getting picked out of his crowd."

"Did he resist?"

"No. He raised a little minor hell. A couple of the people who were sitting with him in your hall wanted to come along. I told them I'd take all that came to jail and separate out the one I wanted there. The rest stayed upstairs messing up things in your hall after Amesworthy told them to stay. Some of them have bar soap and they're writing on your windows."

"What are they writing?"

"I don't like to repeat it," he said. "You know how gentle I am."

"Sure you are." I opened the back door again and went across to Judge Fred's chambers.

11

ED AMESWORTHY SAT in a wooden chair in front of Fred Fred's big desk. I thought he was sweating a little even though the courthouse was morning cool from the rain.

Judge Fred's office was decorated with pictures of deceased judges who'd once sat on the Mojeff circuit court bench. Now that there were two new superior courts trying local cases some courthousers were waiting to see if Fred hung dead superior judges' pictures up also, but no superior court judge had yet died and both were young.

I'd known the latest pair of deceased circuit riders, Judges Steinmetz and Harner. I nodded to them courteously.

"You going to record this, Judge?" Amesworthy asked, trying to sound threatening.

I looked down at him. I guessed he weighed three hundred and fifty pounds packed in, on, and around a five-foot-nine frame.

"I can record our discussion if you want it done. You tell me. Are you representing the crowd upstairs, Mr. Amesworthy?"

"Not really. A couple of them asked if I'd come along and so I did."

"I'll have someone find my court reporter."

He thought for a moment and then shook his head ponderously. "I'm not requesting that you have the session recorded. I'm only here with those upstairs as a kind of observer. I'm not part of their action group."

"Whatever. Are you and your people here today on any matter now pending before me in Mojeff County?"

"Not exactly. I heard what they want to do is raise hell about a death penalty sentence you imposed in Floyd County. They had a meeting on it at the Wolfer farm last night and then drove up here early this morning."

"To be legal the only place we could talk about such sentencing would be in the courthouse in Floyd County. Mojeff County would be an improper venue. Even if it wouldn't be completely improper it's *forum non conveniens*. All the records are down in the Floyd clerk's office."

"I understand that, Your Honor. I also agree. I'm not sure they understand that even though I've explained it."

"You being with them, observer or not, I think you should be the one to tell them again," I said. "I'm not going to hold any hearing or listen to anything on the Wolfer case in this county."

He inclined his head. "I'll try talking to them again, Your Honor." He leaned toward me. "I really came along as a kind of messenger, this being a good opportunity. The senior Wolfer, Mr. Damion Darius, would like to talk one on one with you about his son up on death row."

"I doubt I should converse privately with Mr. Wolfer or anyone else concerning his son. I know from a letter he wants his son out and he's offered himself in prison as a substitute, but the law doesn't work that way. We lawyers know that don't we, Mr. Amesworthy?"

He ignored the question. "Maybe you should be the one to tell him that after hearing him talk?"

I shook my head. "No way. Check the rules and the law out for him, Mr. Amesworthy, you being both family and a lawyer. There may be methods for him to do many more things to benefit his son and even ways where he can appear legally in front of me. Go research it."

"I could maybe bring Mr. Wolfer here in secret if there's nothing to help in the law books," Amesworthy offered boldly. "Or, better, I could arrange for you to come secretly to the family farm in Floyd County. Mr. Wolfer has lots of friends up here in Mojeff County that he told me he'd personally ask to vote for you if you could be reasonable about this and do him one single, small favor."

I shook my head. "I don't want and hopefully won't need his political help. I drove past the Wolfer farm recently. It looks more like an army camp than a family farm. I'd not want to visit inside there unless I went with a full battalion of regular army troops."

"The folks I know who live on the Wolfer farm are good people hand-to-mouthing it in lean times. They're farm folks who've been wronged by the damned government in its many branches—state, federal, and county. Those branches of government have taken Wolfer land, jailed people for unpaid taxes, and sent police into the farm to harass us. You once had the reputation for being a fairer man than you now have been on the bench, Your Honor."

I was unfazed. "That's pure bull, Mr. Amesworthy. I try to be fair and hope I mostly succeed. I think there may be big trouble coming at the Wolfer farm. If I were you, living there, trying to practice law from there, I'd move on before such trouble swamps you."

"I'm okay," he said, looking another direction, but hearing me.

"I'd move on," I repeated loudly. "And with nothing more here in Bington to do, maybe you might move on out of Bington today. Try federal court, Mr. Amesworthy,"

"I've tried the federal courts before," he said, still not looking at me. "There's nothing there for the common man these bad days. My people are the patriots of this twenty-first century, Judge."

I said: "Good for them. What I'm going to do now is wait half an hour. If your people are still occupying the upstairs I'm going to call area newspeople, point out that your group's in the wrong county, that the case that interests you and your people was originally heard, and remains, in a nearby county. Then I'll find anyone left around my hall upstairs in contempt and put them in jail if they refuse to leave."

"You do what you have to do, Judge," Amesworthy said softly. "I came to pass on the message I've given you."

"I thought that might be the way of it. One more time, Mr. Amesworthy: You went to law school, you studied hard, and you got yourself admitted to the bar. Some judges tell me you're smart. Best show it."

He shook his head, still not meeting my glance. "The Wolfer folks have a right to counsel."

I thought he was afraid.

In half an hour the crowd was gone. I sat in Judge Fred's office and watched the black trucks, most of them pickups, all with the number 23 on their doors or sides, pull out and away. Some went away easily. Others squealed their tires in frustration and anger, disturbing Bington's morning tranquility.

Larry, Curly, and Moe sent up a single courthouse janitor. He took one look at the hall and fled to make his report.

I sent a note downstairs that said if cleanliness wasn't restored by next morning I'd invite the newspaper and radio to come take a look. In a short while a group of janitors came to the third floor and began work.

Sheriff Jumper came to Judge Fred's office with Preacher while I waited. Both watched. Jumper was jubilant that there'd been no trouble.

"I stopped one guy with a cased rifle," he said. "He was maybe looking over that empty store across from your courtroom windows. He wasn't carrying any bullets for the rifle, but I bet he knew someplace close where he could get them."

"What caliber was the gun?"

"I thought about that also. It was a twenty-two rifle and not a thirty-thirty, but it had a sniper scope on it. Expensive target gun. You screw the barrel on to the stock. It was all packed in a tiny suitcase, but I'd seen them things and cases to hold them before. I went inside the store building he was near. There's a window up there that looks into your courtroom windows. Is it okay with you if I get some deputies and janitors to move your bench about two feet east and that much closer to the back wall?"

"You bet it's okay with me. Anything else?"

"Yes. I got a man coming to see you from the FBI this afternoon. He'll be along about closing time. I called him this morning when all them people showed up and occupied your third floor."

Preacher nodded at me, liking what he was hearing and also always in favor of Jumper.

It suited me also. "All right."

When Jumper left I asked Preacher, "Did you learn anything about labor problems at Macing Drugs right now?"

"There are always problems there because the union is a company union and the Macings openly run it. Another national union is trying to get in just now to represent the workers, but the Macings will just raise the pay again and keep the union in their ownership. I talked to Big Bill Williams. He said he and you are old friends. He might tell you more in person." He shook his head. "That's probably what Libbie Macing wanted of you, Judge. She'd carry you away under one luscious arm and then make you take over as the Macing union leader. Lots of time for you to screw around."

He laughed and I joined in. I didn't laugh hard.

"Would you call him for me and tell him I'll stop by?"

He nodded.

I got other news in the early afternoon. I was sitting behind my desk watching the town out the window and waiting for negotiations between the parties to complete before hearing the case of *Smith* v. *Smith,* a dissolution wherein substantial property rights were in question.

I was watching business when both Preacher and Evelyn Haas entered my chambers.

They wore extra-large smiles.

"You tell him, Evelyn," Preacher said.

"Your primary opponent awaits audience with you," she said. "He wants to say a few words and give you your personal copy of a letter he's just delivered to the various local media: newspaper and radio and the Louisville paper and TV stations. Preacher and I both would like to be in here when you receive him and read his message."

"Bring him on in," I said. I thought I knew what was coming, but I wasn't sure.

They exited and then returned quickly with Lance Tacker. He stood in front of my desk, shifting from foot to foot, a bit nervous. He wore a sport coat, a conservative tie, dark slacks, and black loafer shoes shined to perfection. I nodded at him. He smiled carefully in return and handed me a letter-sized piece of paper.

I inspected him once more before I read his letter. He was a nice-looking young man. I'd heard he was enthusiastically dating a pretty young lady who worked in the county treasurer's office on the first floor. Some of the people down there had told Preacher it was serious.

He'd not been born in Bington and his father, mother, and two much younger sisters lived in Indianapolis, a city sometimes frowned on by Bingtonites. I'd heard nothing but good about him and had no intention of looking around for anything bad.

I read his letter. It bore today's date. In it he stated that he was withdrawing his candidacy for the office of circuit court judge as of the date of the letter. He gave no reason.

I smiled.

"Can I inquire why, Mr. Tacker?" I didn't know him well enough to use his first name. "I'm sure my people here want to know your reasons also."

"Because you ought to be the circuit judge and not me. Maybe I'll be a judge someday, but not now, and not at this age. In ten or twenty years I'll maybe think on it some more. I did some checking around in the last week or so. The other area lawyers and judges like you and I guess I like you also although I've not yet had much business in your court."

"It will come with time," I said. I waited, knowing there was more.

"Some angry-sounding people came calling on me in my office in early February. After lots of hot talk, they said they wanted to back me." He shook his head. "I was flattered then, but I soon got over it. What they really wanted was to buy or rent me."

"Chemical and drug-company people?"

He hesitated and then nodded. "The two Macing brothers were there. They had some other people with them, but they were in charge. They promised they'd get the Macing workers to vote my way. They said they'd give me money and the Macing lady did bring me some cash later." He smiled and continued: "She patted my head and told me I was cute."

"She used to do that with me twenty years ago," I said. "Made me smile, but only after I checked my head for holes."

He nodded and went on. "I heard you're no longer friends. I used the money for posters and some ads. You never had any ads or posters and so it made me feel queasy when I saw mine on telephone poles with all the sheriff posters. The Macings got people to put up the signs. Some other people came around and said they were sent by the Macings and that they also wanted to help me. They seemed mostly nuts-and-bolts. They sure don't like you, Judge. You'll need to watch out for them. I thought some of them could be dangerous. I decided that I didn't want to be anyone's boy at my age. I keep hearing where I go to church that the Macing owners are crooked and that people won't work there if they can get any other job. Some of the folks who came to see me in my office were relatives or friends of a man you sentenced to death after he was convicted of a double murder in a jury trial in Floyd County."

"Yes."

"Some of the others who came and offered help are from a church I'd never heard of out in our county. I got curious and drove out there two Sundays back. I stayed for the service. I'll never go back again. It got crazy. There were people jumping up and down in the aisles, there was crazy trumpet and guitar music, and the preacher tried to act like he was a god."

Preacher said softly: "That heavenly minister has fourteen disciples, Lance."

"I looked in on them once years back," I added. "I've never forgotten it."

I examined Lance Tacker again and couldn't remember ever being as young as he was.

"You don't owe me anything, Your Honor," he said softly.

"I know that. But I'll say thanks."

"Shit," he said. "You'd have whopped my ass."

I recognized the FBI agent when he entered my office. He'd been one year ahead of me in law school. One remembers the ones before and, not so easily, the ones who come after. We'd been acquaintances only, both of us serious in our own way about going to law school, both of us working hard, him on scholarship with a job in the law school library, me at various odd jobs in order to eat and survive.

Only a little time for beer and dalliance.

I had sometimes beered and dallied. He had not.

I remembered conversations with me had irritated him and so, after a while, I didn't talk to him at all. He had no time to talk anything but law.

On this day he wore a good suit, dark and conservative. His dress shoes were polished so that I could see them reflect my walls and overhead lights. He carried a black raincoat over an arm. In his free hand he carried a full-sized black umbrella.

I remembered his eyes from law school. Then they had been bright and questing. Now they seemed mostly bored.

Outside the window of my office the rain had ended and the sun was bright again on the roofs of the old buildings that made up downtown Bington.

I directed my visitor to a seat. I sat behind my desk across from him.

He reached across the desk and formally handed me a card. His name was as I'd recalled, Elmer Glavine, office in a federal building, FBI. I remembered things I'd heard or recalled about Elmer: *summa cum laude,* Order of the Coif, top of his law class, one year before mine.

I'd not been top of mine and had no regrets.

"I remember you, Robak," he said.

"And I remember you. My recollection is you went straight from school into one of the biggest and best of the law firms in Indianapolis."

He nodded. "I worked in Indy for a time, but I never got to where I was allowed to sign my own letters. I did research for the big boys in the big firm for a couple of years. I was well paid, but the partners did the talking to judges and juries. I got tired of that about the time my marriage broke up. I was working eighty-hour research weeks and had no time for a wife. Soon I didn't have one."

I didn't remember him being married. I shook my head in careful sympathy. If one doesn't want to work damn eighty-hour weeks then one just doesn't.

"And so you're now the circuit judge here in Bington?" he said.

I read something in his voice that sounded like disapproval. Okay, he'd excelled in law school and I'd survived. Maybe he had a right to be unhappy because our lots in life were subtly changed as far as any imaginary pecking order.

"That's right," I answered without belligerence.

"When we were in school together I thought you'd have trouble passing the bar exam. I mean, you weren't stupid or like that, but you were hardly ever in my library. And you drank and partied a lot."

"Passed it first time." I remembered something more out of the dim past and so I asked: "How about you?"

He grimaced as if in pain and sat silent and insulted. I continued to remember an old vague scandal. Despite being number one in his class Elmer had failed the bar examination. It had been a state problem at the time and it had soon been remedied administratively with Elmer's exam regraded as passing. But such original failure would surely have had an effect on an elite law firm that had already hired him.

"Your sheriff told me that you were the guy who sentenced the youngest of the crazy Wolfer brothers from Floyd County to death. Is that the way it was?"

"Yes."

"Such sentence caused my office a lot of difficulty. We think old man Wolfer might act better and be less bellicose if he wasn't under the strain of having a son on death row."

"The way it happens is this, Elmer: You hold a sentencing hearing before you decide. I found no reason not to sentence Wolfer to death and many reasons to impose the penalty. I'm interested that you tell me it caused you and your organization problems. What problems?"

He looked at me, his eyes gone unreadable. "Forget I said it. I shouldn't have. We'd be out there in the cold wasting our time watching the bastard Wolfer patriots anyway."

"Patriots?"

"That's what they proclaim they are, patriots, citizens, free men."

"Can you tell me a few things about them?"

He shrugged. "Maybe. And only for a few moments because I'm very busy keeping the area lid on the Wolfers and doing a million other things. Your sheriff and I are acquainted and he asked me to come visit you. He's a living-legend lawman and so we're under orders from regional offices and Washington to keep him happy. Ask away."

"The people on the Wolfer place drive mostly black trucks. Many, maybe all, have the number twenty-three painted on the side doors in Arabic numerals. Does that number have a meaning?"

"We believe so. Remember Oklahoma City?"

I nodded.

Elmer watched me and I watched him in return. I thought he was trying to stare me down, kid style.

"It's because of that," he said.

Outside, as I glanced away and out my window I saw the man I'd seen watching from the courthouse wall several times before. He was intently looking up at my windows, concentrating his stare on them. He saw me looking back, but stayed full stare.

Elmer began again: "The Oklahoma City bomb went off on April the nineteenth; fourth month, nineteenth day. Add the numbers together and you get twenty-three. The various citizen and patriot militias have since then adopted that number on their calendars to memorialize the day. Other bad things also happened on April nineteenth. I won't waste time listing for you what they all were. Look them up if you're interested."

"Would you please walk over here and take a look out my window," I said. "There's a man down there who seems to wall-sit a lot and watch me. He probably saw you enter the courthouse today. Can you identify him?"

He moved languidly over and looked out. He got suddenly more interested.

"I know that bomber bastard," he said softly. "I didn't know he was around this part of the country. I've not seen him around the Wolfers. He must be sneaking in and out of a back way. He's been a lot of places where there's trouble, but we've never been able to tie him in directly to anything. Just exactly what kind of shit are you into here, Robak?"

"I was named special judge in Sweetboy Wolfer's murder trial. That you already know. He killed two girls, ages eleven and twelve. Both were small for their age, baby girls. They were tortured and died hard. Wolfer cut out some of their female parts after death for either later consumption or admiration. He then got caught. I did his trial. The petit jury convicted him of murder, but hung in the punishment phase. I took over. I sentenced him to death. His people flooded the courtroom that night and I had a courthouse full of hate when I pronounced the sentence. Now a judge in Floyd County, where the murder trial was held, thinks the Wolfers and their friends would like to kill me so they can get themselves a new and perhaps friendlier judge." I smiled just a little. "I, of course, object."

He shook his head. "Killing the trial judge after the fact likely wouldn't change things."

"You know that and I know that. The Wolfers apparently don't believe it's that certain. Six months ago someone did a number on my wife, slipped her an unknown Mickey Finn in a, so far, undetectable way. It made her sick enough to die, but she didn't die. Now she's under care in a nursing home here in Bington. Lab samples taken at the time she was admitted to the local hospital thereafter vanished. All this may have been set up by the Wolfers as a special punishment for me. Revenge. I can't tie it to the Wolfers, but it might have been them."

He shrugged. "If you do tie it to the Wolfers then contact your local prosecutor. Have her, as a courtesy, contact me. My phone number's on the card."

"Are your people now watching the Wolfer place?"

"Only from outside and not all the time. The Floyd sheriff keeps watch for us and tells us what goes on." He shook his head. "There are maybe five hundred to a thousand little hate groups like the Wolfers all over this country. The Wolfer family leader used to be a mining engineer, mostly coal, in eastern Kentucky. He got shut down by the Bureau of Mines when there was a cave-in and his mine was determined afterward to be a death trap. He moved over here into Indiana. That was a long time ago. His mine disaster killed a dozen people. He never got charged. He's a devious man, a planner who thinks he can do all."

"I see."

"We have a contracted airplane fly over the Wolfer farm and take photos for us every once in a while. I could loan the photos to your sheriff if he, not you, wanted to see them. Your neighboring county mounties also help us. They check the trucks. Since Oklahoma City we're leery of trucks. We don't think the Wolfers are active just now as such things go. They're making decent money selling their eggs. There are enough dollars coming in to buy them food, more farm fertilizer, illegal guns, and legal axes.

"There's also enough money coming from somewhere so that they're trying to buy out their neighbors and are offering cash."

He shrugged. "As long as they just posture around, play at being patriots in the woods, and stay quiet, we'll also stay quiet. We won't step in and take over their farm for taxes owed, for one thing."

"Maybe they're becoming unquiet."

"There's no reason to believe that."

"They sent a legal emissary today who tried to talk me into a private meeting with Damion Darius Wolfer."

"I doubt you should do that from what you've told me, but it's up to you." He nodded, his eyes as cold as the last past Indiana winter.

"I don't do private meets, but various law-and-order people believe the Wolfers will lie in wait for me or do something soon to make me a forced visitor at their farm."

"All you have to do is stay alert. I might have my people follow behind you once in a while if your sheriff requests it, Robak."

"No. That would be of no good use. Local officers already follow me. They also watch my home and my courtroom. Things are crazy enough so that I've sent my sixteen-year-old son to live with a relative in another state. I also had to put my wife in a nursing home. Only a few people know where she is, but by now that could include the Wolfers. I'd like to get some federal help if a real need arises."

He shook his head and his eyes were strange. "After I got out of law school I read some stories about you in newspapers and sensational magazines. I believe you've spent most of your career after law school running around this part of Indiana acting like someone out of a bad Perry Mason movie."

I nodded: "I take it that means no help from you. That's all right, but it's also enough of my time wasted for the day, Elmer. Thanks for stopping by."

He watched me.

"Just say goodbye," I said. "You're not listening to me. You're somehow playing my superior, remembering our law school grades. You maybe think I'm some sort of bumpkin. That means we're not going to be of any help to each other."

"Robak, you're a penny-ante state-court judge who thinks he's a minor deity. How'd you like to talk about subtly requesting federal help for your personal problems in front of a federal magistrate?" He shook his head, now gone quickly angry and red faced.

"Most of the magistrates around this area are partially there because state-court judges like me backed them for the appointment." I remembered his old nickname from years back. "I turned down the chance to be a federal magistrate myself two years back. You can check it. I'd probably like it if you ever got me in front of a magistrate, Elmer Fudd."

His face went from red to white. I stood up from behind my desk. "Just move on out. We're not passing out honors here or grading each other's bar exams administratively. I need to plan on what I can do to help keep me and mine alive."

"Now see here, Robak."

Evelyn Haas chose that moment to open the door. I thought she'd had her intercom on and had heard at least part of the conversation.

"Leaving, Mr. Glavine?" she asked pointedly.

He picked up his coat and held it tightly. He swept out past her.

When he was gone I said: "You had your intercom on and listened to our every deathless word?"

She blushed pink, looked down at my desk, and then looked up at me defiantly.

"Of course I did," she said.

"I think this day's about over for me unless the Smith dissolution is now ready to try," I said to her.

"They settled the case."

"I want to think some. If someone comes and needs me call me at home. I'll be there. Have them let the telephone ring once and I'll call here."

"Your wish is my command," she said.

Mo didn't call or come back to the house that night. I again thought I knew where he was, but that was all right and certainly not my business. If cat things were as I thought then I was delighted.

I ate my light evening meal and sat on my favorite couch again. This time I left the television off and tried to think about the world and me. No one had tried a direct attack on me since the 30-30 six months back on the house. No one had shot again at me from a secret place and no one had tried to stop me or follow my car or catch me when I ran.

Why?

At dusk I looked at the outside thermometer beyond the kitchen window. It was fifty plus. I unlocked the window lock and then opened the window a tiny amount. It was getting dark, but I could see a large flock of birds winging up from somewhere over my river-view hill. They settled in a big tree near my house. That seemed okay because it was time to roost for the night.

In the growing dimness the area dogwood trees were beginning to lose the best of their fine spring blossoms.

Something alien moved near the top of my hill. Maybe it was a floater in my eyes. I watched the spot carefully for a time, but saw nothing more.

I had not gone out and checked around my double acre for a while. I took up the phone and found there were no messages. I then called in that I was going outside to explore.

I waited until the light in the west had turned the same color as the rest of the night sky.

Bington's city lights vaguely outlined the edges of my hill as I exited the basement door. I locked the security lock behind me. The lock made a grating noise, but it was a soft one. The shotgun was fully loaded and there was a shell in the chamber.

The ground was soft.

When I reached the top of my hill I could see downward. The river stood out, vaguely light against dark, a long chain of moving water. The muted city lights from below stood out dimly against the dark.

There seemed to be nothing. And yet something I heard or felt made my heart race and my breath come fast.

I eased down to sit on the cold ground and to let my eyes grow more used to the night while I watched my city of Bington below. The grass was wet. The old pants I wore would either have to go to my laundry bag, the cleaners, or the rag bag.

Somewhere I could hear faint noises, but I could see nothing. Nevertheless I heard a repeating sound again and then again, like metal sliding against something soft.

I crawled toward the sound trying to slow my rapid breathing.

Someone or something was doing a task inside the earth below and near me. What I guessed was that a watcher sat in a open hole in the earth and smoked a cigarette, holding it low. I didn't see its light until there was a glow as he drew on it near ground level. I then could see a bit into his hiding hole. Thereafter, because the wind was blowing toward me from his location twenty feet away, I could smell the cigarette smoke.

I stayed still and attempted to guess what was going on.

Someone was digging a tunnel. No other house was close to me so the tunnel had to be to my place. I remembered the tiny bits of earth I'd seen when running. Maybe they'd first started digging at that spot, then become aware that I'd soon discover them and so had moved their excavation to a new and better spot.

Whoever watched from the top of the tunnel flipped his cigarette down the hill.

I moved carefully back until I hit something that made a sound underneath me.

"Who's there?" the man called.

I was up and running over the crest of the hill. I turned at the top and fired my shotgun wildly toward the opening in the earth. I then ran on to the house.

No return shots came. I heard no one following me.

In minutes Jumper was on the scene. We inspected the tunnel entrance together close up, but neither of us entered the hole. We were agreed on that.

Deputies combed the hillside, searching, using bright flashlights, but nothing remained other than the hole and its insides. The diggers had fled into the night.

"They were doing a good job tunneling from what I can tell without entering their damned hole," Jumper said. "The entrance is shored up with timber. They likely hauled the excavated earth away before morning every day."

"Elmer Fudd told me the main Wolfer, called Double Damn, the head of the clan, used to be a mining engineer across the river in Kentucky. I remembered that when I came outside and heard something."

"Elmer Fudd?" he asked.

"That's what some used to call your FBI friend when he was in law school. That was during some of the same time I was also in law school."

"Because they liked him?" the sheriff asked, not understanding.

"No. I think it was because he used to hog class-assigned law journal articles. He'd read and then hide the articles in the law library from others so that no one could know as much as he did. That was because he wanted to be, and stay, number one in his class."

"Some of the other area FBI agents don't have a lot of use for Elmer, Judge, but far as I know he's mostly okay."

"Elmer's not a completely happy man. Today he wasn't happy because he'd decided I was a penny-ante state-court judge."

Jumper shook his massive head. "You're a bit more than that, Don and I will tell him so. You have a knack for staying alive for one thing. Tomorrow I'll borrow some men from the state police

174

bomb squad. They'll look inside your tunnel and see how far it goes and how close it is now to your house. They'll be extremely careful while trying to examine what's inside. Mostly they'll be interested in the intentions of the diggers. They'll shoot some pictures and then close the tunnel off."

"Guess about intentions?"

He shook his head and his twisted body moved in waltz time with the shake. "Maybe they'd have tunneled into your basement, come through, and then hauled your sorry ass someplace to deal with you privately. Or maybe they'd have set off a big bomb while you were still sleeping or were eating your morning Wheaties. Blown you and your house into many pieces. Or maybe they'd have come inside and had tea with you."

"Yeah."

He whapped me on the back. "Keep the faith, Jedge."

"Thanks for coming, Jumper. Did Preacher tell you I've no opposition now in the primary?"

"Saw it in the paper this afternoon," he said. "Don't count on running unopposed in the fall. The Macings will now likely try to get the other party interested in fielding a November candidate by giving them money, but you'll win by a landslide in the fall."

"Promise?"

He nodded. "If we can keep you alive. Why do the Macings hate you?"

"Because I don't follow orders no matter how much I'm offered."

"Watch your ass," he said tersely.

"I may have to take some chances. I think maybe it's time to take chances if they're going to come tunneling in after me."

"Check with me first before you do anything." He stood up and put a hand on my shoulder. "Not because I'm dead set against it, but you may need my best advice."

"Yeah."

12

IN A DREAM during the night I saw my long-dead dog, a small Welsh terrier named Tip. He was surrounded by full-grown cats, hundreds of them. He was barking and growling, not liking the feline company.

Ann Sembly, the cat lady, was ordering all the animals: "Play nice."

A group of men, perhaps as many as thirty of them, approached through mist and fog toward me from a hole in the ground. They were armed with automatic weapons. Some of them had axes. I watched Tip, the cats, and Ann Sembly.

Tip wagged at the men, wanting to be friends. He'd been a great dog until he'd been a dead dog, killed by an arrogant strong-arm robber who'd entered my house.

The cats acted like cats and ignored the men. Ann Sembly cocked her long gun.

There was danger for all of us, but I wasn't able to do anything about it, not even run.

I clawed at the pillow hunting my shotgun and then I awoke.

I slept again, this time with better dreams. Jo and I gamboled in a sunset time, finding each other sweetly, making gentle love, but there was, as always, no pleasure and no completion.

When I awoke anew it was dawn on Tuesday the seventeenth of April, just two days before the anniversary of the Oklahoma City bombing.

I wondered how the Wolfers and friends would celebrate. Maybe they'd figure a better way to blow me up.

I didn't believe that the Wolfers were going to send their black number twenty-three trucks out to bomb the surrounding world even though some of their ilk had done it before.

But they were going to do *something*. That something likely would have to do with me.

For some reason, on what looked from my window to be a fine April morning, I woke and was angry at the world.

I lay there in my bed and thought on revenge. I couldn't do some of the things I wanted, but still I wanted them done.

I was somehow a small step closer to discovering what had happened near Thanksgiving time last fall and why it had occurred. I tried to recall what suddenly had made me feel that way, but there was nothing I could reach out and examine and so no one to plan against.

My dog Tip was long dead, killed by a sadistic robber who was also long dead. That badass had later personally tried to kill me, but I was alive.

Was I angry because of the Tip dream?

The world around me is and will remain full of badasses.

I needed names. I needed to plan.

In the dawn, with the outside temperature in the high forties and growing warmer with the risen sun, I ran. The feeling of anger faded.

I ran past fields of goldenrod and trees approaching full leaf.

Again no one followed.

I did my morning visitor worship with adorable Jo.

Her nursing home neighbors mostly lay *quiet* on this morning, many of them behind closed doors. So it was to be another fine day? So what? At eighty-plus, or maybe ninety, who cared about fine spring weather? Piss, if you can without pain, on the golden years.

All each new day meant for the old and ill was it might be a fine day to die.

Later I ran back, moving fast, keeping close watch, shotgun held tightly to my chest at a kind of port arms which helped me run without falling. The morning was bright with sun and I encountered nothing new on the running trail, although I imagined eyes watched me from concealment.

If they wanted me so badly why didn't they try to take me by force? I was puzzled.

My southern Indiana world moved closer to summer with each new day.

I looked for a further sign that new watchers and/or tunnel makers had been near the abandoned sawmill again. The tiny dirt crumbs were still there, but they were old. I stood for a moment thinking more on them. Why were they there? I put my hand down and felt them, using my index finger to probe the ground around where they lay. The ground was hard. No one had dug there and then replaced the earth.

I had a momentary vision. What had likely happened was that a someone had come from the hole in the ground above the tunnel. That person had matter-of-factly cleaned out his trouser cuffs and dumped dirt while he watched stupid Judge Robak's house and smiled about a future happening at that residence.

No dirt would ever now be added or subtracted. I guessed a second time at another possible origin of the dirt. Maybe head mining engineer Double Damn Wolfer or one of his subordinates had laid a surveyor's line for the diggers to follow across from the hillside to the dirt point. Then they'd turned the tunnel right and into my house.

Yeah. That could also be it.

The state police bomb squad Sheriff Jumper had said was coming had not yet arrived. They also hadn't arrived by the time my police escort came and I departed for court.

There were two police and two sheriff's cars escorting me this day. Double the guard on Robak.

We peace and police officers think someone's soon going to try to blow your ass off, Judge.

Such made me nervous.

At quarter of nine we arrived at the courthouse. My third-floor deputies were already manning their metal detectors, alert and ready. I noticed both deputy sheriffs now had cell phones for quick communication with Jumper's nearby office.

One of the deputies told me that Evelyn Haas had called in and said she'd be late.

The other deputy then told me that I had visitors waiting to see me, two brothers and a sister, the Macings. They were in the library and good Preacher had gone to fetch them coffee. The deputy was impressed.

That deputy also reported solemnly that all of the three had passed weapon check.

I arrived at the library door about the same time that Preacher did.

"You want some coffee?" he asked. He was jiggling an ornate tray I'd never seen before.

"No."

"How about me for company and as a witness when the Macings spit, strike, and curse you?"

I hesitated. The Macings weren't likely to cause problems.

"Not right now. Maybe later. Stay close."

I followed him inside the law library.

The two Macing brothers were seated on a leather couch. They were dressed in expensive business suits, wore highly shined shoes, and sported handsome ties. When I'd known them in their younger years they'd both been fair tennis players and golfers, but were already heavy drinkers.

Now all things for them had literally gone to pot. The suits were well made, but they couldn't hide the signs of ruin.

Libbie occupied an easy chair. Her skirt was short and her legs were long. She, although sharing the genes of her brothers, had not gone to pot at all.

I counted her legs. Yep, two of them just like always.

I smiled and sat down quickly in a conference chair. That way I avoided shaking hands. I did decide I would shake legs if Libbie extended one.

"Good morning, Brothers Macing. And good morning to you, Miss Libbie. You're looking particularly fine." I gave her a nod and smile as her eyes met mine. I could read nothing in those eyes and had the idea she might be here under minor protest. "Before we start let me say I can't talk to you about the case set for later this morning. I'm sure you know that."

Beauregard Macing seemed to be the spokesman. He nodded to me impatiently and began: "We know that. What we wanted to speak to you about has nothing to do with the pending share-holder lawsuit, Judge. What we'd like to do is get a few things straightened out between you and the Macings as a family. We'll admit to you that we tried to buy you some opposition in the primary next month. That's our right. It's also all we did against you."

"Not all," I replied. "You've also been consorting with people at the Wolfer farm in Floyd County and also with angry people from one of our area churches."

"We did talk with various anti-Robak groups seeking political help." Beau shook his head as if he realized that such talk had been wrong. "They are enemies of yours and it was a place to go for support."

I nodded and waited. I was certain there'd be more.

He looked down at the floor and then up and surprised me. "As to your wife we're sorry she became ill and remains that way. Libbie has told us you have several times expressed suspicions that some compound from our Macing plant might have caused your lovely wife's problems."

"I thought such was possible," I answered, trying hard to show nothing. "You run a drug company. Something my wife was exposed to caused her to suffer a strange illness."

"We want to now admit it might have been an experimental chemotherapy drug from our plant which caused her the problem," Beauregard said evenly, surprising me more. "It's possible that something we were experimenting with in our plant near that time did it. We do much cancer research. One of our research people, retesting quite recently, came down with symptoms such as we're told your wife experienced. He was an older man. He died within three days."

"What were his symptoms?"

"I was told high fever, blood pressure spikes, immense joint pain, and sudden organ failure: kidneys, lungs, then heart. Our plant doctor and several other physicians treated him before he died. The man who died was sixty-four years old. The doctors reported he died of a coronary infarction. It's on the death certificate."

"How could my wife have come in contact with that kind of hot stuff?"

"We have no theory on that. Our sister remembers seeing your wife at a country club golf banquet the night before the onset of her illness. Maybe a tiny bit of the drug got out of our plant with Libbie or others of our research people who were at that same banquet. We counted and there were nine of our people at the country club that night." His eyes left mine. "We're not sure of any of this. But we're suspicious enough about the happening to want to make amends to you and your wife, sir. We want to pay for your wife's care to date and also for her needed care in the future. All this would have to be privately done. No legal complaints, no investigation, and no lawsuits."

I looked inquiry at Libbie, but Libbie declined to look back at me.

"What else can you tell me about what happened to Jo?"

He shook his head. "I will answer no other questions."

"I must take your proposition as you've given it or leave it?"

He inclined his head.

"Then you must let me have time to consider what you've told me," I said. "I'll get back to you as quickly as I can. One more thing: Could this drug make its way accidentally from inside your plant again?"

"No way. As a part of a chemotherapy combination of drugs, after experimenting, we found it too deadly to use or save. It offered no hope as a cure and so it was destroyed. Chemotherapy drugs must not kill the patient; they must kill the cancer. Nothing of the drug now remains." Beau Macing looked at his brother and sister and all three nodded.

"I'll think long and hard on it," I said again.

They looked at one another, found agreement, and arose together.

I saw them to the stairhead and onto the elevator.

"Thank you for coming to see me," I said. "I really do appreciate it."

"Our lawyers will be along in a bit on the other matter. Libbie will be with them."

"Fine."

The brothers nodded once more. Libbie stared straight ahead.

Pee on thee, Robak.

I went to my office and sat thinking for a time. Their story was not impossible and had plausibility.

I tried it on and thought about it for a while. I doubted I had all the truth or even most of it.

But what I had, after all, was more than I'd had before.

Why the theft of Jo's specimens?

I mulled it over for a time without success.

Preacher interrupted. I took a walk with him into the courtroom after I'd donned my black robe. The two of us examined the ceiling for additional water damage.

All seemed about the same. April had been an unusually dry month so far.

"There hasn't been enough rain yet," Preacher said, peering at the large discolored ceiling area.

"Does the floor register under the spot in the ceiling still open and close?"

"Sure. When it gets real hot the commissioners send a janitor up here to open it. We watch and wait until he's satisfied and done. Then we close the register again. All it does is let the hot air below rise."

"And isn't there another register just like ours below on the second floor?"

"Sure. It opens up on the commissioner's room."

I remembered something else. "Do we still have that room divider we sometimes use in here to separate called and uncalled jurors?"

"Yes. It's against a wall in the probate commissioner's room."

"Let's go get it and bring it in here."

"I can have a janitor do it for us," he grumbled.

"I want us to do it."

He was mystified, but together we pulled the lightweight room divider inside the courtroom and leaned it against the wall near the discolored area.

"Now, if it starts raining on a weekend and the wall is up so that most of the water comes down near the register area, I'd like the register open and also the register on the second floor open."

He didn't see it for a moment. Then he did and both smiled and nodded.

He said: "It's past the middle of April and you know it usually rains a lot in Bington during our Aprils, but so far things have been drier than a still being watched by federals. So maybe the hole won't breach even when it does pour rain. Things could just stay the way they are for a while." He nodded at me.

"With the registers open on floors two and three, plus the room divider stopping water from going far on our floor, where will most of the water from the ceiling flow?"

He smiled widely. "You know where it would go, you scoundrel."

I tried to look insulted, but failed.

"Now tell me what the Macing family desired out of the circuit court judge?"

"They made me a kind of proposition."

"I hope it included some late-night visitation with the female Macing."

"One more time, friend: She's not my lady."

I'd noticed Preacher's suit coat ride up as he pointed at the dark ceiling. I saw he was carrying an oversized western-type revolver in a holster hooked to the back of his belt.

"What's the gun for?" I asked. "What's going on? Are you going to shoot someone?"

"Yep, all three of them damn county commissioners. Then we won't have to worry about watering them down." He nodded. "But I'm not shooting them right away, Jedge. Truthfully, Sheriff Jumper swore me in as a special deputy along with a goodly number of your local lawyers. Bad people get this side of the hall, with the weapons alarms I could maybe shoot them before or after they shoot you. We can discuss whichever time frame you'd prefer."

"Shit," I said softly.

"Shit's what you told me that nursing home where Jo's a resident always smells like and also what you do most mornings if you eat regular, Jedge. It ain't a word you ought to say right out in this fine but not yet leaky courtroom, even if you are the judge of it. Tell me more about the Macings."

"Not now," I said. "How many lawyers do we have who are now running around carrying guns?"

"Most of them. I heard about ninety percent. A couple begged off because their wives raised hell with them. The bar had a private meeting and decided they're used to you now. They don't want to have to break in a brand-new judge even if he would surely be smarter and quicker than you."

"Shit," I said again. "Now I'll be afraid to rule on a motion in open court for fear the loser will figure out what a stupid bum I really am and shoot me through the ears to end my misery." I found I was touched and felt my eyes start to moisten. And I also found it easier to believe what the lawyers were doing than to believe the Macing tale, which just might be real.

"True," Preacher answered solemnly. "Live with it, Jedge. I hoped the federal people would get interested in what's happening around here. It's not normal for the feds not to want to stick their nose into everyone's business, and you gave them a real opening to do that. You say you knew this FBI guy in law school, and when he came to see you he was wearing a chip as big as a horse barn on his shoulder?"

"That's a good way to explain it. He seemed angry and upset at me for being a judge. His grades in law school were lots better than mine."

I thought more about it and was no longer certain why such treatment had so angered me.

"Maybe what I said to him sounded too much like me giving him his marching orders. If I'd been smarter I'd have let him ask the damned questions and then also let him give the orders instead of me trying to decide things up front for him."

"I think we ought to call Jumper over here and talk to him more about other area federals. The one who came to see you yesterday surely isn't the only federal agent around," Preacher said.

"I'd be happy for any help. That farm and fort down there in Floyd County has a lot of troops. Sooner or later they're going to show up around here in force."

"Jumper wasn't in when I stopped past the sheriff's office. A deputy over there said he was out late last night and that I should ask you why. So now I'm asking about that and renewing my questions about why the Macings talked to you."

"On Jumper, I had a serious problem close to home. Jumper made the problem go away. Now I've got a trial set nine-thirtyish, but I'll bet my dinkus, after conferring with the Macings earlier on something else, that the trial doesn't happen," I said. "So there'll be lots of time for me to tell you my last-night problems once we get past seeing about this morning's trial."

Preacher seemed puzzled.

I enlightened him a little on trials by lifting my arm and exhibiting my watch. "It's after nine and there's nobody waiting out there in our hall. No experts, no witnesses. The hall would likely be teeming with them by now if there was going to be a trial in less than half an hour."

He said: "Gene Smithham and the big butter-and-egg lawyer from Indianapolis who represents the angry, mostly rich plaintiffs against the angry, double-rich Macings are in the jury room talking. Maybe they've got their witnesses in the library with them. And the Macings may still be lurking around somewhere in the courthouse."

"Possible, but not probable," I said. "They took the elevator down and said only Libbie would return."

We waited.

I watched through the courtroom back-door window glass during the ensuing silence. I saw someone female arrive by elevator and peek quickly through the courtroom window. Preacher caught the movement also.

I knew who the returnee was. Beau Macing had said Libbie would be back and she was.

"Would you step out and see who that is, if she makes it through the weapons detector?" I asked Preacher.

He nodded and went out. I opened the top file for the Macing case and began to read it again. I knew all the recent papers almost by heart. Thunder, lightning, and much, much bull. Lawyers who write legal complaints are among the greater fantasists in our weird world.

Preacher came back wearing a tiny grin. He closed the courtroom door firmly behind him so we couldn't be overheard.

"It's your old and new sweetie, Miss Libbie Macing. Back for me to give more coffee and also to see you for the second time today. She said she was first looking for Mr. Smithham and so I escorted her to the jury-room door." He shook his head. "She didn't ask a single thing about you. But she sure walks nice and smells nice. Lucky, lucky you. She makes an old setter like me into half a pointer."

"I keep telling you she's not my lady, Preacher. We were an item twenty years ago when I was a poor virgin lawyer boy. That was about the time you were beginning to sneak around on wife number one. We aren't into anything now."

"Yeah, okay," he said, either not believing me or playacting like it. I thought he might be a bit miffed because I'd not let him sit in on the earlier Macing conference.

I settled into my seat behind the bench, turning my legs slightly away from underneath so I'd not knee my loaded, abbreviated shotgun. I looked at my watch again. Nine-twenty.

I said: "Would you please go to the library door, knock hard, and tell all those assembled there that I'm out here on the bench waiting for them?"

"Yeah, okay," he said again. "Virgin lawyer," he muttered heavily as he passed me and then, more softly, "Virgin judge. Hasn't been screwed yet this morning."

"Hold up a minute, Preacher. To add to your suspicions would you also inform Miss Macing that I'd like to talk with her after we're finished in court this morning?"

He nodded, his mouth now open slightly.

I could hear doors opening and closing as I sat behind the bench. The room was warm and last night's crawling around on the hilltop had made skin allergies pop up. My wrists itched and so I scratched like a farm boy who'd taken a nap in poison ivy.

Anthony Pellingham, attorney for the plaintiffs, entered first. He was accompanied by one of his associate attorneys, this one female, auburn-haired, thirtyish, and extremely handsome. I smiled gently at her and looked furtively down at my gown, glad I was wearing it, and yet still hoping my fly inside the robe was zipped. There had been a time as a young lawyer when I'd made final argument before a jury without zipping my pants up all the way and I remembered it always, even when I wore a robe over my clothes.

Smithham brought a single associate, a young man dressed in a well-tailored suit. That young man led Libbie Macing. She held lightly to his left arm.

"No trial today, ladies and gentlemen?" I asked, knowing it was so.

Pellingham said unsmilingly, perhaps not liking what my unseemly haste had caused: "No trial hopefully ever, Your Honor. We're going to try to work this thing out by proceeding to arbitration. We've even been able, this morning, to agree on an arbitrator."

Smithham nodded formally. "We agree with all Mr. Pellingham says."

I nodded. Some judges don't like lawyers coming before them on a set trial date with changes in the plans. Those judges look grim and prim and raise hell, but I couldn't help a smile because I was delighted.

"Good for you, gentlemen. I think both sides will be better served. Do I need to sign anything for you? I've been informed my court reporter won't be along for a while."

"If the court will kindly write or dictate a docket entry showing that we appeared, that the trial date was continued by agreement, and the case will go to arbitration by agreement," Smithham said. He then named the arbitrator. It was a name not known to me.

"I will so note."

"And congratulations, Your Honor," Smithham said.

Pellingham looked surprised.

Smithham nodded at him and said: "Of course you'd not know, Pell, but yesterday the judge's primary opposition announced he was dropping out of the May primary. He had no chance of winning, but now our good judge here won't have to waste time campaigning. He has no fall opposition and I'm told by many who are in the know that he'll draw none."

"We're done, then, ladies and gentlemen," I said.

"Are you also done with me?" Libbie asked.

"Not quite. If you can spare the time?"

She smiled impudently and then stepped forward until only I could hear. "I've the time and the place."

"I'll excuse the rest of you then, lady and gentlemen," I said, looking around Libbie. I lowered my eyes and scribbled their entry on the docket sheet in front of me. Usually I'd have waited for Evelyn Haas and then dictated it, but I wanted to do this one myself. I wrote the entry slowly.

I could hear receding footsteps. When I raised my eyes the attorneys were gone. Only Preacher and Libbie Macing remained.

Preacher nodded. "Would you like me to leave the courtroom now, V. J.?"

I ignored the question. "Preach, do you know an area labor person who drives a black, newish Chrysler?"

"Not offhand, Your Honor. But I'll bet I can make some calls and likely find out."

"First let me ask Miss Libbie about it. Do you know any labor leaders who drive black Chryslers?"

"No," she said, her eyes gone from warm as sex to cold as a winter storm.

"You had nothing to say when Brother Beau was talking earlier. Do you have anything you want to add to what he told me?"

"No."

"I assume by that you then admit that something from your drug plant did almost kill my wife?"

"No. I admit nothing."

I turned back to Preacher. "Go see what you can find out and then also find out what you can for me about any current labor problems around Bington."

"Why don't you ask Miss Libbie about that also while she's here," Preacher said. "They always have labor problems at their plant," he said. "It's said such is a way of life at Macing Drugs."

Libbie's face was red. "I have no answer for you or your hired help and I resent your questions and their implications. I'm out of here," she said.

I nodded permission. "As you probably should be. Tell your gate guards not to expect me at your door, Libbie. And I think that the most likely person to have accidentally or purposely caused my wife's sickness is now present before me in this courtroom."

"Should you ever try to come to my door I'll have the guards take a whip to your backside."

I saw Preacher smile at that. I lowered my eyes and said nothing more to her.

She was gone with a swish and a smell.

*   *   *

I retreated from bench to chambers and sat there alone and disconsolate. I realized that my manners needed upgrading. Bad as Libbie was, if there'd been no intent, I'd not been right in accusing her.

No one else came this morning, no one sought a dissolution, no one appeared wanting to engage in argument about something done or undone, no one appeared with a thick sheaf of papers for the judge of the court to inspect and then hopefully sign.

I had set no other case today as a second setting because I'd been certain the Macing matter would begin.

Most mornings were busy with ho-hums for at least an hour or two. Today, when I wanted my time in the courtroom to be hectic, it was not.

I heard Evelyn come in. I then heard her on the telephone talking to someone in friendly tones, so it wasn't a law-book salesman. I thought it was probably one of her bridge-player friends.

I went softly to my door and peeked out. Evelyn sat at her desk talking, her back to me. Her purse gaped open. I could see a small automatic pistol in the jumble.

I returned silently to my chair, brushed at my again-wet eyes, and looked out the window and examined my town of Bington.

There were more flowers growing in the courthouse lawn than there'd been on any of the days before, thousands of them now. On the hills up from the river there was a full federal treasury of golden dandelions plus a dozen dogwood trees still in bloom: purple, red, and white.

I could also see the fine houses built on Main near downtown. There one could sit on an elegant porch and watch the passersby.

I looked the town over.

I noted only one thing out of the ordinary. One of the Wolfer trucks must have become disabled yesterday. It sat across the street from the courthouse. The hood was raised and the man who sometimes watched my office from the courthouse wall was tinkering with the engine. The sun showed the number 23 on the truck door.

I thought one more time about other angry attackers who'd used a truck, a big truck, to blow up the federal building in Oklahoma City. They'd loaded their truck with fertilizer, diesel oil, then added a detonator and timer to set it off. They'd parked it by the federal building and walked away.

The Wolfer trucks I'd seen were small trucks, pickups mostly. I believed they had plenty of what seemed to be the same kind of fertilizer used at Oklahoma City available on their armed farm. I decided I'd thought on that too much already. The Wolfers wouldn't try a bomb like that. It was too apparent even for an angry leader nicknamed Double Damn.

Or was it?

It was too damn quiet.

I thought about calling Sheriff Jumper. Outside I could hear a phone ring.

Evelyn buzzed me.

"There's a man on line one who says he was to call you and I was to let him through even if you were on the bench and in trial. He said to tell you it's Billy Bob Konkle and he's Deputy Bob Konkle's father."

"Thanks, Evelyn," I said. I picked the receiver up and said, "Hello Mr. Billy Bob."

"Can you help my son for sheriff this time?" he asked, without preface. His voice was raspy and demanding. He was low eightyish and I'd heard gossip from the courthouse-wall sitters that he was fighting lung cancer by smoking two packs of high tars a day. He was a hard campaigner retired by the voters last election after seven terms on the county council. I'd also heard he'd given up farming his four hundred acres of rich land, renting the land out this year. He still showed up at some political things, haggardly slapping backs, shaking hands, and damning the other rascally party to hell and gone.

Jumper's first term as sheriff had been chaotic. He'd led un-popular raids on beer-and-booze parties along the Indiana side of the Ohio River. He'd issued strict rules ordering kids to be picked up and detained for parental pickup if they transgressed the laws of the state. Some locals hated him, but I believed he'd get more votes than all twelve of his opposition combined.

"I can't this time, Billy Bob, but likely could and would four years from now. Bob's a bright young man and he'll go far if he stays away from women and booze."

"Wouldn't we all." I could hear him sigh raggedly. "I ran for sheriff one time before I got elected to the council," he said. "Got my ass beat good by an incumbent who couldn't catch cold. I guess I want my son to be sheriff mostly because he wants to be sheriff. You owe me, Don, but I'll let you off the hook for this election if you promise to take good care of my boy for me. I likely won't be around next election so I'm calling in things due now."

"I don't believe you won't be around, B.B. Our party needs you and your friends. I'll back your son all I can up the line. I know I owe you, but this time I also owe lots to Jumper. He's backing me."

"I heard that. I also heard that your opposition quit. Can Jumper win now and in the fall?"

"I believe and hope so. All you really hear out there bad against Jumper are loudmouths who want to party out in public and parents angry because their kids got caught doing things everyone knew were against the law."

"I think he can win also," Billy Bob said. "That's why I'm pulling in my horns this time. Bob's going to pull out of the race Saturday and back the Jumper."

"You sly old fox," I said.

He was silent for a moment. "That's dead true. Stop by and see this sly old fox when you can, Judge. Maybe don't wait real long."

"I promise."

13

Evelyn Haas entered my office as I hung up the phone.

She sat in the nearest chair to my desk and said: "I've some things I know that you ought to know."

"Tell me." I decided not to ask her why she was carrying a gun in her purse. It just might be to shoot obstinate law-book salesmen and not to protect me.

"A couple of times a month for maybe four months I've had calls that sounded legitimate wanting your wife's mailing address. I then would give them your home address, but some of the callers want to know where she can be personally reached because they know she's no longer at home."

"And what do you tell them then?"

She smiled without humor. "I advise them to use the home address."

"That's fine."

"What I wanted you to know is that I've had no calls now for almost two months."

I thought on that for a moment.

"My guess is that the curious callers have found out her address. Maybe it's time for you to consider moving Miss Jo somewhere else on a dark night, boss."

"First-class idea. They probably are watching close and would know immediately where I moved her just now. But thanks for telling me." I thought some more. "Why not this, Evelyn? Call out there and ask that lady in charge you play bridge with to change her to another room."

She smiled and nodded. "Will do. One more thing. I used the copy machine and made you a copy of your very latest hate note. I found it in this morning's mail without a postage stamp. Normally I won't and don't copy you, but I think you should see this short note."

She handed me a single sheet. I read it and then placed it in front of me.

It read: "You're dead and/or your wife's dead on 4/19." There was no signature.

I called Preacher into the office.

I handed him the short note. "This arrived in our mail today. It's unstamped so someone smuggled it into our mail pile. How would they do that?"

Preacher read it and shook his head. "Let me think some on it and try to figure out the hundred ways it could get into the court's regular mail."

I then told him about Billy Bob Konkle and he grinned. "That old bastard could have had an eighth term if he'd had the strength to stand at the polls last Election Day."

There now being time I also related what had happened the night before. As I talked Preacher's eyes kept getting bigger and bigger.

"Jesus." He got out his big revolver and inspected it. "I guess I better load this damn thing."

Evelyn snickered.

"Maybe that wouldn't be a good idea," I said. "The gun's pretty rusty and could blow your hand off. Maybe clean and oil it first."

The pair exited and I could hear them laughing in the outer office.

The sheriff appeared in the office an hour later. He was, as usual, bent both sideways and over from his old road-patrol injuries. He never mentioned them to me and I had little knowledge about whether he was in any pain. Some who knew him said he lived in constant pain, but was too proud and too mean to show it.

He said from my doorway: "You're lucky to be alive"

"Tell me about it."

Preacher stood behind him and so I motioned both of them in. They closed my door behind them and sat on the couch.

I got up and politely opened the door a little so Evelyn could listen in if she desired.

"The tunnelers were about finished with digging. The state boys figured the end of their tunnel was within two or three feet of the side of your basement. Someone would likely have broken through and got inside your house late last night or set off a bomb in it early this morning or maybe tonight. It was a good tunnel, well dug and strongly shored, a tribute to its talented builders."

"I saw only the outside of it. Were there any explosives inside?"

"Not yet. But there was a case of dynamite hidden in the weeds near the entrance and there were maybe more cases in the dirt trucks people saw pulled over on the lonely road below you. I think they were going to come in after you, take you prisoner, then blow up your house once they were outside and on their way. That would have kept things confused for a while what with us looking around for your poor, blown-up body in the wreckage."

"Oklahoma City celebration."

He nodded, catching my meaning.

I handed him the note Evelyn had given me. "This came in with the regular mail."

He looked it over.

"What do you plan to do about all this?" Preacher asked Jumper.

Jumper shrugged. "You tell me. We're watching. We're guarding. There are people all over town who might be from the Wolfer farm, but probably aren't."

"Did the state police find anything interesting in the tunnel itself? I mean something that could identify the diggers?" I asked.

"No. And the dynamite we recovered was probably stolen from a construction site off an interstate near Indianapolis. At least it fits the description of what was taken there, same brand."

I said: "I can't think of anything to do other than watch and wait. If I'd been able to sneak away after finding the tunnel last night then maybe we could have caught some of the diggers. As it is I can't identify anyone, not even the guy who was smoking on guard. It was too dark." I thought for a moment. "But I want you to know I'm getting hot."

"No doubt. You know who they are, don't you?"

"Certainly. The tunnelers were off the Wolfer farm."

"Well, you sent their high-class leader's boy up to death row just because he butchered two little girls," Jumper answered.

"And I'd do it again, Sheriff. It'll likely be another ten years before they execute that child torturer. What bugs me is that's a long time to expect people like you and the locals and the state officers to guard me and mine and also a long time for me and mine to sit waiting to see if anything bad is going to happen to us."

"Watching you is part of my job," he said.

"Your job, but maybe not that much of a priority for the next guy."

Preacher broke in: "The judge went to law school with the FBI man who visited yesterday. I guess they didn't get along in school and aren't going to get along now. The judge has also been acting strange with women. He just was very gruff with one of the best-looking ladies around Bington. She left mad at him and his damn virginity."

Jumper watched the two of us with a smile, but without full comprehension. "What's this about?"

I said, "Libbie Macing needs to think about what I said, Preacher. She believes this town is hers, paid for in full, and that I know nothing while she and her brothers know damn all. It must have bugged her when she found out my primary opposition had dropped out. The question I asked her about the black car visitation probably also surprised her."

Jumper said: "Forget Libbie Macing. Your federal friend Elmer called me again this morning. You got cussed and discussed. I did my best for you, but without a lot of effect. You are not a sweet citizen."

"How much do you remember about Oklahoma City, Jumper?" I asked.

"Some. I read what was in the papers and then heard more details later from some of the ATF guys who were down there after the fact."

"That's probably more than I know. I do know they have enough fertilizer at the Wolfer place to build themselves a lot of bomb trucks. And now we know that they have or had some dynamite with which to set it off."

"Do you believe they're putting bombs together there, Judge?"

"I doubt it. I think they're using the idea they might be building bombs to hide something else. Besides, the farm's in the next county and not in Mojeff County." I got up from the desk and went to my window.

"Come see this."

Jumper came and looked down. Preacher peered around him out the glass.

"See the black truck, number twenty-three on the door down there? I think they expect us to come and check it over."

"I can do that," Jumper said. "In fact, I think I damn well will."

"Good plan," I said. "Then take a close look around the courthouse and wherever else you can think of and see if there are any other parked trucks or other vehicles that belong to the Wolfer folks. Such vehicles might be another color than black and there likely won't be number twenty-three on it. Vehicles might have a flat tire or the hood up. Check any vehicle that appears disabled."

"So you do think they're aiming at this courthouse?"

"Doubtful, but not impossible. You've got some friends north. Call them and have them do some checks around the prison where young Wolfer awaits."

"We shall do just that," he said. He shook his head and then added, "We'll have a long look both today *and* again tomorrow." He examined me with interest. "People told me when I retired from the state police and got elected sheriff here that you'd been one crazy lawyer and now one crazy judge. What are you going to be doing while I'm doing what I get paid for?"

"I'm not sure. I might take a couple of my friendly armed lawyer deputies you swore in to protect my aging ass for a drive and look around. Maybe that'll give me an idea about what's going on, but I doubt it. I'm leery of trying anything direct like driving past the Wolfer house. Somehow I think they'd like for me to do that."

"I think an even better idea is you just go home and hole up until Saint Oklahoma's Day is over," Jumper said. "Then I'll know where you are. I'll send a flock of deputies along with you. I know what I said before, but—"

"No matter how many deputies you send, the Wolfers can field a larger army," I said. "I don't want to be any place where they know I'm there. So no to my home. But I'd like you to watch my house some, Jumper."

Evelyn chose that moment to tap loudly on the door and then open it.

"Sam King just called and wanted the judge to come over past the office. He said he needs to talk to you about something that's not pending in court."

That made me nod. I looked at Preacher and the sheriff. "Would you gentlemen like to accompany me? I'm hoping Sam may have discovered the whereabouts of a person involved in the missing hospital lab reports concerning my wife."

There were five of us in the law firm's conference room.

Sam King had the floor.

"Her name is Amy Ringer. She lived in Madisonville all her short life until she moved here to Bington a couple of years ago. She's my color, pretty, very young, and extremely timid. I saw and dated her a couple of times when she was here in Bington. Cute lady and straight as a Christmas package. She worked in the hospital lab, but wasn't a technician. Instead she kept things clean, took care of incoming and outgoing mail, sometimes working with others. She mostly did the cleaning jobs. I talked to the people at the hospital. She was good at what she did and she had an interest in learning more. The hospital had offered to pay for some night lab courses at the university. She'd had a couple of pay raises. One day last November she just didn't show up for work and then never showed again." He looked at the sheriff. "She may have misdirected a lot of mail or taken it along with her when she left."

"Someone could file criminal charges here or in federal court against her, but no one has as yet," Jumper said when there was silence from the rest of the room.

"She's now back in Madisonville," Sam said. "I don't know her address, but I can likely find out just by asking. I asked about her around the courthouse over there and some African-American people told me she had been out visiting in L.A., but was now living at home. She's unemployed, but is looking for a job. How about you people let me contact her, maybe look her up, and then see what I can get out of her?" He looked around the room. "From knowing her my bet is that something or someone made her up and vanish."

"Okay with me," I said. "When are you going to try?"

"This afternoon. I have a short hearing in Madisonville."

"Could I ride along with you and see if she'll talk to me?"

He thought about it. "If she won't I may have to leave you sitting in the car when I talk to her."

"Whatever," I said.

Madisonville was easy driving distance from Bington especially with Sam King behind the wheel. He drove a small BMW convertible and he could move it.

On the way we slowed just before we passed an Indiana State Police car waiting behind trees down a side road. The trooper in the driver's seat and Sam waved companionably at each other.

"He sits there almost every day and bags a couple," Sam said. "I always slow down a little for him. He told me one time he was going to move his watching spot and get me."

"I bet he doesn't," I said.

Sam nodded in agreement. The world loved him and he, in turn, loved the world.

There were places along the road where I could see the Ohio River up close. I watched for them. The river and I were brothers, he big, me small. I knew inside that I'd never leave him or my Bington town that he muddied each spring.

Today the sun was shining and the river was rising a tiny bit from rains to the east. I could watch all this happen while Sam drove.

Madisonville was now a town of about ten thousand inhabitants, smaller than my Bington. The two towns shared the river, with Madisonville getting its water after we'd used it at Bington. The towns were bitter rivals. Sometimes there were fights at the high school football and basketball games.

The courthouse there was old and built of fire-red brick. There was an impression, looking at the three-story building, that it leaned just a little to the north. My county engineer had told me such was true.

"It's the river," he told me. "It was way up into the courthouse when it flooded in 1937. Some of the building settled north."

We parked.

"You want to wait for me out here?" Sam asked, once we were out of the car.

"I could maybe go upstairs and make a social call on the circuit judge. He and I are old acquaintances. He was the judge in that poison case that I had over here with Kevin Smalley."

"I remember. I also know the circuit judge's on vacation. Rather than starting rumors going around Madisonville about you being with me how about you take a seat on one of the benches out in the yard, watch the river from there, and maybe whittle a while."

"You're ashamed of me," I said.

"Not exactly. What I have to do inside won't take a lot of time and will work better if you're not with me."

"All right."

"Are you angry?" he asked carefully.

"No, Sam. It's this whole situation. These damn Wolfer people do what they want and I sit and wait." I waved a hand. "I'll stay out here with the river, but damned if I'll whittle."

"You got something against whittlers?"

I shook my head and then grinned.

He shook his head also and opened the door of the courthouse. I found a spot on a bench in the yard.

I sat. A couple of other idlers watched me curiously for a time, but then gave up, even if I had appeared on their scene with a big, African American man.

I drowsed a little in the warm sun.

Sam reappeared and I came back up to life.

"Bingo," he said. "I called and we're going to see her. I explained your situation and she said she'd like to talk to you also."

We got back in his car and he drove slowly and carefully through the streets of Madisonville until he found the street for which he searched. We parked near where a big gum tree's roots had jumped up through the asphalt.

A thin girl sat on the tiny porch of a metal-sided, assembled home. She examined us from her folding chair and I could tell she was frightened. When we gained the porch she motioned us into two other folding chairs and we sat.

Sam introduced us. She kept her head low and never let her eyes meet mine.

"Some things vanished from the Bington Hospital around last Thanksgiving," Sam said.

She nodded. "I know. I took things because someone told me to and I was scared. The men didn't tell me exactly what they wanted. I just gave them all the mail for about a week. I think they then mailed some of it on."

"What men? How many of them?"

"There were three men, but I only saw one of them up close. The other two would stay outside. From my window I could see out to the parking lot. The two men sat in their truck and waited for the one with the knife scar on his nose."

"A bad scar?" I then asked.

She nodded.

"Did they pay you money?" Sam asked.

"They told me they would, but they never did. If they had I'd have put it in a church door or thrown it in the river. What they did was they scared me bad." She looked down and made a small, hopeless gesture. "They told me there were a lot of them and that if I didn't give them the outgoing mail or if I told anyone they'd taken it they'd kill me and my family." She nodded at Sam and I could now see tears in her eyes. "I believed them."

"What color was the truck?" I asked.

"Black. It had a number twenty-three on the side." She looked at both of us forlornly. "What can I do now?"

I nodded at Sam.

"Do nothing now," he said. "Would you recognize these men if you saw them again?"

"I would for sure on the one with the scar, maybe on the other two."

"Stay away from Bington and in Madisonville for now," Sam said. "Those people who threatened you are also after the judge. They're hot enough after him that they're unlikely to look for or bother you, Amy. One day soon I'll tell you more about things. For now, just be careful."

She looked at him. "You'll be back?"

"Just me alone, Amy."

They smiled at each other and touched hands.

We drove back to Bington. I thought on it and found the whole thing puzzling. If the Wolfer followers wanted the mail stolen then did that mean they knew my Jo had been poisoned?

It had to be. Or did it?

Sam drove back more slowly. I thought he was trying to figure on it also.

The Bington Union Hall was owned and occupied by a large number of local and area unions. There was a parking lot in the rear and there were cars parked there.

One of the cars was an almost new black Chrysler Concorde.

"Do you know anyone here?" Sam asked as we neared the door of the hall.

"Probably," I said. "If I get us into an office let me ask the questions."

"Sure."

We entered. There were offices down both sides of a hall. A greying, straight-haired lady of perhaps fifty summers frowned at us from her desk in the middle of the hall.

"Is Bill Williams here?" I asked.

"I'll check. Who shall I say is calling?"

"My name's Don Robak."

"And your name?" she asked Sam.

He smiled and gave her his name amiably.

She nodded and rose from behind her desk. She took a cane and used it to support herself as she slowly walked. She entered the third office down the hall and in a moment she came out and beckoned to us with the cane.

"Mr. Williams says you damnable lawyers are welcome. Come on back here."

At his door I looked in and saw Bill Williams. His nickname was Big Bill and it fit. He was maybe six and a half feet tall and he weighed somewhere between three and four hundred pounds. At one time he'd been a professional wrestler, but now he was over fifty and retired from all that action and drama.

I'd represented him a long time ago when he'd had a fight with a strike breaker hired by the Macings. A city judge had lightly scolded him and then found him not guilty because he'd acted in self-defense. He'd then shook hands with both Bill and me.

It had been one of my better moments for that year.

Bill shook my hand, hiding mine in his strong, larger one, and then thumped me lightly on the back. Then he did the same to Sam.

"Come in and sit down," he said.

We did and Bill continued to smile at Sam.

"I saw you play for the IU's a few years ago. You were a breath of fresh air for them poor Hoosiers."

"Thank you, Mr. Williams," Sam said. He was always polite and his smile was always affable.

"Is the almost new black Chrysler in the parking lot your car, Bill?" I asked.

He nodded. "End-of-the-year clearance and they took in my old clunker and gave decent trade. And I've been expecting you because of a call from Preacher."

"Do you ever visit the Macing estate in your black car?"

"At times. They don't much like for me to come there because they think their company union members will think we're into plotting things together." He shook his head. "Which we are. I work for the union, but the Macings own the union and the workers, all the way. In one way that's not too bad because they live in fear of a bad strike and workers in the plant get pretty good benefits. So the Macings discourage me from driving to their horse farm, but sometimes they also order me to visit. That's what it was most recently."

"Were you ordered to visit the Macing place sometime in the last four or five days?"

He thought for a moment. "It was a few days ago. The same day someone shot into their place, but earlier. There'd been minor trouble about a worker dying on the job, plus a couple of workers being fired, and so I was called to come immediately to their place. I thought it was about the dead worker, but it wasn't."

"You went there and conferred with the brothers?" I asked.

"Brothers, sister, and some guy I'd never seen before. Four people."

"Tell me what this stranger looked like."

He shook his head. "Why? I mean, you know I'll happily tell you whatever you want, but I'm curious and guess I need to know the why of it."

"People have shot at me, Bill. Someone got something that was poison into my wife. She almost died and she still isn't right. Someone tried to tunnel into my house with a case or two of dynamite."

"I'd not heard that. I'm sorry, Don. This guy was big and he didn't say much. His name was Wolf or Wolfer or something like that. He was pushing sixty years old. He spent most of his time listening. The meeting was about you, Don. They were planning to organize my union people to get voters out to vote against you in the primary next month." He looked over at the wall and then back at me. "I told him they could organize all they wanted, but that I intended to vote for you, that we were friends, and that you'd been my lawyer. They didn't like that too damn much. Things got a little ugly and they asked me if it would be okay for them to wire around me until after the primary." He smiled as he remembered.

"What happened then?" I asked.

"I told them such was fine with me. Then I also told them the word would get out about the Macings trying to win an election and whoever they were backing would get his ass chewed and spit. I just frankly told them that in my opinion no one would or could beat you."

"What'd they say to that?" I asked.

"They talked among themselves, the three men and the woman with, again, the stranger not saying much of anything. Then they asked me to leave and I obliged them and left."

"Did you hear any more about it?"

"No. Afterward I read in the paper that your opposition quit, Don."

I smiled. "He did do that."

205

"And the Macing lady she'd try to tell them when things got suggested, how you'd take them personally and what you'd do."

I found the idea of Libbie evaluating me for her brothers and Wolfer interesting. Maybe she could have twenty years back, but not now.

14

FROM MY OFFICE I called a senior judge I knew well. He was retired from the bench two counties north and now personally ran a security company guarding large office buildings, apartment complexes, and malls in his hundred-fifty-thousand population county and the larger ones around it. He was a large, angry man and a first-class judge.

I explained my problem once his secretary had located him.

"You mean these idiots want to kill you so they can get themselves a new judge?"

"Dead right," I said and he laughed, but only a little.

"And you want me to come and sit in for you for a couple of critical days while they're trying to find you to get the killing done?"

"Dead right," I said, chancing the answer because we were friends.

"Can I bring help? Like maybe four of my best people?"

"Make it six large and well-armed ones."

"I'll be at your courthouse at eight A.M. tomorrow."

"Make it eight-thirty," I said. "I don't want you spoiling my folks down here."

He laughed again and I laughed with him.

"Stay dead right," he said.

"Watch yourself. These folks are likely to shoot first and check your identity later."

In the trunk of my car I had a sleeping bag. Sometimes, when I felt Jo needed me I'd slept in the bag on the floor beside her bed at Green Home.

I rolled and folded the sleeping bag up, trying to make it look like a bunch of sheets and blankets, and put the mess on the passenger seat of the Ford.

I'd dropped Sam off earlier at his office. I now parked my Ford in the sheriff's lot.

I planned to leave it there for both tonight and tomorrow night. Sometime today I would pick up the sleeping bag.

I entered the sheriff's office and told the radio deputy, who didn't recognize me, that my car was parked in their lot.

"And you are?"

"Don Robak."

"You a special deputy?"

I smiled at her. "I'm a judge."

She reddened and then nodded her head. "I guess it's okay then."

"Just tell Jumper I parked it there."

"Yeah," she said, still not sure about me or my place in the high-sheriff's world.

I walked back upstairs in the courthouse and found Preacher sitting in the courtroom. He was watching the ceiling and also the weather outside.

"Do you want to put the movable wall in deluge place?"

I'd thought some more on that and I shook my head. "It doesn't sound as funny to me as it did when I first thought about it. It's our courthouse just like it's the commissioners' courthouse and it's no place for practical jokes."

"I agree. Nothing much sounds funny just now, not even thoughts about the three wise men."

We took Preacher's car. I was certain my plate number was widely known to the Wolfers and their associates. Plus my sleeping bag was in my car and I'd need it later.

The afternoon had grown warm and there were ominous clouds in the April sky. I wondered if this could be the day we'd have a downpour and the black hole of Bington would open into the courtroom.

Preacher's car was black, a nine-year-old Cadillac with about thirty thousand mostly local miles on the odometer. Before he quit drinking Preacher had bragged that he only drove it to the bars and home.

We picked up Kevin and Sam at their law office and we four drove about Bington. All seemed normal. We saw no groups of hostiles gathered together with guns. In fact nothing appeared ominous. We eventually went up the hill and looked over my house. There were marked sheriff's vehicles parked at several street corners near the house.

Someone female in sheriff's brown uniform colors waved and we waved back.

I said: "I just don't want to settle in there. That could bring on a battle. If they don't spot me after watching my house they'll look for me elsewhere and they'll have to break up in smaller squads."

Preacher nodded.

We turned around in a neighborhood cul-de-sac and I motioned for Preacher to put on the brake and he did.

"Think about this for the safety of your own asses, gentlemen," I said. "The Wolfers somehow managed to get a letter into our courthouse mail today. It says I must die or my wife must die by midnight tomorrow night. The Wolfers have got someone at the courthouse, inside or outside, a someone who reports what I do."

"Could be anyone," Kevin Smalley said. "Even wall-sitting watchers go in and out."

I nodded.

"Lots of people have threatened you in Bington and elsewhere, Don," Smalley said, probably personally remembering some of the threateners. "It's part of your local charm and stories are told about it on the tourist bus trips. Why do these Wolfers bug you so much when earlier baddies didn't?"

"Maybe because I'm sure the Wolfers were involved in Jo being poisoned. Maybe I'm just getting older. Another thing: I've not seen anything of my friend Mo or his catty new friend for a time. That friend owns a place just west of the Wolfer farm. She's the one I told you guys about, the one with lots of cats. She's also the lady the Wolfers sued because of those same cats. Maybe we could get the answer to that question by driving to her place and taking a careful look around. But I know where I've got to be when the looking's done and it's late-night time tonight and tomorrow night."

"Where would that be?" Sam asked.

"Under cover. Watching and hiding. And doing it armed and ready, close to Jo." I thought for a moment. "With a gun, preferably a high-powered rifle with a laser sight so that even I can shoot accurately. And by myself until I'd need someone."

"We're going to help you whether you like it or not, Judge," Smalley said.

"Too many people watching might spoil it," I said.

"I know where I can borrow several high-powered rifles with laser sights," Sam then said.

"Where," I asked.

"Easy. Stored at my apartment. I belong to a shooter's club. Some of the others have small kids at home and so they leave their guns at my place. I've got a dozen guns there and three or four of them have laser sights."

"Will any of your friends raise hell if we borrow them for a day or two?" I asked.

"I'm sure not, but I'll call and get permission."

"Let's get them later," I said. It sounded like an order. "We'll do it when we come back. We won't get much help from lasers in daytime when the other side can see us also."

Kevin Smalley smiled and said: "He's not as dumb as he looks."

Sam shook his head. "Yeah, he is."

Everyone laughed but me. And then I did also.

I shook my head. "You guys stick with me and one or more of you may wind up hurt or dead."

"I'm enlisted for the duration," Smalley said. The others nodded. "I just hope it's a short war."

"Shit," I said.

"You keep saying that and nervous as I am I might do it," Preacher muttered.

And so we drove south toward Floyd County.

I got out of Preacher's well-aged car and waited until my two lawyer friends also got out. We then directed driver Preacher into a kind of hiding area we'd noticed across the road from the cat farm; it lay behind an old chewing-tobacco sign that adorned the single remaining wall of a collapsed barn. You had to go behind the wall to see the car.

Preacher was older, had heart problems, and so would stay with the car and wait for us. If anything started up and we didn't get back to him fast he was to go to Floydsburg for help. He now was armed with a twelve-gauge shotgun and also carried his aged pistol. The pistol had been cleaned and loaded and might or might not explode if he fired it.

I offered him my seldom-used cell phone, but when he professed there was one in his car I took mine back.

We three climbed up and over the northwest corner of the cat lady's fence and proceeded east in the general direction of her cabin. I'd called her telephone number several times on the cell phone before and after we'd left Bington, but there'd been no answer. I'd had an operator check the line and she'd reported that it appeared to be in service.

That worried me some. I didn't like the idea of coming to her farm to look around, but it seemed something that needed to be done.

The land was quiet around us except for birds. They chirped at us from ancient trees, alarmed at our invasion.

Some of the tree limbs where they roosted were already green with half-grown leaves. That allowed the birds to hide and mostly chirp anonymously.

Behind us the land sloped downward so that I could see for miles west, the direction away from the Wolfer farm. Behind us was a land of houses and barns, cattle, fences, telephone poles, and plowed fields, a civilized, agricultural land. I saw nothing behind us that alarmed me. In the area we were now crossing observers on the Wolfer farm also could not see us. We were protected by the lay of the land. We were walking up the backside of a hill. I remembered that Ann Sembly's cabin was over the top of that hill, but I couldn't remember the exact line. Once we arrived at the top of the hill and started down toward that cabin then we could be seen from Wolfer property.

That worried me more.

The farmland that lay behind the cabin had not yet been planted with anything. In places the spring weed growth already was over ankle high.

I doubted Ann intended to plant many crops. Her land was like the Wolfer land, and so not much good. Maybe some catnip.

Near the crest of the hill I stopped, hunkered down, and got low enough so that all I could see was Ann Sembly's cabin and the area around it.

What I saw alarmed me. The cats were there, cats by the dozen, but only a few whirligigs now fought the wind to duel with cats. Most had been kicked down or pushed over. Many of them lay crushed on the ground. I slowly raised myself a fraction. Across the road on the Wolfer side there were more cats, two dozen or so. Those cats were dead and strung carelessly over the Wolfers' barbed wire. There was a sour smell to it all, a smell of blood, animal feces, and sudden death.

The sky grew darker as I counted cat corpses. More than twenty.

The door to the Sembly cabin was battered in and several of the windows were broken. It looked abandoned, but as I watched

I thought someone came to the window and looked cautiously out, perhaps waiting for the arrival of the person who'd called on the telephone several times.

It seemed also possible that the inside watcher was Mo or Ann Sembly, but I stayed low and quiet because out in the front yard there was something else I'd not noticed at first look. It was a single human body. Someone had covered it over with blankets the color of the ground so that it perhaps wouldn't be seen or recognized for what it was by a passerby on the county road. From my vantage point it was apparent what the lump was. I could see a hand sticking out from under blanket edges nearest me. The hand was bloody and the fingers were stiffly pointed in my direction. What clothing I could see on the body was camouflauge. I was encouraged by that. It was a large hand and it was also white. Therefore not Mo, and not Ann the cat lady.

I'd been a step or two ahead of the others, but Sam and Kevin were now up to me and also kneeling and watching silently.

Sam nodded solemnly. "Someone's shot. We need to call for some law."

"Want to use my cell phone?" I asked.

He nodded. "Okay."

We slid a few feet backward from the top of the hill.

"You want me to call?" he asked.

"Sure. Tell him what you see and that I asked you to call."

I'd called the sheriff's number in Floydsburg often enough from special judging so that I remembered the telephone number. I told it to Sam and handed him the phone. He punched the number in, talked softly, and then handed the phone to me.

"The sheriff down in Floydsburg wants to talk to you," he said. "I thought he would."

I took the phone. "George, this is Don Robak."

"What's going on, Judge?"

I described the scene below for him.

"A dead body? This is on Ann Sembly's farm?" he asked. "I know that crazy cat lady."

"So do I and it's her place for certain. First farm east of the Wolfer place. There are also a flock of dead cats strung on the Wolfer fence."

"I'll send some people. Try to wait where you can't be seen. And be careful. If anyone threatening comes your way then run and run fast. It may be a little while before I get a car there. Those crazies on the Wolfer place are out of their corral. We found a bomb in an old car parked close to the jail down here. Nothing hooked up to set it off yet, but there was a lot of fertilizer in the trunk and a lot of diesel oil mixed in it. We found it because your sheriff called and he'd found another half-ass bomb in a station wagon up there, same setup, no detonator attached yet. Now sheriff's officers and state police all over this part of southeast Indiana and northern Kentucky are checking cars and trucks parked near courthouses and federal installations. They've also got extra guards up north at Michigan City where the Wolfer son is held. They're now stopping and holding all people in trucks with a twenty-three on them."

"Have your people be careful when they enter the Sembly farm," I said.

"Sure. Is there a why?"

"I think there may be someone or several someones in Ann Sembly's log cabin and I don't think she's one of them."

"Yeah. Okay."

I turned the phone to off and put it in a pocket.

I sat on the warm ground and thought more on the present situation. I'd once been, but now was no longer, a soldier. Sam and Kevin also had military experience; Kevin still wore a miniature Silver Star medal ribbon from an old war in his suit lapel. Sam was now a captain or maybe a major in the National Guard, a weekend warrior. But we weren't trained, equipped, or armed to fight a daytime battle. The laser-sighted guns might be of help if we had them, but they'd be more help at night. And I had no right to get my friends or myself into a firefight.

Coming here had been a stupid idea. Now it was high time to get away.

"Let's all stay down and out of sight," I said. The sky above grew dark and then lighter. "If we see anyone other than the sheriff coming then we're going to bug out fast. Let's move back a little closer to the crest of the hill, being double careful."

At the top again we saw that the cats that were left near the cabin appeared to be in a state of shock. They wandered here and there, shying away from the cabin door, snarling and purring.

It suddenly began to rain, soft, then hard, then soft again. The wind blew the rain into my eyes as I tried to keep watch.

The cabin was only a hundred yards away. I wanted badly to see who was inside. Maybe Mo was down there and hurt. Maybe Ann Sembly was inside.

A man exited the cabin's ruined door. He was dressed in camouflauge hunter's clothing and he was armed with an oversized rifle.

More men exited the door of the log cabin behind the first one.

There eventually were ten of them. All of them wore camouflauge gear. Two carried automatic rifles with long, banana clips. Another man, with a helper following behind him, was armed with what I recognized from my wars as the parts of a Browning automatic rifle. The rest had rifles and shotguns and belted pistols. Some of the rifles had magnifying scopes.

The leader was Damion Darius Wolfer, Double Damn himself, about six four tall and three hundred pounds, big as a barn, strong and angry because the damned world wasn't obeying his commands.

Angry mostly at me.

Seeing him made little drops of perspiration roll down my back.

He stared around, looking intently up our way at the top of the hill. I hoped he couldn't smell me.

I lay very still. I realized they'd likely been waiting down at the cat lady's ruined cabin for someone, that someone being me plus whoever I brought along. They'd either guessed and/or hoped I'd show up. Maybe someone had recognized me or my car when I'd visited the cat lady's farm along with Mo before.

A final Wolfer soldier exited the cabin. He was almost as large and strong-looking as Damion Darius and he pulled a man who'd been crudely blindfolded along behind him. My memory from a five-year-old trial told me that the grinning captor was another of the older Wolfer sons.

I also recognized the prisoner. It was my pal from the FBI and law school, Elmer Fudd. He looked like he'd taken a beating. His clothes were torn and disheveled and they were not the same clothes he'd worn to visit my office. I could see what I thought might be blood or dried mud on the blindfold he wore over his eyes.

"You four stay here and watch the cabin," Double Damn ordered and pointed. "I still think he'll come back here. Our informer said he'd left with some lawyers driving an older black Cadillac and also said they might have guns," Damion Darius continued loudly. He shook his head. "The way I'm told he operates he almost has to come back here. He's both curious and stupid. The rest of us will go back across our boundary road and take with us this federal asshole we caught snooping. I think we need to have a full patriot's meeting and discuss what to do with him. Live or die. If Robak does show up then you four catch or kill him and whoever's with him. If you need help fire a couple of shots. Or call on the cell phone although other people may be listening in, so better to fire shots than call."

He turned away, raised a leader's hand, and most of the men and the prisoner followed behind him.

We waited for the sheriff's car, watching carefully. Wolfer and his followers soon vanished into the trees on the Wolfer tract. The four men left behind conferred in low tones I couldn't overhear and, when rain came again, reentered the cat lady's cabin.

We waited.

A time came when the sky above us lighted up a bit like the sun had come back out. All the world around us became confusion. Two explosions came first and then one slightly larger. All ripped at our ears. They came from a place beyond the Wolfer woods. We looked and saw some of the trees in that woods were now on fire. A light shock wave rolled over us and I slipped and fell and then rose. I was unhurt but I felt warm. The shock wave had been hot.

"Somebody set off something over there on the Wolfer place," Sam said.

Smaller explosive noises continued. We could see nothing because the explosions were happening behind the woods. I believed that people might have died.

The four men left behind to wait and watch for us bolted out of the cabin door and ran hard toward the road and the Wolfer land. I stood up so as to see what was happening better, not caring now if they saw us.

Coming almost directly toward the four Wolfers who'd abandoned the cabin were our two, Mo and the cat lady, leading one more person, a man. They looked to be all right and were running well, but were too close to the Wolfer party.

"Fire your guns down at the Wolfers," I called. I fired my shotgun without sighting, knowing such was mostly useless on account of the distance. I could hear the two lawyers shooting with their rifles. One of the four Wolfers miraculously fell and was picked up and dragged across the road by the three others. There the men sprawled themselves on the ground, saw us, and shot back.

Mo saw what was happening in front of him. He turned to his right without missing a step. He pulled the cat lady with him and the other man hesitated and then followed. Soon there was a good distance between the two groups on the Wolfer property. At the fence Mo used something and cut a pathway in the wire, then led Ann Sembly and the man through it. No one fired at them and I thought the four Wolfer men had not even seen them.

There was another small explosion from inside the Wolfer farm. Then a fearsome thing happened. A big man came running out of the woods on fire. He was screaming and using his big axe to strike at whatever lay in front of him. He fell and rolled. Then he rolled more slowly and soon rolled no more. His shirt and pants continued to burn and I thought I could smell him dying, but I knew that was unlikely.

Sam called the Floyd sheriff again and tersely reported the new happening.

The sheriff told us to sit tight because deputy sheriffs and state police were close, and indeed, some patrol cars did soon appear on the roads.

We joined Mo and Ann Sembly near where Judge Fromm and I had looked back into Wolfer Fort. The man with them was Elmer Fudd of the FBI. Mo and Ann were slightly scorched, but looked to be uninjured. Elmer had a first-class black eye, a serious head cut, and an arm he carried as if it were hurt.

Elmer nodded at me.

"Troublemaker," he said, but then he grinned. He poked me easily on the shoulder and I poked him back, both of us smiling.

"What happened?" I asked Mo.

"Best get us out of here," Mo said. "There's going to be all kinds of hell on this one." He looked back across the road and I looked with him. A part of the wall at the back and side of Wolfer Castle was in ruins. The building itself still stood although the back showed much damage. "And I'm cooked a little and so is Ann."

Ann Sembly gave me the smallest of smiles. "There are people who are likely dead over there, a few in trade for my dead cats."

A deputy from Floydsburg came up to me. "The sheriff's on his way. He'd like for you to wait and be here to talk to him, Judge."

Elmer nodded at me. "Go if you want, Judge. I'll talk to the sheriff. And these people who seem to be your friends likely saved my poor old administratively graded ass."

We shook hands.

"I apologize for saying that," I said. "I was frustrated, is all."

"I accept the apology and return my own," he said. "I keep reliving law school too damn much. Maybe this will give me a new thing to live."

I gave Elmer and the deputy one more nod. "Tell your sheriff I had to leave. Some of the people here with me got burned in the explosions. He can call me or I'll call him later."

"Okay."

The five of us walked down the road toward where Preacher had parked the car.

In minutes we were back in Bington. The courthouse was closed, but Preacher had a door key. We went to the jury room, which had no windows.

"It's over," Sam said. "All blown to hell." I could read relief in his voice.

Ann Sembly smiled and Mo nodded.

I shook my head. "Maybe, but more likely maybe not. I want one of the laser-sighted rifles as soon as I can get it. I'm going to get close to Jo's room. When it gets dark I'm going to visit or call in and see if they've changed Jo's room number. If they have then I'll locate outside near her room and keep watch. You people go on, but sleep at home so I can call and find you."

Mo nodded at me.

"What happened at the cabin, Mo?"

"We were sleeping. They got up close to us and started shooting into the cabin. We went out the trap door and into the tunnel. The best place to hide when we surfaced seemed to be the Wolfer chicken houses. We were in one and men with guns brought the beat-up guy in and strung him up on chains."

"He's FBI," I said. "He didn't think the Wolfers were going to be trouble."

"When they hung him up the Wolfers who brought him were telling him they were most likely going to cut off his head with a big axe. Then they said old man Wolfer might eat him. A little later things started blowing up and we got out of there, bringing him along."

Ann Sembly smiled again as if she knew more than the rest. I shook my head at her. She nodded.

"You people need to go get some medical help. And like I told you long ago, Mo, you don't want to make statements or answer questions."

He nodded and took Ann Sembly's hand.

"You know what I think happened?" I said. "Lightning hit something. Does everyone believe that?"

Everyone, including Mo and Ann nodded, some slowly.

"Wait here," Sam said to me. "I'll get you a gun."

I waited.

After a while, with a laser-sighted gun and my sleeping bag, I headed for Green Home.

15

AT GREEN HOME I watched in the daylight and later in the dark. I first lay behind trees and a cemetery wall that hid me from easy sight. I wasn't alone. In the graveyard around me were many old friends.

Senator Adams, my first partner, was the nearest to Green Home.

I said to him: "If you will, Senator, please watch the front of the building."

"And if you will, Judges Steinmetz and Harner, please watch the sides of the assisted-living and nursing home."

And so they did.

I watched along with them. In between we talked of many things, mostly the sour shape of the world we knew or had known.

Once I left my hiding place and ran to Green Home. I inquired of the night shift about Jo's new room number, but it had been a busy day and so no room change had yet occurred. I was told that when they could they were to move her five rooms farther down from the entrance, same side and would do it that night. I waited a while and watched until they began the room change.

Jo slept through it.

I ran back to the cemetery. All seemed the same.

The weather was cool, but not cold. There was a light rain for a time, an April shower. I got into my sleeping bag. It was rainproof. I stayed dry.

Nothing happened that day. Nothing happened that night. At midnight it became the nineteenth of April, the witching day, and so I watched even more carefully. A couple of times in the early morning large town trucks appeared in the nursing-home drive to deliver supplies.

I also watched workers known and unknown arrive. I also saw doctors and nurses and attendants I knew.

Nothing suspicious happened. Not all day of the nineteenth.

During the day I called Sheriff Jumper and told him exactly where I was.

"They got a real mess down there at the farm-fort in Floyd County," he said. "Some dead, more hurt. Deputies and state boys all over the place without needing search warrants, some of the officers Catholics and Jews. I talked with the Floyd sheriff and he's delighted. Maybe the Wolfers will give up on you now."

"I hope so."

"I'll be along your way soon. I've already got people watching the roads."

"Thanks, Jumper."

"That FBI guy called in here singing your praises. You're no longer an asshole."

"That's good."

During the long day I also called my legal friends and Preacher. They reported all was calm. No one had tried to do anything in or to the courthouse.

Both lawyers said they would be on the scene before dusk and Preacher said he planned to park somewhere in the parking lot in his car. Other members of the bar were also coming to guard Green Home.

I waited some more.

The Wolfers *did* come about 11 P.M. There were about two dozen that I saw. Later I learned there was another truck that entered from the north. The ones I saw came rolling out of two four-by-fours painted olive drab. The invaders had light weapons, rifles and shotguns.

As they dropped out of the truck I saw laser lights touch around them, mostly low to the ground. I heard shots. I was far enough away so that I couldn't add my own rifle fire.

Men screamed and cursed. About half of the men managed to scramble back over the lowered four-by-four tailgates. When they did that the laser spots left them and concentrated on those who were still on the ground.

Those men were now firing back.

I saw Double Damn and tried to shoot my rifle at him. Every time I got red light onto his body I pulled the trigger. Nothing happened. My rifle failed to fire. Nothing I did helped.

The senior Wolfer had, by now, vanished into cover. His men were yelling and screaming, some trying to surrender. The trucks that had fled the scene were half a mile down the road.

Someplace up by Green Home I heard the sound of an explosion. There was a noise and a brightness.

I feared my Jo was dead.

I found Damion Darius Wolfer laying amid evergreens near the edge of a pond about a quarter of a mile from Green Home. He had crawled under low limbs to hide or rest and so I almost didn't see him.

The April night was cold around me, colder by far than it had been the night before. I'd noticed the cold but I grew warmer when I saw Wolfer. At first I thought he was dead, but quickly found he wasn't. His eyes came open as I approached. His hands reached out and searched, but there seemed no gun to find. His axe lay far enough from him so that I didn't worry on it.

I'd left my own defective rifle leaned against a tree.

I pulled Wolfer roughly out of the spruce branches by his boots. There was dim light. I figured he weighed a hundred pounds plus more than I did so I had some trouble getting the pulling job finished.

I saw a wetness on his dark windbreaker. I believed and hoped it was his blood.

Somewhere out there my Jo, plus sheriff's officers and friends of mine, might be injured, maybe dead, for the Wolfers had fired shots and set off an explosion.

"Help me," he whispered. His eyes watched me. "Help me, bastard Robak. You surprised me and mine with those red-light guns. Now it's your legal duty to help me."

"Sue me," I said. "I know you tried to kill my wife once before. I don't know exactly how you hurt her or why you did it, but I know you did it. And maybe you got the job done tonight."

He shook his head, smiling, liking my anger.

I reached down and lifted him by his shoulders so that I could pull him farther out. I put his back against the trunk of a nearby cut tree. He allowed me to do that without much groaning.

I let him loose and he turned like a cat and tried to crawl-walk to his axe. I stopped him with a shove and he caught at me with his oversized hands. The left one came high and tightened around my right arm and his right one sought and missed my throat, but hung on below, trying to cut and tear me open with long, dirty fingernails.

"Damn you, Robak."

The wetness on his jacket rubbed against my clothes and I saw he'd caught a slug in his upper chest and maybe another farther down on his lower body.

"Let go," I ordered, but he would not.

He slid closer to me, muttering curse words. He looked into my eyes and said: "The missing pieces of the two little girls, Robak. My son cut them out for me. I ate them long ago. They were tasty."

"You're shit, Wolfer. Your fort's bombed and burned. Your people will scatter when you die. And you will die."

"She said you couldn't kill, Robak. Was she wrong?"

I saw that he was in pain and I pushed my fist hard into his stomach so that it made him scream.

His rough right hand slid over to my neck and I let it. He hadn't enough strength to do real damage, but his nails were sharp. He released his grip quickly, sensing his own lack of strength, and cuffed openhanded at me. The fingernails scratched my face. He was trying for my eyes. I stiffened my fingers into a kind of hand spade, a thing I'd been taught in an old war. I smacked the spade hand into his belly hard and then did it again. He screamed both times. When his right hand dropped a little away from me I repeated the blow once more, this time as hard as I could.

He screamed once more.

"Kill me," he said. "You've made me hurt so bad inside I want to die."

He stopped fighting then, but he spat at me. He fought to get breath. Then he closed his eyes.

He said: "Kill me, Robak."

"Die on your own."

I watched and he still moved. I thought if he stayed alive tonight he would soon try again. We lay there, both breathing, me heavily, him gasping slowly, each breath a whine of pain.

I arose, got the axe, and came back to him.

After a while Jumper Jimp called my name twice. "Robak. Robak!"

I answered: "I'm over here on the ground, north side of the pond."

He came close and helped me to my knees and then my feet. He shone his flashlight on me.

"Your throat looks like raw meat," he said. "It's bleeding some."

"I'm all right."

"You'll do hospital time before I believe that," he said. He turned away from me and lifted Wolfer's head and then checked with inquiring fingers here and there.

"We won't need this bastard driven back to my jail in leg irons and manacles," the sheriff said, his voice sounding satisfied. "It

225

hasn't been a real good few days for the Floyd County Wolfer militia."

"Fine with me."

"You do this to him?"

"We had a fight and I had to use his axe. You'll have to inquire into what killed him with whoever does the autopsy. He had me by the throat and I fought him. Someone shot him a few times before that. It wasn't me because my gun wouldn't fire. He tried to get the axe, but I got it." It seemed enough to say and it was all I was ever going to say.

Jumper gave me a happy smile. "Even if you're the one who axed him it's open-and-shut, Judge. It's good old self-defense."

"I need to get to Green Home. Something exploded around there when I was tracking."

"I heard it. My boys picked up some Wolfer bandits running back to the north. One was carrying some dynamite sticks."

At Green Home there were two sheriff's vehicles with gum-ball flashers spinning. Deputies guarded the front door. When I tried to enter, a uniform who looked familiar stopped me.

"My wife's in there," I said.

"There might be more bombs," he said, still holding on to my arm.

"My wife's in there," I shouted. I thought he recognized me for certain. I shook his hand off and pushed my way around him.

At first there was little damage. In the great room the fake fire burned. The old lady who usually sought her dog there was absent.

Then there was much damage. Walls were pushed crazy and windows were glassless.

Back where Jo had lived there was great damage. The old woman who I thought prayed to die seemed to have found her reward. She lay on her floor, finally silent.

Jo's former room was mostly gone, but I could get around it and on down the hall.

The roof had fallen in over where Jo's new room was. I could smell the acrid odor of the explosion like nitrite smells I remembered from wars.

Her clothes were still in her new closet. My heart beat faster. I got farther inside and heard something.

The voice was faint, but I recognized it. It called hopelessly: "Robak. Don Robak."

I called out. "It's me, Don Robak."

The voice came louder. "My head hurts. Am I dead again?"

I pulled at lumber and wall siding, finding an opening. I couldn't move some stuff, but I managed enough for an inward opening. The heavy stuff was piled atop the sturdy hospital bed, held securely. I lowered myself to the floor, one knee bent and higher than the other. I pushed and tore things away, finding it hard to locate a place to shove the debris.

I could see under the bed and there she was.

My Jo. Her head had a bruise and there were scratches on her arms and legs.

Her voice was a little garbled, but I made out the word. "Time," she said.

I changed my balance point and found I could reach under the bed a bit. I patted her hand and she sighed and crept closer to the bed's edge and to me. I could see her eyes and they were wide open.

They seemed more aware.

I moved closer and she moved closer.

"Kiss me," she said with words I could understand and believe in.

We managed it.

16

THERE CAME A day in mid-August when candidates from other parties could no longer file for office or be filed by their political organizations. On that day I had an ounce and a half of Dewar's in a large glass of water and ice. I was no longer a candidate for reelection. I was, on that date, an electee.

I'd run all right in the primary, not top of the ticket, but not bottom, either. It was nice to know that I'd not have to worry about the general election.

By that date a number of things had happened.

Various federal and state groups had gathered like vultures upon dead animals and investigated the explosion(s) at the Wolfer camp and the invasion of the nursing/assisted-living home.

The farm death count stood at five with twenty-seven injured.

The favorite theory was that lightning had set off the first (and perhaps the only true) Wolfer explosion and the other happenings had fed off the first explosion so as to cause a half-explosion and a half-fizzle.

No explosions occurred elsewhere except for the later dynamite explosion at Green Home, which had killed two.

I disqualified myself from any and all county hearings. Other area judges and special prosecutors did the State of Indiana hearings. The federals did their procedures in Washington, D.C. No one subpoenaed me to testify as a witness in the federal hearings. The federals did try to subpoena Reverend Mo and Ann Sembly, but neither could be found and served. Eventually the hearings ran out of things to hear and so ended. During that time the newspeople avidly sought Reverend Mo and Ann Sembly because the lone area FBI special agent, a man injured on explosion day by the Wolfers, had made Mo and Ann into heroes in his testimony. He swore that neither of them could have had anything to do with causing the disaster. He also swore that without their aiding him in escape he likely would have been killed. I read later that he'd been transferred into a far more important job in Washington with the Bureau. I smiled when I read it.

Six armed invaders of Green Home were shot, five of them in the legs and feet on the grounds near Green Home. Twelve more of the approximately fifty invaders were arrested. Only the most senior Wolfer had died, along with one aged patient. I was called as a witness before a grand jury and testified that I'd fought, but didn't believe I'd killed him. The coroner then testified that one of two bullets in his body had been the cause of death. The killing slug had entered his lower left chest and couldn't have come from my unfired rifle.

Most people, when my secret testimony given before the grand jury quickly got around, went out of their way to nod and smile at me. Most of the rest, with one major exception, were at least respectful.

The Feeps foreclosed in late May on the various and many tax liens. Such ran most of the remaining inhabitants off the Wolfer lands. An angry someone, perhaps a neighbor, ran a farm tractor or a many-wheeled truck, or both, through the heavy wire fences. There were soon a dozen ways to enter and exit Wolfer land. Some people claimed that Wolfers and friends still camped on the land, but no one could show any real evidence that such was so. Rumors I heard had the remainder of the family mostly in Mexico.

I waited until all newsworthy things about the Wolfer farm tragedy grew calm. I wanted badly to make a call to Libbie Macing, but I wanted all else done and the federals gone.

Jumper was renominated. The closest of his pursuers ran more than five thousand votes back and the total votes cast for all his opposition were less than Jumper's total.

Two of the three incumbent county commissioner stooges, Larry and Moe, were seeking renomination. The third incumbent, Curly, had two years to go on his term.

Both Larry and Moe lost.

My longtime friend Judge Fromm dropped dead from a massive heart attack during a June Floyd County dissolution trial. I went down for visitation and served in my black robe along with other judges as honorary pallbearers at the funeral. His court reporter told me he'd had no problems with his ulcers after using the new medicine, but that likely the long years of fighting to live and eat had weakened "him's heart."

Sam King and Amy Ringer got engaged in late July.

The Wolfer lawyer, Ed Amesworthy, died on the farm.

Red Chuck's parents reconciled.

Rumors spread that Macing Drug Company would be absorbed by a huge French and German conglomerate.

The black hole of Bington never opened. When new commissioners took over first of the following year, they did major repairs to the roof and air-conditioned all of the courthouse.

I put out signals that I would like to see Reverend Mo.

I waited patiently and then I waited impatiently. It became late August and the weather went hot and dry.

The woman who answered the phone at the Macing estate had a cool, British voice. She asked my name and I supplied it.

I wasn't certain Libbie would talk to me, but after a while she came to the phone.

"Congratulations on being a winner and also what in hell do you want?" she asked.

"I think I'd like to take a look at this great exercise room of yours you've told me about," I said.

There was a long silence. "Go far away," she finally said. "And don't call here again. I'll get in touch with you when I decide to tell you what you're going to do."

"Then also don't call here, Libbie. And don't watch my house nights."

She laughed and said: "But I have to call and watch."

She was still calling my home number almost every night and not blocking her number. And I would see her car sitting on a close-by street at night. From her parking spot she could watch my house. I didn't answer the phone when she called.

"In addition I want to talk to you, as commanding officer, CEO, and madam president of Macing Drugs, about my wife and her ongoing problems and the rising costs thereof now that she's better and they have specialists working with her."

She was silent again for a moment.

"You're a nut and a half. I won't talk to you about your wife's troubles. You can call Beau at the plant for that crap or you can converse with your doctors. Or you can sue us. I wasn't in favor of telling you anything or offering you anything, but I wanted to see your upset face when you heard the news that we'd likely done it. And my damn brothers wanted the problem over."

"So you won't talk to me at your place on your terms?"

"You've got someone listening in on an extension, haven't you?"

"No one, Lib," I told her. It was a small lie, but I saw no reason to be truthful with her. My bailiff Preacher was listening. He didn't know why, but I'd asked him to listen without telling him more. He'd smacked his lips like he was doing a taste test on Jack Daniel's and then nodded.

"Sure," he'd said.

I could envision Libbie at her phone. She was a woman with great curiosity mixed with high intelligence, She also owned not an ounce of pity for the world around her. The world was there for her to manhandle as she wished.

But what did I know? Why did I want to see and talk to her?

She was a woman of confidence. She believed no one could interfere with her.

"Okay," she said. "But come now, this very moment, instantly. Don't try to plan something. Don't bring anyone or anything along with you. Come now."

"You'll have to promise me your fence and gate guards won't get me inside your place and then take a blacksnake whip to me."

"I was angry on that day and I had a right to be angry. I never said anything to the guards. A whip might do you damage and I don't want that. They'll let you inside."

Before I drove to the Macing estate I cheated a little by entering the courthouse. There I removed the economy-sized shotgun that I kept under and near the bench in the courtroom. I also took a pocketful of shells. I then secreted all under the passenger seat in my aging Ford, tying the shells loosely in a handkerchief. The shotgun fit neatly and couldn't be seen unless someone bent down all the way to near floor level.

I likely wouldn't need the gun to get inside the Macing estate, but it might get me out past the guards if things went poorly and I was able to make it back to the Ford. I'd try to make sure that things went well.

I drove. On the way I passed the Redeemer church. It was dark. I knew things were a problem there and that the last minister was still around Bington openly hating and baiting me.

I then drove on past the trailer park where my friend Earl Hardiman and his daughter Alma June lived. There were lights on in the trailer, but I didn't stop. I'd heard one of the neurologists at King's Daughters' had taken an interest in Alma June and that she was doing better.

I stopped in front of the entry gate. I measured the distance with my eyes. It was only a short rifle shot from the fence to the mansion, too short to only do chip damage.

A burly guard opened the gate for me. I recognized his face from the courtroom. He was someone who'd pled out a year or two back to a lesser charge in a plea bargain over a house burglary. He must have liked the courtroom result because he smiled in the car window at me.

"Nice to see you outside the courtroom, Judge. Park right up front of the house in one of the spots there."

I did. I knocked on the door.

The British maid answered the door. Within a few moments I was with Libbie in her exercise room.

Libbie was dressed in a leotard that looked as if it had been crafted from thin, fine tiger skins. It was low and loose at the neck so that when she bent I could count nipples, one, two, peekaboo.

She had lots of expensive professional apparatus set up around a forty-by-forty-foot room. At one end of the room there was a hot tub, at the other there was a twenty-by-twenty-foot swimming pool. All around the rest of the room there was equipment.

"Want to work up a sweat together, sweetie?" Libbie asked.

I shook my head. "Not now. I need to talk to you about Jo first."

"I've heard from my spies you've been able to take her out overnight a few times." She shook her head. "Does she remember, you know, love things?"

"Why do you ask that?"

"Because I hold prior ownership and a forever mortgage."

"She remembers. I have hopes that soon she'll spend more time at home, three days a week, then four, and someday permanently if things go well."

Libbie shook her head disapprovingly. "I don't like the idea of that."

"Tell me some more about how you feel and then tell me what you plan to do about it."

She shook her head and frowned. She focused on me again. "I think you're wired."

"I'm not. You can look. I'll even take my clothes off and you can be dead sure."

"First, take off your shoes and let me see them."

I did. She felt inside the shoes, banged them on the floor, hefted them high to see if they seemed overheavy, and then set them in a corner.

"Take off the rest," she said. She was now excited, but I wasn't.

I took clothes off. She examined them inside and out and then she examined me.

"How do you keep your stomach so flat?" she asked, touching me.

"I run. I don't drink martinis and eat the olives. I keep thinking about you and my wife Jo. My feeling just now is that you'll try to do something else to her," I said.

"You still believe I tried to kill her?" she asked, taking a step backward.

"Yes. You did that. It took a while but now I know that you did the poison job on her. I'm convinced beyond a reasonable doubt."

She smiled and I became dead sure.

"Now, I want you and maybe your brothers to pay big money to Jo for having injured her. I'll use that money to buy her a room like you've got here so that she can help make herself well. I also want your promise in writing that you and your hirelings will never bother Jo again and also won't try to harm me or my son."

"And if I gave you that promise would you believe it?"

"If it was in writing and in my safe-deposit box I'd try to believe, but I'd also keep watch."

She shook her head. "No way, Don. First, I'll never pay Jo a penny. All you have as evidence is what my brothers and I said to you in a private meeting. We'll not repeat what we told you that once and we've pretty well covered it up, so sue away and try to find the evidence we gave you in your library. Should you try to get the police or the sheriff to arrest me on some silly criminal charge, I promise you I'll make bond and start big trouble for you. I'll spread our affair twenty years ago before your judicial disciplinary people and say for a complaint you've been after me to resume it. I'll claim anything and everything. I'll hire me a dozen witnesses." She looked at my face. "And if you bring your little Jo bitch home you can try to keep watch and we'll see what happens."

"Why?"

"Because I own a lot of this damned world and have the inherent right to whatever I want in it."

"You're sick and wrong, Libby. Maybe we could talk and get your brothers to put you in a treatment place with high walls. They've got to have guessed what you did and that you did it on purpose. It'll save you from going to prison."

"I'm not sick. What's mine is mine. You're part of my property; I may have let you stray from me for a time, but when I want you back then you'd better report."

"And so I'm still your property even though we've not been lovers for twenty years?"

"Yes. You had a chance to renew the love thing a few months ago, just before your silly primary. When you fully understand me in the near future, then our troubled times will be over." She perched hipshot against an exercise machine and smiled happily at me. For most men she was a dream. For me she was now a nightmare. "You see, I don't absolutely have to destroy your fine, little wife, but that's up to you."

"Tell me exactly what it is you have to have from me and mine, Lib. A day, a week, doing your bidding and getting my back clawed? A night with you in New York or San Francisco now and then? I want to know."

"No. No schedules now. I'll tell you what's needed as time goes by and I have a chance to plan, feel, and then decide what will happen."

"Think on it, Lib. Make me angry enough and one night I might bring a gun and blow your crazy head off. Or maybe bring rats and snakes. You don't like them."

She smiled. "You can't do anything. It's not in you to do it. If I tried to kill you with a gun or knife, me against you, you might be able to fight back. I told the Wolfers that when I hired them on and gave them lots of money, but they were always stupid clods."

"They used your money to try to buy out their neighbors."

"I don't care how they used it, but I'll ask you not to talk about rats and snakes. You know I hate them."

"You hired someone to shoot into my house?"

"No. I did the job myself with a rifle that my long-dead daddy had from an old war. I was gone in my little red car a moment after I shot."

"But you were with your brothers when someone shot at one of them and used the same gun?"

"I hired a friendly, money-hungry, off-duty guard, a good shot. I let him use my gun. He wanted me, but he settled for money. I didn't want anyone hurt here at our place."

"And how did you feel about it when you were shooting at my house?"

"Terrific. And now I don't want you bringing your little wifie home much. So don't do it."

"I have to do what's best for her and me."

"Leave this house, then," she said. "Eventually you'll learn to do what you're told." She smiled and I couldn't read her eyes. "I'm in no hurry."

"You think you're safe. Is that the way of it, Libbie?"

"I'm safe. If those axe people had done what I said you'd have tried to enter their farm, been caught, and then I'd have ransomed you with enough money for them to start two wars."

I shook my head. "They'd not have taken your money for me. They want me dead." I thought of something else. "One thing more, Lib. You built a storage building over near Madison-ville after a church on that land burned."

She smiled. "I remember that. It was one of the many ways I made money for my Macing company and why my stock will be worth two or three times what it was worth soon. The land was worth more for storage than for churching. So I had some Wolfer people burn the church."

"The minister of the burned church was the man who let you into my house on the night in April you came to call."

She smiled. "That's funny. He sure looked like a damned butler to me."

"What was it you gave my wife?"

"There's no name for it. It was something I concocted, a liquid we tried in chemotherapy, but it turned out too hot."

"And how did you give this stuff to her?"

"I patted her on the head and gave her a little spray of it at the same time in the ladies' room."

"A little spray?"

"It was enough."

"Thank you for telling me all this, Libbie. I'll put on my clothes and be moving on now."

"Go. I don't want you around tonight. I wouldn't let you get close to me if you tried. I get mad when people talk about rodents and snakes."

"Yes. You do that." I thought for a moment. "Why didn't you marry one of your three men?"

"A man might steal some of the power. I want all of it." She watched me and a tiny tear appeared in the corner of the eye I could see. "But I do love you, Robak. A lot."

17

ON A COOL nonelection Tuesday in November, not quite a year after my Jo had been poisoned and nearly died, I sat at a conference table in Green Home with my friend Dr. Hugo Buckner. We conferred with a lady neurologist from Louisville who wore glasses and seemed to like to stare over the lenses. Also at the table was the head nurse for Green Home, and my Jo. Every once in a while Doc Buckner would smile at me.

"Didn't I tell you this could happen, Don? Didn't I?" he kept asking.

He had told me several times, but neither of us had really believed in miracles, nor had there been a true, full miracle. My Jo now knew me and knew her son. She could talk and understand some things. She was not fully recovered and there were times things were fuzzy for her, but she was improved. Her tremors had mostly vanished. Somehow the explosion had dynamited her partway back to my and our world.

Outside our meeting room I could see Jo's fellow patients passing. They were all old people. Some had canes or walkers. Others rode in wheelchairs. Some of the people knew what was going on and were excited about it. They would lift clenched hands for good luck and smile in at us.

Jo would wave back.

People came to Green Home as patients in need. From the home they then went to other places. They went to full-care nursing homes and to hospitals. Some went places to die and some died at Green Home.

No one had been cured and then gone home. No one had stayed alive. No one had become well.

I smiled also. The lady neurologist had just told us in her positive voice that she believed we could try living at our home three days a week now, then four if three worked out, then five and six and finally seven days if all went well.

I promised the neurologist to help Jo. I talked about a live-in lady to help Jo while I was in court.

Jo was to continue some of the medicines they'd used with her, but decrease dosage until final stoppage. Those drugs would be monitored by Doc Buckner. She was to continue her rehab exercises and continue seeing her speech therapist. She was to walk with me three or four times a week, such being every other day.

And I was again mainly to "watch and help" her. There were gaps in her thinking and reasoning powers. I must help her navigate through the rocks and shoals.

I knew she'd never be as she'd once been.

Son Joe was in school, but I would give him the news later at home. I would use care. What was happening was good, but not all good.

When the meeting was done I shook hands with everyone but Jo. Doc Buckner whapped me on the back one more time and we grinned like the fools we were.

"Didn't I tell you?" he asked one more time. "Now you take good care of her."

"I'll have to."

"Yes. It won't be easy."

I nodded farewell at Doc and escorted Jo back to her room. We kissed with enthusiasm outside her door. She liked to kiss and so did I. Her kisses were sweet.

Some of her memories of things that had happened in her past were gone. Other things were only dimly remembered. Parts of her had been stolen away and I knew there would be times when she'd cry and I'd find no way to stop her tears. I also knew that one day she might die unexpectedly as a result of the unknown damage done.

I would do my best.

"I'll come tomorrow and we'll walk," I told her at her room door. "I'll visit Thursday and come for you Friday morning and we'll walk again. Then we'll go home for the whole weekend, not just for a single night."

Time wasn't clear to her, but she understood a little about it. I'd bought her a new watch and she liked to consult it, but she read the minutes and hours without understanding them.

"Ummm," she said, watching the watch. We kissed again and she temporarily forgot her manners and groped me, but no one saw. It was difficult not to grope in return, but I would wait.

I wondered if she would grope others who came to see and visit her. I looked at her and she was beautiful. She might.

I feared for her, my son, and myself.

I'd watched a man move into our neighborhood two days back. I'd first seen him as he sat in a car and looked at my house and the new houses being built around it. Then he'd driven downtown, me following, and entered a realtor's office.

He could be a Libbie's man because I knew he'd moved to Bington to work for the Macings. That meant he'd been hired by Libbie.

For what?

Other people, including Libbie, watched my house.

Libbie had told me she'd wait for my decision until I brought Jo home.

Libbie was sick and, in her way, she was sick because of how much of the world she owned. She was sick also because she believed she owned me. It wasn't a sickness I'd intentionally in-flicted upon her. The sickness she had was caused by her absolute power, by having so much money that there was no longer a real way of measuring it.

I would watch and guard my injured Jo and try to keep her well, knowing that she could be harmed by Libbie or her hirelings at any time. I'd made up my mind that would be my way.

I'd not seen Mo since April. I wanted to see him. He'd not called or written. I'd left word among his friends here and in Madisonville that I wanted to see him. He'd vanished along with the cat lady and the remaining live cats.

No police were looking for him and I thought that he knew that by now.

Several times I'd driven past the cat lady's farm, but it was abandoned. One lonely whirligig remained standing.

I left Green Home and drove into downtown Bington following my late afternoon plans. I parked my Ford in a city parking lot and walked east on Second Street, a few blocks up from the Ohio River. The weather was becoming cooler, but on this day it was still low fifties, a fine fall day, with Christmas less than six weeks away.

A special judge sat behind the bench in my courtroom on this afternoon. Lawyers had picked a jury yesterday and today they were trying a case before that jury. I was therefore on semivacation. And I would, when I brought Jo home, take extra time away from the courthouse.

I made my promised call to the sheriff's office from a store where I was known and so could use their phone. That store was a block away from my destination.

At the junction of Second and Court, in front of the big Acme feed store, I spied the Right Reverend Raybin McFee. He was leaning into a hot, public sermon, his voice loud, spittle flying. The feed store had a raised cement step that ran the length of the front of the store. Many with the Jesus call preached there and a church-going feed-store owner allowed it.

Raybin had a crowd of fifty or so, more than he'd been drawing at his church on summer Sundays before he'd been asked to leave it. I'd heard I was the butt of many of his outdoor sermons, as were the federals and the Floyd and Mojeff County peace and police officers. According to the preaching of McFee we'd plotted together, all of us. The result of the plot were the deaths and injuries of God-fearing farmers on the huge Wolfer co-op farm in Floyd County, killed or hurt by a rigged explosion. Raybin then added that men who'd come to Green Home for a social call and to pray for the residents had been shot at and wounded and one of them had been assassinated by guess who.

Raybin McFee, to correct these wrongs, wanted me/us dead or, at least, inside a maximum-security prison.

I thought he saw me at the back of the crowd and I also thought I saw him smile a little. He had no fear of me on this day. Two of the largest of his five remaining apostles flanked him.

I'd heard that his church on the hill was shut down, but that he still was allowed to live in the fine house on the church premises until a new minister was found. I'd been informed that most of his flock were actively seeking such new preacher and that they no longer supported Raybin because he'd been visiting the Wolfer farm on the day of the explosions and had been singed some on private parts of his body. He'd come out the front door of the farmhouse building not wearing any clothes and in the company of one woman and one girl child who also were unclad.

I was certain that Jo, if she now remembered any of my past concerning McFee, would not have given her approval to my coming within sight and challenge of the good reverend. But I had come.

"There's one of the blood-spattered leaders of this outrage watching and grinning in contempt of God's laws," shouted Raybin McFee. A few people turned around and saw me and I waved to them. I wasn't grinning.

"You're full of beans and worse, as usual, Raybin," I called back.

Reverend McFee pointed his finger at me. "You are a damn murderer and an abomination before God," he called.

"At least I have my clothes on and am not trying to carry on with a nude woman and a nude girl child on a warm day," I called.

Many of the people laughed. The McFee story had spread through Mojeff County like wildfire.

As more people looked in my direction McFee whispered hurried directions to his two close guards. He'd publicly hoped I'd show up, dared me to come and face him, and now here I was daring him in return.

Upstairs, in a building across the street from the feed store a concealed camera rolled, filming all.

I knew the filming was happening because I'd hired the camera-people.

The three holy men walked toward me. I tried to look frightened.

Two large plainclothes deputy sheriffs fell in, one each at the side of the two large apostles.

By the time McFee got to me he was by himself. Just him and me. I intended to let him have the first blow for the cameras above. He was strong. Not quick, but strong.

"Here I am, Raybin," I said. "Enjoy."

He looked to the left and then to the right and saw he was alone.

He ran.

When I got back to my house Mo had finally returned to Bington.

A place for the cat lady and cats had been found in the Smoky Mountains. She and Mo had an arrangement, but they'd returned for a time. She wanted to look at her farm close to the Wolfers' land again before making a final decision. She was, he told me, present there now.

I sat with him in my kitchen. I was so glad to see him I was almost ill. I poured a quart of Diet Pepsi into a giant iced glass.

"No one's looking for you around here."

"I know. Maybe one day they might be."

243

"I doubt it," I said.

"Some who knew where I was telephoned and told me you wanted to see me."

"I did and still do. I wanted to see and talk to you because I now know the answer as to who poisoned Jo and who had your second church burned."

I watched his eyes change.

I told him about my meeting with Libbie.

He asked several times if I was certain of what I was saying. "Yes."

"And so she did this because she and her planners thought that my church property was more useful to the chemical plant than other property they'd looked at?"

"Yes. And cheaper. She didn't set the fire personally. She ordered it set. Thereafter we took their land-purchase money, added it to the insurance money that I still hold for you, Mo."

"Again, how sure are you?"

"Dead sure."

"And she personally used some drug to try to kill Jo?"

"Yes. She told me straight-out, Mo. She told me also that Jo would die if I brought her back now to our home. She said I could do nothing to change that and that no court would hold her without bond if I told others what she'd admitted to me and tried to make a case against her. I agree it would be that way. She'd file a petition to let to bail and then she'd post the bail, no matter how high it was. She'd hire lawyers by the dozen. She'd hire liars to testify. She'd have my butt in traction. We'd have a local circus if things ever got to trial. And truly, with all her money and power she's beyond my law. No evidence would ever be enough."

"All you're telling me is true?"

"Exactly true. Of both offenses she's guilty beyond any reasonable doubt."

"Good words." His eyes sought mine in the half-darkness.

"Words to live and die by." He looked away and then back. "Do you know she's sitting in her pretty red convertible watching your house tonight?"

244

"I know she does that. She also calls me. In an attempt to make her cease I've gotten some farm boys I know to capture me some rats and snakes. I've spread rat and snake food up where she parks and I've let the snakes and rats loose. She watches but her car windows are shut. I've had people watch her with binoculars. She has a gun in the rear of her car. A rifle. She keeps something in her lap and now and then looks at it and fondles it. I think it might be some kind of container holding a poisonous drug."

"What drug might that be?"

"I'm not certain. Perhaps it could be something new she's concocted in her lab especially for my family."

"And her brothers?"

I shook my head. "They won't speak to me about Libbie."

He nodded and we sat there for a while.

"She is beautiful."

"Yes."

"Maybe she need not die?"

I shrugged.

He shook his head and I saw tears in his eyes. "I guess I'll go out of your house now and take a night walk," Mo said. "I will pray and then tomorrow or maybe even tonight I may drive up past the land where I once believed I'd build my last church. Good land, but something bad has happened or will happen in the future there."

I looked at him and read meaning in his eyes. I had no desire to stop him. I'd already entered my decision for Jo and Joe and myself. I knew I might never sleep well again, for Libbie had loved me and once, a long time ago when my world was young, I'd loved her.

"Whatever, Mo."